Rock Star Mom

The Rock Star's Wife, Volume 4

Melina Druga

Published by Sun Up Press, 2024.

Content Warning

The Rock Star's Wife series is about sex, family, and rock & roll. It has elements of chick lit, romance and erotica and is best compared to *The Vagina Monologues* for frank talk about sex and its consequences. The series follows Cassandra from her teen years into her 40s as she navigates relationships (both romantic and platonic) — all with music playing a prominent role.

The series is comprised of eight books and four holiday stories. Each book has its own theme and is a standalone story.

The Rock Star's Wife series contains coarse language, sexual encounters and adult themes, and is intended for mature audiences.

Dear Diary

I broke my own rules.

I said I would never own a house in the suburbs, but I do. With a dog and cat to boot: Scooter, the incompetent watchdog, and Maisie, a middle-aged mouser.

I asserted there was no such thing as love at first sight – until it happened to me at a Fourth of July weekend cookout two years ago.

I swore I would never give a man with brown hair and brown eyes a second glance, but I did. Now, I never look at other men.

I said it was unlikely I would ever get married, but I did. Twice. To the same man, a dude with brown hair and brown eyes who I fell in love with during a car ride we took in the middle of a Fourth of July weekend cookout.

I vowed I would never have children, but one month I had a huge surprise. Her name is Megan.

I said I would get out of my hometown of Sterling, Illinois, and I did. There, I succeeded at something. But I said I was moving to Chicago. Nothing mattered more than that goal. Until something did. Someone. His name is Nat. He's the dude with brown hair and brown eyes who I fell in love with during a car ride in the middle of a Fourth of July weekend cookout and married twice and own a house in the suburbs with.

It's strange how life takes us on paths we least expect.

Oh, and one more thing. I said I would never marry a man whose work takes him away from home, making me a part-time, single parent. Well, I broke that rule, too. Nat's a rock star. He's on the road for weeks or months at a time. He does it because he loves it, and it pays our bills. Right now, he's the only wage earner in our household. I had a job as an HR assistant, but I quit right before Megan was born to pursue a dream. I want to be an erotica writer, but so far I haven't made one cent. I keep trying.

I'm glad you're here to take this journey with me, even if my new roles keep me from writing as often as I once did. My name is Cassandra Hardwick. Today is September 3, 2004. Welcome back to my world.

Chapter 1

The Sound of Sibling Rivalry

September 3, 2004

"I'm so glad you were able to come to Minneapolis for Brandon's gallery opening," my sister Vanessa says. "It's a really big deal for him, but his family isn't very supportive. They don't think being an artist is a real job."

I shake my head and reach for one of the sandwiches Nessa prepared for us. "That's a shame."

"You used to be one of those people," she says, tone critical.

"Because Mom and Dad thought that way. I didn't know any better. You know how our family can be about education and jobs that support people."

Brandon worked odd jobs in the past to pay the bills, but his passion is art. He made connections at his new job as a collections specialist at an art museum, which started a chain of events that led to a commission for a mural downtown and tomorrow's gallery opening.

My gaze drifts past Vanessa to the adjacent sunroom where Brandon shows Nat the part of the house that serves as the art studio.

She glances over her shoulder then back at me. "Remember when we used to be competitive as kids?"

I shake my head. "No. You were competitive. You're three years older, so you were always better at everything. You know how annoying and frustrating that was? It wasn't until I became salutatorian that I finally beat you at something. After that, everything has pretty much been equal."

She leans against the kitchen counter. "No, not quite equal. You're still competing with me."

I furrow my brow. "What do you mean?"

"Look at your life choices over the past two years. I ended up with a creative man who initially wasn't my type but that I really click with. You've done the same thing."

I laugh. "I hate to break it to you, but we met through his sister. I didn't go out purposely seeking a musician who wasn't my type so I could emulate your relationship."

"And what about your vow never to have kids? You swore up and down you'd never do it. Ever."

"Well, you know. People change. Things happen...backstage."

"Uh, huh," Vanessa says bouncing seven-and-half-month-old Megan on her hip.

The baby giggles before sticking her fist in her mouth.

A second later, Vanessa's face goes pale. "Wait. What do you mean things happen backstage?"

My gaze drifts to the sunroom. "Shawna and I drove up to Milwaukee to see Dramatic Sneezer in concert. They were the opening act. The set was maybe 40 minutes, but for security reasons we couldn't leave when we planned. Nat and I missed each other. It'd been New Year's since we last laid eyes on each other, and we couldn't keep away from each other. God, I remember how gorgeous he looked that night. We couldn't wait until we made it to the hotel. We tried, but it was hopeless. A lot of sports teams play in that arena, so there are showers. We went in there and," I indicate Megan, "things happen."

I squirm, pussy wet from the memory of that April evening.

My sister shakes her head. "Geez, Cassie, you're gushing. If anyone can make sloppy sex in a shower sweaty dudes use sound romantic, it's you."

"Who said anything about sloppy? It was one of those mind-blowing fuckings where we forgot everything except how fucking fantastic it feels."

Noah and Parker, my eight- and five-year-old nephews, run into the room, and I silence myself with a piece of sandwich. What's that saying about little pitchers having big ears? Do pitchers have ears? I've never seen a pitcher with ears. Anyway, the boys might hear something they shouldn't whereas Megan and Kendra, my one-year-old niece, are clueless.

"I still have you beat by two kids," Vanessa says over the ruckus.

Damn, still convinced I'm trying to emulate her?

I point to my temple. "Yeah, okay. I'll make a mental note. Have three more accidental pregnancies in order to procreate one more time than you."

The boys run out of the room, and for a third time Vanessa follows my gaze to the sunroom. "So, tell me. These mind-blowing fucks, are they a common occurrence or was that evening special?"

"Oh, yeah, happens all the time. Sometimes multiple times a day, especially if we've been apart for a while. I've never had it so good."

Am I bragging? Sounds like I'm bragging. Is being honest bragging?

Vanessa sets Megan on the floor beside Kendra, and the two babies ignore each other in favor of exploring the tiny great room.

"Really?" she says, straightening her back.

"Yes, really. I've had plenty of boyfriends, but it wasn't until I met him that I understood what 'clicking' with someone actually means. As an added bonus, his sex drive is as high as mine."

My eyes drift again to Nat.

"Damn it," Vanessa says, voice rising, "can you stop staring at his ass for five seconds while I'm talking to you? How can you be this horny when you have a baby in the house?"

I toss my sandwich on a plate. "What? I'm a mom, not dead. Megan sleeps through the night. And I really like him in those pants."

She sighs. "I don't get it, but doesn't matter. I like you better this way. You're content, and I don't think I've seen you content since 1984."

I roll my eyes. "Nineteen eighty-four? What happened in 1984?"

"That was right before you started school and that was the first time we visited Chicago. You've been dissatisfied with your life ever since."

I thought I was six, not five, when we first visited Chicago and I decided I was going to move there after college. Oh, well, doesn't matter. I made it to a Chicagoland suburb called Vienna-on-the-Lake, less than an hour's drive from the Windy City.

Nat and Brandon enter the kitchen. Judging from their expressions, they have been discussing either artistic vision or us women.

Nat smiles and places his arm around my waist. "I need a music studio in our house, don't you think, Honey?"

"Where would we put it?"

Every inch of our semi-detached townhouse has a purpose. There's no spare space on the ground floor, and our basement isn't much larger than the furnace it surrounds, although Nat sometimes plays down there. I'm not sure why. Acoustics are terrible. Our only spare bedroom is my office where I toil most days attempting to write my first novel.

"Well, we won't be living there forever. If we have another kid, we'll need to move. We'll want a detached house and a swing set in the backyard."

Vanessa smirks, and my stomach turns. The last thing I want to think about is pregnancy and childbirth. I'm enjoying having my body and sex life back.

"Yes, I'm sure we will want a larger house someday," I say, betraying nothing.

My sister claps her hands together. "I hope you're hungry. Brandon and I found a fantastic Greek restaurant not too far from here. Not as good as our family's place, of course, but enough to make you homesick."

Our family, specifically our older brother Chris, owns Costas' Place, the only Greek restaurant in Whiteside County. Other Greek restaurants remind me of home, but they never beat Yiayia and Papou's recipes. I'm looking forward to tonight. It feels like forever since my sister and I hung out.

"I CAN'T BELIEVE MAROULA eloped," I say, ripping my pita bread in half. "It's not tradition to elope. I bet Thea Ilena and Theos Khristos are pissed."

Maroula, our double first cousin, grew up with her older sister, Persephone, and her older brother, Phillipos (Phil), two houses down from us. We saw them nearly every day. Our mothers are sisters and our fathers are brothers. We all look like siblings.

"*You* eloped. And a couple months later you had this sweetie," Vanessa says, pinching Megan's cheek and eliciting giggles.

I stab my lamb. "People expected me to buck tradition. I said it all along. But Maroula, she always followed the rules."

Maroula and I were born 14 days apart. She drove me nuts when we were teens, always reminding me that we weren't allowed to do X, Y or Z. It was like hanging out with a narc.

At least she married a nice Greek boy, Stephanos Voulgaropoulos, an ear, nose and throat doctor from Moline that she met at Western Illinois

University. He knows the language and culture, so they can pass that down to their kids. Wait a minute. Oh, you don't suppose?

"We hired a babysitter for tomorrow," Brandon says, putting an end to any discussion of Maroula's motives. "I want to thank you again for driving all this way for my debut opening."

Minneapolis is nearly six hours from Chicago if there's no traffic, but between traffic, potty breaks and lunch, it took eight hours to get here. I'm going to dream about highways tonight, I just know it.

As for the babysitter, that's a foreign concept. In Sterling, family helped family, and Nat's family does the same in Vienna-on-the-Lake. I've never left Megan with a stranger, except that one time the neighbor watched her in the yard for a few minutes so I could go into the house. Does that count? No. Oh, well.

"Oh, no problem, man," Nat says, grabbing Megan's hand to prevent her from throwing food on the floor. "I know it's not the same thing, but I know what it's like to be starting out and finally getting that break that proves to you that all the hard work hasn't been for nothing. Next time Dramatic Sneezer's in Minneapolis, you'll need to come to a show. Backstage passes."

"Backstage, eh?" Vanessa says. "I hear all kinds of exciting things happen there."

The hair on the back of my neck stands on end. Does Nat know what Vanessa's getting at?

He smiles and shakes his head slightly. "Usually, it's pretty dull."

Phew, no clue.

"Well, I hope you won't find the gallery opening dull," Brandon says, leaning back in his chair. "I know it's probably not your cup of tea."

Vanessa smirks. "Yeah, there's no showers."

I give her a stern look. At least I have an interesting conception story, unlike most people who had it happen in bed or on a couch or in the backseat of a car. Boring.

"Why would an art gallery ever have a shower?" Brandon says, wrinkling his brow.

"Never mind," Vanessa says, taking a forkful of pilafi. "Let's order dessert. We'll compare them to our aunts."

"Yes," I say, "we'll compare...desserts."

I'M AWAKENED FROM A light sleep by the sound of banging followed by a woman moaning. I lift my head and remove the covers from my ear. What the hell? Is that the TV downstairs? No, it's coming from the master bedroom next door.

Nat's arm hangs over my side, the same place it was when we fell asleep. I push his shoulder, making him mumble.

"Wake up," I say.

"Leave me alone," his says, groggy.

"Wake up."

"Leave me alone. I'm tired."

"Please."

"We were on the road eight hours. We argued three times about stupid shit. I want to sleep."

"Want to make it four times? Listen."

I can't see him in the dark, but—

"Ow," I say, eyes watering. "You hit me in the eye with your nose."

"That's what you get for waking me up." Something hits the wall. "What is that?"

"Sibling rivalry."

"What?"

"Never mind. I'll explain in the morning." I rub his underwear. "Fuck me."

"What?" He pushes me away. "No. I was asleep a minute ago."

"You heard me. Fuck me, then go back to sleep."

"I must be dreaming because you were as exhausted as I was."

"Nope, you're very much awake. I'll jack myself off if I need to, but I'd rather have your participation."

"Participation in what?"

"I've already told you. I want you to fuck me."

"Goddamn. I want to sleep."

He hasn't stopped me rubbing his underwear. The ruckus in the master bedroom hasn't stopped either. I need to show them how it's done.

Despite his protests, his cock quickly hardens. Maybe if I pull it through his fly, I can get fucked and he can be lazy. I stick my hand though his fly.

"If we're going to do this, we're going to do it right," he says, grabbing my wrist. "Get naked."

We quickly undress. My eyes adjust, and I make out the shape of his body in the dark. He runs his hand up my inner thigh, making his way to my sensitive spot and rubbing it with his thumb. I'm juicy.

While we engage in foreplay, Vanessa and Brandon go at it like a couple in a porno flick, their mattress creaking in time with every moan.

Whump, whump. Aaaah, aaaah.

I rest my thigh on Nat's hip, and he slips in. Usually, we don't start with scissoring – too slow and gentle – but this is what happens when your lover is half asleep. Problem is I don't want him to make love to me. I want him to fuck me.

Don't get me wrong. It feels nice. Incredibly nice. I close my eyes and whimper. Our lips touch, and his tongue darts in my mouth. Oh, oh, oh my! His cock rubs exactly the right spot. Oh, yes, it feels fantastically nice, but nice isn't going to win this competition.

We flip over and, interlacing my fingers in his, I squat on his cock. I pump, smiling mischievously when he groans, and clench his hands so tightly my knuckles hurt. Good thing I keep in shape. Otherwise, I'd never be able to pump with the intensity necessary to make him groan loud enough.

Thwack, thwack. Ooooh, ooooh.

"Come on, big boy, give it to me. Give it to me!" Vanessa says in the master bedroom.

I laugh. They watch way too much porn. If you're fucking correctly, you're moaning too much to speak.

After several minutes of squat thrusts, the day catches up to me. Tired, I place my shins on the bed and, placing my hands on his chest for support, lift my hips so high his cock nearly slips out before grinding down. This results in a loud groan. Excellent. Take that, Vanessa. I hardly hear your man at all!

I lay on Nat, kissing him passionately. Yes, I know, kissing defeats the purpose of what I am attempting to do, but my thighs smart. A slow, gentle screw for a few minutes is what I need to recharge. This is one of the most enjoyable positions for me, although, shit, I love them all.

Smack, smack, smack, smack.

What the hell is going on in the master bedroom? My sister must be into some kinky shit.

Nat takes over the thrusting. I moan in his ear and enjoy the ride. Then I remember to lift my head and project toward the headboard so my moans can be heard in the master bedroom,

Just when I could cry, we flip over. He thrusts vigorously. I clench the fitted sheet, wrapping my legs around his hips and my arms around his back.

The master bedroom has gone quiet. They must be finished. Good. They can listen to us.

I'd like to say I'm loud simply for the sake of winning this competition, but when he thrusts like that, I can't help but moan in ecstasy. My nails dig into his skin, and I shout when he cums.

Exhaustion catches up to Nat, and he lingers inside me before pulling out. He attempts to make me cum, but his finger circle my clitoris slower than usual. How can fingers be tired? Oh, well. Doesn't matter. I'm so sensitive, this shouldn't take long. I close my eyes and focus on how it feels.

A baby starts crying but, since Megan and Kendra are only half a year apart, I can't tell who. Nat's fingers stop mid-motion. I open my eyes and lift my head. In the near darkness, we stare at each other.

"I'll go," he says.

"No. It's my sister's house. I better go. You can finish me off when I get back. I'll be as quick as I can."

I reluctantly get out of bed and put on my robe.

WHEN I REACH THE NURSERY, I find Vanessa holding a fussy Megan.

"I'm sorry we woke her up," Vanessa says, "especially since she's sleeping through the night now, and you had that long drive today. Brandon and I got a little carried away. I'm jealous because you still have a sex drive after having a baby. Mine did a nosedive, and I hate it. I want my old sex drive back. I wanted to prove we have the better sex life, but it's a ridiculous thing to be competing about. It shouldn't be a contest. It's a very personal thing. So, again, I'm sorry. Our cries were for dramatic effect."

"It's okay," I say as cum starts running down my leg. "Ours weren't."

She shakes her head. "What? How is that possible?"

"What do you mean?" I say, nonchalantly wiping the cum before taking Megan. "We really enjoy it. I mean, *really* enjoy it. Our libidos feed off each other."

Vanessa checks on Kendra, and I put Megan into the travel crib.

"How long do you think that'll last?" she says.

I shrug. "I don't know. It's always been that way. We were made for each other."

"Brandon and I were made for each other, too. But raising kids is exhausting. I get my sex drive back just in time for us to have another baby and the cycle starts all over again."

I touch her arm. "I'm sorry. Maybe it'll come back now that you're done having kids."

"I hope so. I really do."

We make the short trip down the hall in silence.

"Goodnight," we say in unison.

I enter the guest bedroom, flush with victory, and crawl into bed, sighing when I discover Nat's asleep. I snuggle close, bare flesh touching, and close my eyes. Shit, it's been a long day. I haven't cum, but Megan spoiled the mood anyway. I yawn. Maybe in the morning.

Chapter 2

A Day in the Life of a Rock Star Wife

September 23, 2004

My ankles near his ears, Nat thrusts one final time before pulling out and collapsing on the bed.

"I'm going to miss that." He rolls onto his side and places his hand on my cheek. "I'm going to miss you."

My chest tightens, and I swallow. "I'm going to miss you, too."

We kiss, and I run my hand down his arm, squeezing his bicep.

The morning fuck – a slower, gentler continuation of the bedtime fuck – happens with frequency in our household as if we're trying to make up for all those months Nat's not home. But we can never actually make up for when he's not home. It's a delusion, a delusion we indulge because we love our shared daydream.

I know how this works. I chose this life, remember? The album (Dramatic Sneezer's third, *Snow on the Sun*) dropped. He needs to promote it. We have bills to pay.

Leaving the warmth of my arms, Nat begins his morning routine. I stand in the bathroom doorway and observe him shave, remembering with fondness the first time I watched him groom. He stayed the night at my apartment and used my razor and floral scented shave gel.

He rinses his razor before turning with a smile. "How long have you been standing there?"

"Just a little while." I come into the room and squeeze his shoulders. "Looks good," I say, referring to his partial beard of shaving cream.

"Sexy. Isn't it?"

I resist the urge to laugh. "Oh, the sexist, but not as sexy as you."

I slap his ass and grab my robe from the back of the bathroom door. I'll probably put on my workout clothes in preparation for later. I workout more when Nat's gone until I get used to his absence. If Megan allows me, I'll do both aerobics DVDs today. Chasing her crawling around the house has become its own type of workout.

BLISSFULLY UNAWARE her father is leaving, Megan sits in her high chair, pounding her palms on the tray and thinking it's funny. Nat moves one of the peninsula's stools in front of her, sits and opens a baby food jar with a snap.

This gets her attention, and she opens her mouth the moment he inserts the spoon in the jar. I hate to say it, but it's almost the same reaction Scooter or Maisie give when I serve them canned food as a treat. They stop whatever they're doing and excitedly run to the kitchen.

"Are you hungry, Sweetie?" he says, lifting a spoonful.

She chomps on the spoon, half the contents falling out, before opening her mouth for more.

He scoops the pureed apples off her chin. "You were hungry, weren't you?"

The toaster pops, and I butter the slices and sprinkle them with cinnamon.

"Is that enough?" I say, placing his plate on the counter beside him. "I could always get out the cereal."

"It's fine. Really," he says. "Don't worry."

How can I not worry? Does he eat well on the road?

"Dadadada," Megan says, demanding to be fed.

WHEN THE TOUR BUS ARRIVES, I follow Nat to the driveway, bouncing Megan on my hip.

"Honey," he says, balancing his suitcase and duffle bag, "I hate to go, but I need to get back to work."

"I understand," I say, placing my free arm around his neck in an attempt to hide the tears forming in my eyes.

I give him one last lingering kiss then let him go. Megan waves bye-bye, bursting into hysterics the moment Nat boards on the bus. She's going through the separation anxiety stage, but her fits don't last longer than a few minutes.

"Well, it's just you and me now," I say as the bus disappears out of view.

Megan responds with incoherent babble, and we go back inside where I set her on the floor. Her favorite activity over the past few days has been crawling to the living room furniture to pull herself up.

She's all smiles, moving around the great room using objects for support, until she tries to move between the couch and the armchair. The gap is too wide, and Scooter's wagging tail smacks her in the arm, causing her to lose her balance and land on her butt.

The moment crocodile tears stream down her cheeks I run to pick her up. Her tears make me want to cry more than I already do. I should cry. Tomorrow will be better and the next day, and before I know it, the tour will be over. This one will be short, two months, and then we'll see him for Thanksgiving. Hell, that's nothing. He was gone nearly all of last year.

I shush Megan and, tears so thick I barely see, carry her upstairs to my office. Well, we call it an office, but it's really a cheap computer desk and a printer stand. If I can get my first book sold, I can start contributing to the household finances again.

I shut the door, to keep Megan in and the pets out, and let the baby explore.

"If I can sell this book, eventually Daddy can stay home longer," I say, turning on the computer.

Megan glances at me, but she's so busy trying to figure out how to stand when there's so little to use for support that she doesn't care I'm speaking.

The computer boots up and, wiping my eyes, I call up the manuscript. I already started querying agents. I'm a bit ahead of the game, I know, but it takes months to hear back from these people, and I'm spending a fortune in self addressed stamped envelopes (SASE in industry speak). I only need to impress one, but my biggest stumbling block is the fact that erotica is a taboo genre for many.

My story involves a committed couple, and I cushioned those sex scenes with a plot and made the characters real people. Hopefully, it's unique enough to spark an agent's interest, but not so unique that it's a turnoff.

My phone goes off in the next room. I must have left it in the bedroom instead of taking it downstairs. I leave the office, crossing my fingers Megan won't be chewing on computer wires when I get back.

I grab the phone from the dresser and glance at the bed. Maisie sprawls on the bedspread, on Nat's side, and knowing I'll be sleeping alone tonight causes a pang of sadness. Well, maybe not exactly alone. A feline might be with me.

I have five text messages I read this morning but never answered plus a new one from Nat. He's only been gone 10 minutes. Maybe he forgot something, and we'll have to go through the goodbye ritual all over again.

It reads: *I love u :) <3*

I return to the office, tears returning – phew, Megan behaved – and sit at the desk.

I respond: *I love u 2 <3 <3*

I set the phone next to the printer and type a few paragraphs. I scrapped together a bunch of old short stories and changed names and details to make them about the same characters. That helped me write this book faster than I probably otherwise could. If I can concentrate, I'll get this draft finished today.

My text message alert goes off. *Ill call u when we get there <3 <3 <3*

I answer: *Stay safe <3 <3 <3 <3*

I set down the phone and glance at Megan before turning back to the computer screen. It's not that I don't want Nat to pursue his career. Rather, I wish we could go with him. It's silly, I know, and the notion will wear off in a couple of days. I'm accustomed to him being gone. He missed nearly my entire pregnancy, after all.

My alert goes off, and I expect a message from Nat but instead it's Maroula.

At the store. Recommendations for a pregnancy test?

Yep, called that one. Didn't I say she eloped for a reason?

I answer: *They all work the same*

"Dadadada," Megan says, pointing to Nat's picture with her tiny finger.

"That's right, Megan," I say, forcing a smile. "That's a picture of Daddy from before you were born. I used to keep that picture on my desk when I worked in an office. Some of my coworkers thought I made him up since he plays in a band, and I had to prove he exists. Isn't that silly? Why would someone make up a boyfriend? I'd let you hold it, but you'll probably slobber all over it."

She eyes me with wide eyes. I have no clue how much she understands. I'm not sure she knows what a desk is yet alone an office, coworkers and a boyfriend.

Arf. Scratch. Arf. Scratch.

Jesus, how am I going to get anything done today?

"Scooter," I say, "down, boy."

Arf. Scratch . Arf. Scratch.

Oh, Goddamn it! I open the door, and Scooter gleefully plods in, looking proud of himself.

I shut the door. He conducts his inspection, nose sniffing loud enough to annoy. He pays particular attention to Megan's face, and I clench the edge of my chair, wondering whether she will laugh or cry. She giggles, and I relax.

Oh, yeah, I have a manuscript to finish:

> His muscles bulging under his flimsy shirt, he leans into her, pinning her between his rugged body and the dresser. She gasps, feeling his hard cock thump in his jeans.

My phone goes off, and I'm ready to give up accomplishing anything today. There are two messages. One from Maroula thanking me – I'll get more details out of her later – and the other from Nat.

Never forget that I love you more than anything in the world. You are the center of my universe.

I burst into tears. Why does he need to travel so much? Yes, I know. I know how this goes. I chose this life, remember? I chose to be a rock star's wife.

Chapter 3

One Small Step

November 20, 2004

In the two months Nat's been gone, Megan and I established a routine. She plays in the office while I write. While I exercise, she practices cruising around the room. On weekdays, when *Sesame Street* airs, I sing along to the number and letter songs. She doesn't care about the program yet, but her eyes widen when the Muppets speak. Scooter hates them and barks as if he thinks he can scare them away. When Megan naps, I clean, and I pay the bills after she goes to bed. Once a week, she stays with Nat's parents so I can hang out with my best friend, Shawna Greene, or Nat's second eldest sister, Nadine Bergstrom, or both. Sometimes we get a visitor or there's an occasion to see Nat's extended family, but most days it's only the two of us.

Megan no longer babbles "dadadada," which has me a bit worried. She's too young to have much long-term memory, and I'm concerned she's forgotten Nat. He talks to her on the phone, so hopefully she recognizes his voice if nothing else.

I sometimes wonder what Megan will remember about her early years. Will she remember playing with her toys in the middle of the great room? Will she remember her furry friends? Will she remember me typing at the keyboard for hours at a time and saying choice words when rejection letters arrive? Will she remember her father being away?

My first memory is of my parents' house in Sterling on the night the *M*A*S*H* series finale aired. I know it was the finale because I remember the closing scene with the big "GOODBYE" made out of rocks, although, of course, I couldn't read yet. I wasn't quite four. I remember Mom crying and Chris thinking it was funny. Greg and Vanessa were there, but I don't remember them. Just Mom crying and Chris snickering. He was 13 and a half and easily amused as boys that age can be.

Dad was away working. He does sales and inspects installations for Huntington & Walter, a company that manufactures shelves and cabinetry. His territory is the entire Midwest. Anyhow, most of my earliest (and, honestly, most of my later) childhood memories involve him being gone. You'd think it'd be the opposite, but it isn't. I remember absence more than presence, and I fear Megan will have the same experience.

She laughs, distracting me from my introspection. She stands in front of the sliding glass door, pressing her hands and forearms into the glass to hold herself upright, and watches the backyard.

Noticing my approach, she looks up and smiles. "Mamamama."

Three squirrels chase each other through the soggy, rotting leaves.

"Those are squirrels, Megan. If we let Scooter out, he'll want to eat one."

I halfway consider letting the dog out but don't want to traumatize Megan should he attack a squirrel and bring the carcass to the door.

"What do you suppose Daddy is doing right now, eh?" I glance at the clock. It's a few minutes after noon. "He's back on the bus. He'll call us later before the show."

I throw myself onto the window seat and wonder if I've simply lost track of time and taken a longer than usual break or if I'm procrastinating because the colder weather made me sluggish.

"Come on," I say, knowing either way I'll need to force myself, "let's go upstairs so Mommy can finish working."

Megan turns. She toddles, same as she always does, but this time she doesn't fall on her rear. She takes a step. A step?! I sit forward and watch her take another. I stand. She takes a third and a fourth before finally falling.

"Bravo, Sweetie!"

I scoop her up and carry her to the coffee table. I'm going to text Nat and tell him. He'll be so proud. He'll— He'll be upset because he'll be home in five days for a break. Five days! He missed his daughter's first steps by five days. I delete my text message and set the phone down. It's difficult enough being on the road. Why add insult to injury?

I'll lie to him. Maybe not lie, exactly. I'll simply pretend the first steps he sees are her "first" steps instead of a re-enactment. I won't be able to do that with other milestones, of course. Her first word that isn't babble, for example.

Keep that hidden, and she might be speaking multiple words by the time he gets home. I sigh.

"Let's go upstairs. I have work to do." I tickle Megan's incredibly ticklish belly. "Maybe you'll do some more walking. Just don't unplug my computer."

She giggles, kicking her feet. I heard that once babies get the hang of walking, they're constantly on the go. Megan already keeps me busy crawling and cruising all over. I have a feeling I'm about to get busier.

HOW IS IT THAT WHEN I was single, that year I lived alone, I ate dinner solo every night and was cool with it? Now, it feels like there's something missing. I set my dinner plate on the counter and am about to sit at the peninsula when my phone rings. A welcome distraction!

"Oh, it's Daddy," I say to Megan, who is half asleep in her highchair, and answer the phone.

"Hey, beautiful," Nat says. "How are you doing?"

"Yeah, I'm okay. The weather's got me down a bit, but I got a lot of writing done. How are you doing?"

"Great. I got a good night's sleep. No problems on the road." He tells me about last night's hotel and the venue for tonight's concert. "Anything interesting happen today?"

Oh, he had to ask that, didn't he?

I smile, remembering Megan's first steps. "Interesting? Hum, let me see. Well, Megan was entertained by a trio of squirrels this afternoon. She thought it was hysterical they were chasing each other."

He laughs. "I love chasing you. I love your tail. What's Megan doing now? Put me on speaker phone."

"Well, she looks nearly asleep, but I'll put you on anyway."

Drool rolls down her chin.

"Hey, baby girl," he says on speaker, "Daddy hopes you're having a good day. I'll see you in five days. That's the number of fingers you have on one hand or the number of toes on one foot."

Megan's eyes flitter open, but she's conked out. Walking must be exhausting.

"She's out like a light," I say. "Better luck tomorrow. I can't wait to see you. Those five days are going to drag."

"I know. I'm counting down the days. But I got to work for four of those days, so it'll keep me occupied. Think you'll wear something special when I get home?"

Wear something special? Is he talking about a sexy dress or something else?

"How special?" I say, squirming in my seat.

"Special like our wedding night."

I laugh. "You want me to wear a dress with a malfunctioning zipper?"

"No, you hot fuck. The other wedding night. Something lacy and see through."

I love Nat so much I married him twice, once for legal reasons and once for fun.

"Oh, yeah, yeah, I can totally do that."

I grit my teeth. Is there such a thing as an emergency shopping trip for lingerie?

"Great," he says. "I'm getting hard just thinking about it."

Wow. No pressure.

"What would you like to see?" I ask, trying to envision what they carry at the local Victoria's Secret.

"Something that shows off your ass."

That should be easy enough to find. I mentally review lingerie options in my head. Megan's foot twitches, reminding me of her first steps earlier today. What do babies dream about? Is she imagining herself walking? Five days. Megan, you couldn't have waited five days?

NOVEMBER 25, 2004

"You realize one of these years we're going to have to spend Thanksgiving in Sterling," I say. "Not so much for me, but so Megan can get to know her extended family."

Nat shakes his head. "You're assuming I'll have off every year. Some years, you and Megan may have to come visit me wherever I am."

I glance at the baby playing on the floor with the pets. Not spend a major holiday with extended family? That's an intriguing yet disheartening thought, but spending a holiday without Nat would be worse. Megan should always spend holidays with her father. Maybe she won't have the typical holiday traditions other kids have, and I need to be okay with that. There's no alternative other than Nat making a drastic career move, and you and I both know that's not happening.

"Maybe we can spend it somewhere warmer than Illinois," I say.

He smiles. "Like the beach."

"Like we did in Miami." I grin. "We had a great time."

He doesn't answer, his eyes no longer on me but on the room behind me.

"Honey, Honey, look," he says.

"Did Maisie jump from the floor to the back of the couch again? She's a cat. They all can do that."

His expression doesn't change. "No, look."

I turn and, sure enough, Megan takes tentative steps.

"Oh, my," I say, "look at that."

Bad acting? Maybe, but I'm more interested in Nat's reaction than watching Megan walk. She's been doing it here and there for days. I shift my stance, so I can observe them both.

"That's my girl," he says, moving to her and crouching. "I'm so proud of you."

Megan beams as if she understands what he's saying and walks into his open arms. He pulls her close, rubbing a hand over her wavy hair, and stands. She's proud of herself, too, I think. Maybe not for walking, but for pleasing him. He kisses the top of Megan's head. There he goes, looking all sexy being a dad.

"Why don't I wear something 'special' today, too?" I say, approaching, pussy wet.

"Today?" His eyes widen with confusion. "We're going to my parents."

"I know," I say with a smile. "But there is everyday underwear and there's sexy underwear."

Megan lifts her head off Nat's shoulder and kicks.

"So tell me about this sexy underwear?" he says, setting Megan on the floor.

Last night, I modeled the lingerie I purchased during my emergency shopping trip, a black panty and bra attached to each other with a chain. Well, two chains actually. They make an X in front of the body with a gold ring in the middle. He really liked it. I mean, *really* liked it. He lasted, like, five minutes.

"Well, I have a satin set and a velvet set. I suggest velvet because of the time of year."

He slips a hand inside my robe. "If you're trying to entice me, I need to watch you dress so I can picture that sexy underwear on you all day."

I touch his side. "You have a deal. How did you like last night's 'special' outfit?"

"Hum." He rubs my ass. "I enjoyed it. That was pretty clear, I thought, based on the huge hard-on. Tell you what. I think we need to start a new tradition. Every time I come home, you greet me with a special outfit."

Every time? I mean, most times it won't matter, but I'm sure there will be times when sex isn't possible or convenient. But why get into all of that now?

"Of course, that's a great idea, but we're going to go broke buying lingerie."

His hand squeezes, drawing me closer. "Doesn't need to be a new one – every time – just surprise me with that fantastic body of yours."

I smile and press my lips into his. He's got a deal.

Chapter 4

Christmas Miracle

December 18, 2004

Add taking a baby to the mall to have her photo taken with Santa to the list of things that sound good in theory but are terrible in practice. How cute, we thought, how adorable it would be to have a photo we can bring out every year and say "look how big you've gotten." That was before we waited in line for 45 minutes.

"I don't remember waiting this long when we were kids," Shawna says.

"Probably didn't. Whiteside County is a lot smaller. Or maybe we just had smaller wish lists in those days."

Megan enjoys riding in a stroller when it's in motion, but when it's stationary, she wants out. Of course if I let her out, I'll be chasing her from here to Nordstrom. I take a stuffed animal out of the diaper bag and hand it to her, hoping it keeps her occupied.

"Remember the hot toys when we were kids?" Shawna says. "Cabbage Patch Kids, Teddy Ruxpin, Koosh balls, Nintendo? Then when we were teens, how people went totally nuts over Beanie Babies and Tickle Me Elmo? What's the hot toy this year?"

"Xbox 360, they said on the news."

She wrinkles her nose. "Going right for the expensive stuff. I'm guessing that costs hundreds of dollars. The Muellers freaked when I asked for Teddy Ruxpin. Like I had any concept of money back then."

The Muellers, Shawna's long-time foster parents, never adopted her. She convinced herself it's because she's biracial, but I think the real reason is because they enjoyed getting monthly checks from the state. Cheap bastards.

"I wanted a Nintendo," I say, avoiding a debate over the Muellers' motives, "but my parents said video games are for kids whose parents don't give a damn about their education. I think I got a lot of clothes that year. The only expensive thing I ever got was my CD player."

I sigh, watching with envy the shoppers who aren't in this fucking line. After this, we need to go to Borders Express, which I still refer to as Walden's, and KB Toys. Toy shopping is another thing we thought would be fun. Why would navigating through narrow, crowded aisles with a stroller a week before Christmas be fun?

"Do you have your shopping finished after today?" I ask.

Might be an insensitive question to ask considering Shawna was a foster kid and there aren't many people on her list, but she has a fiancé now. Her boyfriend, Jason Wright, a Chicago attorney, popped the question around Halloween, and they're planning a summer wedding.

"Almost. I'm waiting for something to come mail order."

Some kid near the beginning of the line shrieks. Hysterics weren't something Shawna and I considered when we hatched this plan. Jesus, I hope Megan doesn't do that when we reach the top of the line.

She's teething, wears diapers and Santa is a stranger with a scary beard. Oh fuck, this was a bad idea, a very bad idea. But we've been in line for so long now. Leaving would be the wise thing to do, but it would mean we wasted our time.

"It's really weird. Since Vanessa and Brandon live so far away now, we might not even see them. It depends on the weather."

"Hopefully it won't snow, and they'll be able to come. I know your parents would be pretty upset if they didn't see them."

The woman in line behind us shifts her shopping bags from one arm to another, hitting me in the back. I resist the urge to give her a dirty look.

"Too bad Nat is missing this," I say, wishing *I* was on the road away from crying brats.

"It must be hard having him away," Shawna says, clearly missing my sarcasm. "I feel so bad for you. I don't know how you stand it."

"The week before he leaves and the week after he leaves are the worst. On the plus side, reunion sex is fantastic."

"And that's how we ended up with little Megan," Shawna says, bending to take the baby's hand. "And we're all happier because of it."

Finally, the front of the line.

We're greeted by a high schooler dressed as an elf. "Ho, ho, ho," he says, hat jiggling.

I feel sorry for the kid. Minimum wage isn't enough to make up for humiliation. Shawna pays for the photo, and I lift Megan out of the stroller and onto Santa's lap. That's when it all goes to shit. She goes from zero to face-nearly-purple-my-ears-are-ringing screaming in 30 seconds.

The photographer, another kid in costume, snaps the photo and quickly puts the Polaroid in a cardboard frame decorated in red and green snowflakes. Apparently, there are no refunds or do-overs. I snatch the frame from the teen as if it's her fault Megan looks as if she's being murdered then hug my daughter, feeling guilty I probably traumatized her for life.

Shawna takes the stroller and our shopping bags, and we flee like thieves from a crime scene, heading straight for the nearest bench where we endure the rude stares of people who think I can't control my own child. There we stay until Megan calms.

"She needs a diaper change now," I say, bouncing Megan on my lap. "Next stop should be the nearest bathroom, but I want to be sure she's happy."

Shawna smooths Megan's hair, a curl immediately springing back. "Well, the picture will still be a conversation starter. Just not how we intended."

"I should burn it, but I'll probably let Nat see it first. I'll have quite a story to tell him. Waited an hour for, for," I don't know how to describe Megan's expression, "murder face. I owe you money for that picture."

"It's fine. That's what aunties are for. You and Nat planning on having any more?"

I give her the stink eye. "You ask me *that* question after witnessing a meltdown? It's a matter of timing and sperm count, and we're being more careful about both. Did you know you're only fertile three days a month? And did you know the more sex you have the less likely you are to get pregnant, sex close together anyhow? That's because the male body needs a day or so to manufacture new swimmers and you need a certain number of them to even have a fighting chance of making a baby. That's where we got in trouble in Milwaukee. I should have asked him to jack off that morning, and I should have counted days. I count my days now."

"And then you don't have sex on your fertile days?"

I laugh. "No, silly. Then he jacks off beforehand and pulls out during."

"Hum. Okay. I'm pretty sure that's not scientific, but it's safer and cheaper than birth control, and I know you hated birth control when you were on it before." She shrugs. "I wondered because some couples discuss it in advance. Jason and I aren't sure what we're doing."

I switch Megan to the other knee. "I think it's best not to think about these things too much. Some couples plan for kids then have fertility problems and stress. Others have oops babies and stress. We've decided what will be will be, but seeing as he's away most months on those three fertile days, I think there's little danger I'll have as many kids as my mother-in-law. Why do you ask? Are you and Jason fighting about whether you're having kids or not?"

She shakes her head. "Not exactly, no. He knows I want a family because I don't know mine. How many kids is the question."

I put Megan back in the stroller and give her the stuffed animal. "Don't stress. I did during my entire pregnancy and it wasn't worth it. A lot of moms relish their changing bodies, take pictures every month, get all excited. That wasn't me. I was embarrassed that people would know I'd had sex, as if I hadn't for years at that point."

Shawna places her hand on mine. "That was your parents' disapproval in your subconscious."

"Probably." I really don't want to think about it and stand. "Let's find a bathroom. Want to help me wrap gifts in a day or two?"

"Sure. I love gift wrapping. I should get one of those temp jobs as a mall wrapper next year," she says as we head toward the nearest department store.

I laugh, grateful Shawna moved from Sterling to Vienna-on-the-Lake nearly two years ago. My other school friends are scattered all over and my only local friends are my sisters-in-law.

"Maybe you should. But then you'd need to deal with all the crazy people like her," I say, pointing to the Macy's perfume counter where a red-faced woman causes a stir.

"What do you mean it's out of stock?" the woman's voice says louder than the other shoppers'. "How can it be out of stock? Christmas is coming."

We can't hear the clerk, but she looks apologetic.

We enter the store.

"I want to speak to your manager," the bitch says. "Call them right now."

"My apologizes, ma'am," the clerk says, face pale. "I'll call right now."

If we don't hurry, the poopy diaper will ruin Megan's cute little corduroys. We silently pass the perfume counter, presumably to listen to the bitch complain about the poor job the store does keeping something or another in stock, and maybe Shawna eavesdrops but I'm deep in thought. Despite telling her not to worry, I'm worried. I'm not naïve. Kids are a deal breaker for many couples. Nat and I never discussed children before I got pregnant. He loves them; I never wanted them. We have Megan now. Life is strange.

GOING THROUGH THE MAIL, I yawn. Since when have the holidays been so tiring? And I don't even have to endure a stupid office Christmas party this year. Megan naps upstairs. Maybe I should nap, too, or at least lie down.

Cards and bills mostly, along with one of my SASEs. My stomach turns. I've gotten so many rejections from literary agents that getting one of my SASEs back has turned into something I dread.

I open the latest letter. It starts off like every other form letter, thanking me for submitting three sample chapters. That's generally what comes before the "unfortunately" part. But this letter is different. Instead of an "unfortunately," it has an "I am please to offer." What? This agent wants to represent me? I actually have someone who likes my story enough they want to try and get me a publisher?

Fuck the nap. I'm calling Nat.

"Hello," he says after five rings.

"Oh." Expecting voice mail, I nearly drop my phone. "I thought you'd be prepping to go on stage."

"I was about to leave the dressing room when I saw it was you. Thought I had better pick up in case it's an emergency."

I shake my head. "No, no emergency. I'll be quick. You can call me back later. I have good news, actually. I landed myself an agent."

"That's great, Honey. When I get home, we'll celebrate."

I know exactly the type of celebrating I want to do.

I smile. "That sounds great. You're great."

"No, you are. I'm so proud of you. I knew you could do it. Your hard work paid off."

I know the type of hard work he will do.

"Thank you. Call me later."

"I will," Nat says and hangs up.

I read all the advice books on how to get published. I know landing an agent doesn't guarantee anything. But if I could replace the salary I had before quitting my job, that would help immensely with the bills. And maybe, just maybe, sometime in the future, Nat won't have to tour so much. That's my long-term goal, although I haven't shared it with him. He loves to tour, I know, but I'm pretty sure he loves me and Megan more.

I set my phone on the counter and do a happy dance.

Chapter 5

One Year Today

January 16, 2005

Can't be greedy, I know that. As a rock star's wife, I can't allow myself to become spoiled. Many musicians' wives don't see their husbands for half a year or more, and it ruins their relationships. I need to be grateful we work at maintaining ours. Nat was home for Thanksgiving, Christmas and New Year's. It's too much to expect him to be home for Megan's first birthday party, too. I smile and put on a brave face.

The party planning store has tons of themes for birthdays, which is a new concept to me. I always thought the theme of a birthday was turning a year older, but what do I know? Megan likes stuffed animals and real ones, so I chose teddy bears and decorated the great room with streamers and bears wearing party hats. Above the fireplace, I hung a birthday banner adorned with bears.

I have yet to change Megan into the cute dress I bought with photographs in mind. Nat's only memories of today will be snapshots. I swallow, pushing down my thoughts.

The party starts at two, but my family arrived early to help prepare food and finish last minute decorating. Vanessa and Brandon came into town last night. They're staying at a hotel and will be over later, along with Shawna and Jason, and my in-laws. Right now, my parents, brothers Chris and Greg, my sister-in-law Penny, and Chris and Penny's kids gather around the kitchen peninsula.

"You need to watch Megan," Mom says while the little one plays on the floor with Scooter and Maisie. "Dogs are dangerous around kids. She could get bitten or worse. And watch that the cat doesn't scratch her. She could get cat scratch fever."

"That's a song from the '70s, isn't it?" I say, even though I know damn well what cat scratch fever is.

It's rare. I looked it up the first time Mom mentioned it.

"I'm serious," Mom says, never once taking her eyes off her granddaughter.

I resist the urge to roll my eyes. "Oh, I know you're serious."

Dad leans forward, elbows resting on the counter. "It really is a shame Nat has to work. This is why we wanted you to marry someone with a stable career, so he's home to help you raise your children."

I suppress a laugh. "You missed most of our birthdays and milestones. I can't remember the last time I saw you on one of my birthdays."

Chris, working his magic at the stove, looks over his shoulder. "I could count on 16 hands the number of times you missed things because you were working."

Dad doesn't look pleased, but he doesn't retort either. He knows we're right.

Mom slaps my hand when I reach for a piece of baklava. "Those are for the party."

"This is my house," I say, taking one anyway, "and the party is for my child, so I'm having a piece."

Mom sighs. "Why must you be so rebellious?"

"Because I want a piece of baklava?"

"Because of a lot of things."

I shove the pastry into my mouth in an unladylike manner and watch Mom's disgusted expression.

Penny hands me a napkin then resumes arranging dishes on the counter. "Greg has a girlfriend. Did he tell you?"

Greg doesn't tell me anything. We don't communicate.

I narrow my eyes at my brother. "No. Who is she?"

"Her name is Katrina," Greg says.

"Katrina what?" I say not believing she's real.

My brother hasn't dated for as long as I've known what dating is.

He stares me down. "No one you know. It's not as if you know everyone. Katrina Franopoulos. I met her when I was getting my master's, and we've kept in touch."

My fingers move toward the baklava to annoy Mom, and she looks ready to slap me again.

"That was nearly 10 years ago," I say. "Who dates someone after 10 years?"

"I do." His posture becomes defensive. "She was only a freshman at the time, and we've both dated other people over the years. We remained friends."

They've dated other people? Correction. He means *she* dated other people. If she's real. I'm leaning toward she's imaginary. Greg hasn't had a social life since moving back to Sterling after achieving his master's in chemical engineering. I'm pretty sure he hangs out with Mom – gotta live at home until marriage like a good Greek boy – and talks about the old country while conjugating Greek verbs.

I'll play along. "So what changed?"

Greg shrugs. "I don't know. We hit it off when we both got cell phones and started talking more often."

They both have cell phones? I don't have Greg's number, and some chick I never heard of has it? Not that it matters. If something happened and I needed a male member of the family, I'd call Chris or Phil followed by Brandon, my uncles, my other cousins, Dad wherever he is on the road, and my grandfathers' ghosts before I'd call Greg.

Chris pops the meal into the oven and turns from the range. "Are you going to knock Katrina up before marriage, too, so Mom and Dad can be three for four?"

Greg's face reddens. "Get your mind out of the goddamn gutter. There's kids in the room."

Chris points to himself. "Yeah, and three of them are mine."

Mom and Dad open their mouths, to complain surely, when Allegra stops running with her brothers and tugs on my sleeve.

"What can I do to help, Thea Cassie?"

"You could help her pick out a dress with a longer skirt," Greg says under his breath.

"Awww, Sweetie," I say, realizing that in a decade Megan will look like Allegra, "thank you for asking. Do you like balloons? Of course, you do. You can blow up a few and put them around the room. Just keep them out of the reach of the baby and the cat and dog."

I hand Allegra a pack of pink balloons. There already are enough balloons, but if the kid wants to be helpful, might as well let her feel helpful.

"Be careful," Mom says to her, "that you don't break any and choke."

Allegra is 10 and a half. I'm pretty sure she knows not to eat broken balloons. I give her a gentle push between the shoulder blades, and she runs off to play interior decorator.

Mom turns to me. "Are you coming back to Sterling to help Maroula when she has the baby in June?"

I laugh. "No. She didn't run to Vienna-on-the-Lake to help me."

"But Nat will be out of town," Dad says. "What else better do you have to do?"

My temperature rises. "When are you going to retire, Dad? You'll be 65 this year. Don't you think it's time?"

Dad grins. "No, not yet. I don't see any reason to retire from something that keeps us afloat financially. Besides, I think your mother prefers me away. When is Nat retiring?"

"He's 28. That's a fucking ridiculous question. Why should he retire when you refuse to leave the road? You apparently love it soooo much. Besides he's the one keeping us afloat financially."

I stop myself before I say anything about my writing.

The doorbell chimes. Thank God, Vanessa and Brandon. I answer, and the noise intensifies when Noah and Parker join Homer and Nestor running around the room. Eighteen-month-old Kendra towers over Megan. Of course, Brandon towers comically over Vanessa.

"Sorry," Vanessa says, kissing me, "we wanted to be here earlier but we got lost."

I laugh. "You got lost in Vienna-on-the-Lake?"

She takes off her gloves and slaps them in her hand. "Don't snicker. MapQuest can be very confusing sometimes."

The downstairs coat closet is full, so I pile my guests' coats in my arms and start for the stairs.

"Oh, hello, birthday girl," I hear Vanessa say, and Megan giggles.

I'm going to get quite a workout today carrying everyone's coats up and down the stairs. I'm storing them in my office on one of those clothes racks on wheels. Normally the damn thing is in the laundry room, and Shawna and I nearly killed ourselves lugging it up here.

When I pass the master bedroom, I avoid looking at the bed. Seeing it makes me think of Nat, and I don't want to be sad when there's company around. Too late. I'm struck with a pang of sadness. I clench the coats to my chest and shut the bedroom door.

THE DOORBELL RINGS. It's 10 after three. Everyone who is supposed to be here is here. Probably one of the neighbors complaining someone parked too close to their driveway. Or Nat sent something for Megan. When we were dating, he periodically sent me flowers. He sent them while I was pregnant, too, as an apology for missing it, I suppose, but the scent made me want to vomit. I never told him I was forced to keep the flowers in the garage. It also could be a door-to-door salesman, but that seems the least likely option considering it's January.

I open the door, and my eyes widen.

"Hello, beautiful," Nat says.

I must be dreaming. I wasn't expecting this at all.

"What the fuck? You said you couldn't be here. You have a show tonight."

I should hug him or move aside or something, but I stand dumbfounded, letting the frigid air into the house.

"We'll reschedule tonight's show. I couldn't miss our daughter's first birthday." He smiles. "Are you going to let me into the house or what?"

I can't believe what I'm seeing or hearing. I allow him entry.

"You cancelled tonight's show?" I say, shutting the door promptly behind us.

"Yep," he says, unwrapping his scarf.

"You never cancel. It's too important to you. The fans'll be upset."

"Too late. This was more important. Where is she?"

I shake off my surprise and point into the room. "Being passed from one relative to another."

The adults quiet when they see Nat. Guess everyone else is shocked speechless, too.

"Why are you always running late for parties?" Nadine says, alluding to the cookout where Nat and I met and he was the last person to show up.

He unzips his coat. "You try and get a last minute flight and see how late you are."

Penny carries over Megan who outstretches her arms, grinning with her four teeth. "Da da."

Nat hugs her, and she wraps her arms around his neck. "There's my girl," he says. "I remember when you came out of Mommy and now look at you."

It's so cute, I might cry. I'm glad we haven't done cake and presents yet. I promised I would take plenty of pictures, but he's here to witness it!

My parents owe me a goddamn apology, Dad especially, for making derogatory comments about Nat not being here. He proved them wrong. Both parents look stunned, but I know no apology will be forthcoming.

Brandon comes to say hello, and Nat sets Megan on the floor to remove his coat. She clings to his leg for a moment before taking off in the direction of the dining room table. I take his coat and head to the closet, wrinkling my nose when I walk past my parents. An apology is owed, but I will not start an argument in front of everyone even though I'm pissed more than ever at my parents' insistence that it's a pity what Nat does for a living.

Mom calls my name. "I thought you said he wasn't going to be here," she says after I stop.

"He wasn't. But you know what he did? He cancelled tonight's show so he could be here for Megan's birthday. Being here was more important than making money."

Mom looks at Dad, and I proceed to the coat closet.

"Geez, too bad Dad didn't do that for us when we were kids," Chris says behind me when I hang Nat's coat.

"I don't think the idea struck him once. Maybe he's a workaholic. Maybe it's a generational thing. Maybe it was too expensive to hop on a plane and fly home. I dunno." I spot Nat in the crowded great room. "I'm grateful for the man I have. He's not here all the time, which is a bummer, but I know we're always his focus."

"You made the right choice as far as picking a guy goes," Chris says, grinning. "I can tell with my big brother intuition. Even if you are eating more streusel than baklava nowadays."

I sigh and roll my eyes.

"THAT WAS THE BEST SURPRISE," I say, hours later, putting my arms around Nat's neck. "Thank you for doing that."

He smiles. "You're welcome, but we'll see how happy you are when I don't come home from tour on time because of the make-up date. And, remember I have a 4 a.m. flight out. I have to leave for the airport at 2:30."

"I know." I nod, glancing at the clock. "But considering I originally wasn't going to see you at all, I couldn't be happier. I really missed you this morning. I hate it when you're not here."

I cringe when I hear myself say that. I rarely voice my feelings regarding him being gone. After all, he loves my independence. I don't need a man. I want one. In his profession, that's valued in a mate. I swallow, hoping he won't notice.

He pulls me close. "I just couldn't miss it. When Megan was born, it was one of the best days of my life. We created her, you and me, and your mini-me is going to be as beautiful as you some day."

I gaze into his eyes. "I love it when you say sweet things."

"I love you."

Our tongues wrestling, his hand slides down my back to give my ass a firm squeeze. I grab the back of his shirt, whimpering as my pussy wettens.

It doesn't take long to paw at each other's clothing. Suddenly, I feel hot. I need to get naked. I need to spread my legs and have Nat's hard cock fuck me until I can't walk straight.

I break the kiss to shed clothing. We're in the middle of the great room, but I don't give a shit. He can fuck me anywhere, in the middle of a crowded public place for all I care.

In one swoop, he picks me up and sets me on the armchair's back. His cock enters with ease, slipping in and out of my juicy pussy. Listen to the noises he makes. Must exert a lot of energy pounding the shit out of me.

I wrap my limbs around him to protect myself from the feeling I'm going to slip off the back of the chair. I suppose it's difficult for him to hold me in place because he transfers us to the area rug. When he resumes thrusting, the carpet fibers tickle my skin. I'm going to have carpet burn in the morning. Not that I care. Clenching the coffee table legs, I moan so loudly I'm practically screaming in his ear.

It's one of those fucks where I literally cry from pleasure. Snapping my eyelids shut, I transfer my hands to his body and, nails scratching his skin, run my palms down his back to give his ass a squeeze. Oooh, I love to feel the muscles tense and relax while his hips do their job.

I hear muffled footsteps and open my eyes to see Scooter plodding toward us. His cold nose brushes my cheek before moving to Nat's ear.

"Scooter, get out of here," he says.

Flecks of dog saliva hit my face.

"Get the fuck out of here!"

Startled by Nat's tone, the dog runs.

Nat thrusts with newfound intensity, beads of sweat forming on his brow. I never fucking had it so good. Oh, who am I kidding? I always fucking have it this good.

He cums, and I let out a cry. My pussy is so sensitive, and I'm so horny, that I know it won't take long for me to climax. Luckily, I have a partner who knows how to please me. I need this release. This morning, I was too lonely to jack off.

I don't want him to pull out, but he does after three or four post-cum thrusts. His fingers tweak my clit. I grab a fist full of rug, body temperature rising and ears ringing. My muscles spasm, and I wish I could cum with him inside me.

It takes a couple minutes for my thigh muscles to relax enough to straighten my legs. Nat lies on the floor beside me, waiting for me to catch my breath, and runs a finger slowly over my collarbone.

"You missed me this morning, eh?" he says, kissing my shoulder. "I just showed you how much I missed you. How about we go upstairs and you demonstrate how much you missed me?"

"Oh?" I smile. "Round two. You're going to be tired when you get to the airport."

His finger moves to my breasts, making circles around each nipple. "I really don't give a fuck."

I smile before taking off toward the stairs, him in pursuit.

Chapter 6

Holy Fuck

July 16, 2005

Jason's best man, his brother Jim, and I are the first people to exit the church into the sweltering afternoon. I wish Nat escorted me down the aisle, but I'm the matron-of-honor and he sits beside Phil with the other bridesmaids' husbands and boyfriends. Jim and I are supposed to focus straight ahead until the photographer gets his precious shot, but I can't help turning and flashing Nat a quick smile.

Nat wasn't originally supposed to be here. It's concert festival season. That means Nat's gone every weekend, often longer depending on the location of the festivals and how many nights Dramatic Sneezer plays. Not this year, through no fault of their own. Jerome's wife, Cassidy, gave birth to their son, Jaylon, three months early. Jerome was planning on being gone for a few months, starting in late August, and a replacement bassist was lined up, but he wasn't able to do it any earlier than what he was contracted for. We can survive for a few months financially, but this hurts, especially because it was unplanned. You'll probably never hear me say this again, but I wish Nat were on the road.

I'm pleased to see the Muellers showed up for Shawna's wedding, but Jason's side of the church dwarfs hers. I let go of Jim's arm and stand in the yard while the rest of the bridal party emerges. It includes Phil's wife, Jennifer, and our friends Jen Hernandez, Jenny Albrecht, and Tiffany Petrova.

Jen married Mike in 2003 and runs a daycare in her house. Tiffany's been living with Dennis for eight years. They are neither planning marriage nor popping out babies. They simply co-exist. And Jenny? You'll find out when she opens her mouth.

Shawna and Jason picked this 200-year-old church, situated in the countryside near the Wisconsin border, because it's old, quaint and picturesque. It makes for a romantic atmosphere and will look fantastic in the photos we took before the ceremony.

By the time Nat exits, a crowd has formed in the churchyard and he doesn't immediately spot me. Other than Phil and Mike, he knows only my friends, and I watch him linger on the church steps, scanning the crowd. A smile appears when we lock eyes.

"Ugh," Jenny says as Nat elbows his way through the crowd, "haven't you grown tired of your husband yet? You act like a couple who just fell in love."

I turn and notice a look of disgust. Jenny was my best friend before I met Shawna in sixth grade, but we drifted apart after she married Derek, the only guy she ever dated, following high school graduation and traveled overseas with him to support his army career. They divorced in 2002, around when Nat and I were heating up, and she's never gotten over it, gets bitchy about life if you get her going. She has four-and-a-half-year-old twin boys, but the best description for her isn't "doting mother" but "bitter divorcee."

I smile, hoping to keep things light. "No. I'll never get tired of him. We click so well. We fit together like two puzzle pieces, like tongue and groove, like a wiener in a hot dog bun."

Her scowl deepens. "You do realize all your references are sexual, right?"

"I can love him and lust after him at the same time."

She shakes her head. "You're the weirdest couple I've ever met."

"Hi, Jenny," Nat says, reaching us. "If you excuse me, I'd like to borrow my lovely lady for a bit."

She forces a smile. "Sure. She is *your* lady."

He takes me by the elbow, and we walk toward the church steps.

Once we're out of earshot, Nat says, "You look so sexy in that dress. I couldn't concentrate during the ceremony. I was focused on you and how much I want to fuck you."

"Oh, yeah?" I say, trying to sound casual.

We aren't fancy people, but Nat looks really hot in his suit. I mean hot as in sexy, but also literally hot because it's, like, 90 degrees. I'm not a huge fan of satin, but temperature-wise I'm okay. Shawna, knowing it could be sultry, selected short gowns for her bridesmaids and a dress for herself with a skirt that zips off at the knee.

The bride and groom appear in the church doorway, pause a few seconds then descend. Nat and I join the guests throwing birdseed on the happy couple. When Shawna and Jason mingle with the crowd, we go back inside the church.

The moment we're inside, Nat kisses me. I respond by wrapping my arms around his neck and rubbing against him. He pushes me against the wall, pulling up my skirt and running his hand up my thigh.

"You're not wearing any underwear?!" he says, breath shallow.

I smile. "I was going to surprise you at the reception or on the drive home. I thought you might like it."

His eyes widen. "Like it? I fucking love it."

I gasp when his fingers part my pussy lips. Grabbing the back of his jacket, I slip a hand down the back of his pants.

"Let's find someplace private," he says, two fingers gliding in and out. "I'm fucking hard. I won't be able to wait until later."

I'm wet and sticky, so it's not as if I can wait either. I nod, moaning slightly from the finger fuck.

He withdraws his fingers, takes my hand and leads me to the altar where a door, hidden from the congregation by a faux wall, stands to the right of the church. On the other side of the door is a small room with an open closet, a desk and a bookcase. There's a window, but it's stained glass. No one outside would be able to see us. This'll work!

Nat takes off his jacket, throws it on the back of the desk chair and pushes the chair aside. I lean against the desk, toss my head back and give what I hope is a seductive look. Separating my feet, I lift one leg.

He kneels and uses his tongue to make me squirm.

"Fuck me," I say, pulling my dress to my waist.

Oh, fuck, I can't stand it. He rises to his feet and drops his pants. I grab his cock and stroke.

"I'm going to fuck you," he says, "because you deserve to be fucked."

I recline on my elbows, he leans into me and we both whimper when cock enters pussy. My feet, still in my orange strappy heels, press against the back of his thighs.

After several thrusts, my arms hurt and I'm forced to lie on papers and a calendar, shoulders sandwiched between a plant on one side and a pencil cup and a picture frame on the other. Damn it, is that a pen poking my back? A letter opener?

His dick rubbing my clit, I squirm and try to maintain eye contact, to watch his expression while he fucks me, but my eyes snap shut.

I feel his weight on my abdomen and open my eyes to see his face inches from mine. We make eye contact, our hot breath intermingling for several minutes before our lips touch. His tongue stifles a moan, and, still squirming every time his cock rubs my button, I clench his shirt.

I'm supposed to be riding with the rest of the wedding party to the reception hall in Chicago, probably right now. I don't give a shit about schedules. I'd rather fuck Nat.

He must read my thoughts because after four vigorous thrusts, he cums and I moan even with his tongue in my mouth.

Our lips part and, cheek to cheek, I laugh.

He lifts his head. "What's so funny?"

"Gotta love spontaneity."

"Did I do a good job fucking you?" he says, grinning.

"Always," I say, grabbing his ass and squeezing my pussy muscles around his cock until he groans.

Holy shit, someone is coming! The sound of footsteps grows increasingly closer. Nat withdraws, hurriedly pulls up his pants and grabs his jacket. I pull down my skirt and put the chair back. The minister enters the room, gasping when he sees us.

"Um, we were looking for the restrooms," I say, hoping the fact we're both disheveled and sweaty doesn't give away what we were doing.

"This is my office," the minister says. "The restrooms are downstairs."

He gives us directions. We thank him and get the hell out.

When we re-emerge outdoors, Shawna, Jason and most of the guests are gone. The wedding party waits on the side of the church.

"Oh, there you are," Jennifer says when I join them. "We wondered where you went. Where have you been?"

Cum rolls down my inner thigh. "Um, Nat and I got hot and … went for a walk."

Jenny glances at me but says nothing. I wonder what she's thinking. Has she figured it out?

"Why is your hair and makeup messed up?" Jennifer says, squinting. "Oh, never mind. You can fix it in the limo on the way to the reception. Are you ready to go?"

"Yeah, give me a minute."

I walk to Nat who stands too close for comfort to Phil for what I'm about to do.

"Your fly is down," I say, putting my hand on Nat's crotch and pulling up his zipper.

Chapter 7

Does the Apple Fall Far?

September 30, 2005

My parents are here. As in visiting. As in annoying me. I love my parents, but why do they want to spend part of Dad's vacation in Vienna-on-the-Lake? I already have a headache. That's not a figure of speech either. My temple throbs.

"You know we wouldn't have to stay in a hotel if your guest bedroom actually was set up for guests," Dad says before taking a sip of his steaming coffee. "Why do you need an entire room for a computer?"

A couple months ago, my agent found a publisher for my book, but it'll be months before I see one cent of my advance. I haven't told my parents I've been writing for the past year and a half because I don't want to hear their disapproval. I may never tell them, especially if sales of my book fall flat. They'll continue to think I'm a stay-at-home mom, which pleases them anyway because it's traditional and balances Nat's "nontraditional" job that they're convinced is destined to fail.

"Yes, well, we have no where else to put it," I say, rubbing my throbbing temple.

"I wish Nat were here," Mom says, not because she cares but because she doesn't like the idea of Megan and me alone. "It was nice he was home for a few weeks, since you have no idea what he's doing when he's away."

I glance at our wedding photos on the wall. There are two. One taken after our elopement in Las Vegas and one from our formal wedding six months later. Does Mom think we're independently wealthy or something and don't have to worry about expenses? The band can never make up festival dates.

"He's paying the bills. That's what he's doing. Touring pays the bills. Recording not so much."

In the middle of the great room, Megan attempts to build something with her Duplo blocks on the coffee table and fails because what does a 20 month old know about engineering?

She hands one of the bricks to Dad. "Papou, one."

Dad sits on the couch and starts arranging blocks into the base of a tower. "Are you teaching Megan the language?" he says.

When my siblings and I were kids, we took Greek lessons in our grandparents' kitchens and sometimes at home. Greg knows the language better than the rest of us, because he's anal that way, but I know enough to understand my relatives or gossip about people.

I shake my head. "No, I haven't even thought about it."

I've been so preoccupied with my writing and Nat's career – not to mention taking care of a toddler, the pets and the house – that it hadn't entered my mind, not even in passing.

Dad continues building the block tower and doesn't look up. "You'll send her to Greek school, I hope. She may only be 50 percent, but it's important to keep our traditions alive and pass them down to the next generation."

"We didn't go to Greek school, and we learned the traditions just fine."

"You were surrounded by family, and you didn't go to Greek school because Sterling has no Orthodox church. You're in Chicago now. There will be Greek schools."

Mom says nothing. She sips her coffee as if nothing is going on. She agrees, of course. I know her well.

"We're in Chicagoland," I say. "There's no Orthodox church in Vienna-on-the-Lake either. I'm not driving 45-plus minutes in heavy traffic just so Megan can take a one hour class once a week."

Dad glances at me, not pleased. "You will teach her then."

"I'm not a teacher. I don't have the patience for it."

"You have to teach her. It's part of her heritage."

I sigh, convinced a lecture is brewing about Nat being distantly related to Hitler if you go back far enough.

"I'll give the Germans credit for one thing," Dad says. "They have a strong work ethic, as do we. Vanessa married an Irishman and what do they have a reputation for? Leprechauns and Guinness."

Um. That's a compliment. I guess. He could have said sloth and drunkenness.

"There's nothing wrong with Guinness," I say, hoping my parents don't see the six pack in the refrigerator.

Dad doesn't say anything, continuing to build the Duplo tower with Megan. I exhale, hoping this conversation is over before my temple explodes. I should take something but if I can't lie down afterward, it won't do a damn bit of good.

Mom sits next to Dad, and Megan hands her a block.

"Yiayia, one."

I take advantage of the quiet to prepare fruit for Megan's snack.

"Megan is so skinny," Mom says. "When you were that age, you were so chubby the pediatrician told us to stop giving you whole milk or else you'd get fat."

I swallow and suck in my stomach. My family is very keen to remind me that I was a large baby – by 1970s standards anyhow – and that no one saw a baby that big before. I was very self-conscious about my girth when I was pregnant, and I'm pleased to be a size 2 again, so the last thing I need is a reminder that I was once fat.

"Well, then we're blessed Megan won't have that issue," I say, taking a Big Bird plate out of the cupboard.

"She took after the Hardwicks," Mom says. "Genetics was good to her in that respect. She is short compared to other kids, though. She inherited that from you both."

I don't say anything, hoping that if I ignore them, maybe when I look up, they'll be back in Sterling. I glance up. Damn. No such luck.

"Planning anything special for Nat's birthday next month?" Mom says, impressing me by actually knowing when his birthday is. "How old will he be?"

But she can never remember his age.

"Twenty-nine."

"Twenty-nine." She tilts her head. "You're both still young. Planning on having more babies?"

I narrowly miss my finger while slicing an apple. My parents have issues with their sons-in-law's professions and their ethnic backgrounds, but they love their grandchildren. Maybe too much.

But really, why the fuck does everyone keep asking us if we're having more children? Clearly, I am not Fertile Myrtle or else I would have conceived Megan sooner and probably had a second one by now.

I shake my head. "I don't know."

"There are pros and cons to everything. I had you and your siblings over 10 years, but it got harder as I went. I encourage you to have yours closer together. You'll have more energy, and they'll have playmates. That's what Maroula plans to do."

"Thanks, Mom," I say, forcing a smile and giving Megan her cubed apple before sitting on the chair Nat and I fucked on the back of on Megan's birthday.

Megan takes an apple and smiles as she holds it up. "Mommy, one."

"Yes, Sweetie. One."

Megan climbs onto my lap and makes herself comfortable. I hold her waist and glance at my parents. Am I going to turn into them, I wonder. I said I wasn't going to end up like Mom. She married a guy who's gone all the time and I didn't want that, but here I am a part-time single parent. I said I wasn't going to end up like Vanessa, marrying a creative man who is not her type, but I did. They say the apple doesn't fall far from the tree. If that's even remotely true, Lord help me.

Megan reaches forward for another apple bite.

"Katrina is a lovely young woman," Mom says, sipping her coffee. "You really should meet her."

I purse my lips. "Why haven't I met her?"

Greg proposed to Katrina, the mystery woman whom I'm still not convinced exists. To avoid the shame, I wouldn't put it past him to make up a woman to counterbalance the rumor I made up about him being gay.

"You haven't both been in Sterling at the same time."

Mom stayed clear of the Greek school conversation, and Dad seems to be sitting this one out. He's fiddling with the Duplo blocks as if they are extremely important. He probably hasn't met Katrina either.

"Where does Katrina live?" I say.

"Addison. Do you know where that is?"

"Addison," I say, clenching Megan as she lunges forward to tap Big Bird's nose on her plate. "That's in DuPage County. Why haven't I met her if she's in DuPage County?"

Mom looks shocked. "Oh, you do know where it is? I had to look it up on a map. The wedding and reception will both be in Naperville."

Did she need to look that up on a map, too? I resist the urge to roll my eyes.

"Naperville? Why not Sterling?"

"Weddings are held in the bride's home. But I wouldn't expect you to know that, considering the circumstances behind your marriage."

Ah, yes, the circumstances. They're never going to let me forget it.

Mom smiles. "You're really going to like her."

I highly doubt it. If she loves Greg, something's got to be seriously wrong with her. I bet it's going to be a really boring wedding. I mean, incredibly boring. I might fall asleep boring.

Chapter 8

Do It To Me

November 15, 2005

"Tell me what you would do to me?" Nat says over the phone.

Wearing only an open robe, I lean against the headboard and spread my legs. When we first started having phone sex, I felt like a 1-900-number operator, saying the words while trying to control my laughter, then I learned what it was like to be involved with a guy who's away from home. That forced me to get good at it.

"Well," I say, trying to sound sexy. "I would strip you naked and kiss you all over, starting at your neck and working my way down. Slowly. When I reach your chest, I suck both nipples, tweaking each with my tongue. Then I continue lower, lower, until I reach your waist and then."

I pause and stick the middle finger of my free hand into my pussy.

"And then?" he says.

"And then I sink to my knees and kiss your inner thighs. My hands massage your balls. I kiss those, too. I stick your dick in my mouth and suck. I move my tongue along the head, focusing on the sensitive spot like you like it."

"My cock is hard," he says in a way that makes me think he means in reality, not fantasy.

"What would you do to me?"

"When I can't take it any more, I help you stand then kiss you. Then I push you onto the bed and eat your pussy until you squirm, your back arching. Then I stick my cock inside you and start fucking you. You're moaning. It feels so good."

His voice is breathy, and I envision him jacking off.

I watch my finger disappear and reappear in my wet pussy, wishing it were his dick.

"Go on," I say, letting out a moan.

He groans. "I love the feel of your pussy hugging my cock. I want to fuck you all night."

Oh, I think my pussy grew wetter. I grin at the thought of fucking him all night. I shift my body, feet propped up on the headboard.

"I'm moaning so loud and your dick is soooo hard. It's felt fantastic before, but tonight it's the best cock I've ever fucked. I hold you close, my arms around your back as you—"

I hear something in the hallway. Stomping. Giggling.

"As I what?" he says, groaning.

"I, uh." I lift my head. "I think Megan is in the hallway."

"What?"

He sounds confused. Not that I blame him. I reluctantly pull my finger out and sit.

"I'll go investigate and call you back. Finish if you need to."

"I need to finish," he says, barely able to speak, "but call me back."

I hang up and toss my phone on the covers. Goddamn the timing. I open the bedroom door, and sure enough Megan runs up and down the hallway in her Rosita Monster pajamas. She likes Rosita because Rosita plays the guitar like Nat does. I guess at Megan's age it's a huge discovery to learn someone else can play the guitar, too, never mind all Nat's siblings can, but I'm getting off the point. If I don't stop her running, she could accidently fall down the stairs.

"What are you doing?"

Megan looks at me but doesn't stop. "Mommy. Run."

"No. Now is not the time to run. It's bedtime. It's sleepy time."

She doesn't stop. Wait until she's in school gym class She'll hate running. I block her and pick her up.

"Mommy, run."

My robe is still agape, and she bumps some uncomfortable areas while struggling to escape my grasp.

"No, run. Sleep."

I carry her into her room and turn on the white-noise machine. We have been trying to wean her off it, so she won't rely on it once she's in a toddler bed, but tonight I need something to lure her off to sleep as quickly as possible. I lay her in the crib and hand her a favorite stuffed animal.

"Go to sleep, Megan. Mommy is going to bed. I'm very sleepy."

I fake a yawn, hoping it'll give her the hint. They say yawns are contagious, and sure enough she yawns a few seconds later.

I run my hand over her forehead and head a few times. Maybe she'll have ringlets like Vanessa and I do when we have hair longer.

"Shush, it's bedtime. Time to sleep."

Megan yawns again and, satisfied she'll stay in her room, I return to my bedroom.

I dial Nat. He doesn't answer, and I know he's cumming without me. I open the nightstand and pull out the fake cock. It's not the one my ex-boyfriend bought me in college. No, this one Nat and I picked out together. There wasn't anything wrong with that other one. Replacing it was symbolic. I sit on it and pump, pretending it's Nat's cock and we're in female superior. My phone rings.

"What happened?" he says.

"Megan climbed out of bed and was running around. I got her tucked in again. Did you cum?"

"I did. I'm sorry. It couldn't wait. Now what are you doing?"

"I'm fucking fake cock pretending it's yours."

"What would you do to me?" he says, continuing the fantasy.

No, not continuing, changing. When we last visited the fantasy, he was on top.

"I've straddled you and sat on your cock, and now I'm moving my pussy up and down on your hard dick."

"I'm moaning and groaning. I grab your ass and hold on. I know you love it when I thrust while you're on top. So I do that for as long as I can."

I pump faster on the fake cock, close my eyes and try to imagine Nat beneath me. "I'm ready to cum."

Since I only have two hands, and need three, I pull off of the fake cock, lie on my back and start rubbing my clit in tiny circles.

Nat talks in my ear, but I no longer comprehend what he's saying. I merely know it's his voice, turning me on more than I already am.

I quickly cum, breathing his name, and insert my finger back into my pussy. Maybe next time I'll put him on speaker phone so I can continue riding the fake cock.

"Did you cum?" he says. "Next time I see you I'm going to give you the largest, most mind-blowing orgasm you've ever had."

"Looking forward to it. I miss your hard cock. I miss you."

"You know I hate being away from you, right? But we both knew this going in. You accepted what I do for a living, and I love you for it."

Whoa, things got serious all of a sudden.

I close my legs and sit. "Yeah, I know. Music is your life, and I would never interfere with that."

"Yeah, but there must be times you wish we had a normal marriage, didn't need to have phone sex because we're in the same bed, that we weren't in different cities and time zones and countries all the time."

I clench the phone. Well, of course, I daydream about those things, cry about them from time to time. I don't want him to miss Megan's milestones or incur my parents' ire, but until they invent the *Star Trek* transporter, this is our lot in life.

"Where is all this coming from?" I say, purposefully avoiding his last comment.

"I dunno. Maybe Megan getting out of bed. Maybe you saying my name."

"Jesus, how much did you drink after the show tonight?"

"Not enough, apparently."

All attempts at deflection failing, I say, "Of course, I want you home, but that's not how our life works. If you had an office job or something, you'd be home, but it would kill you on the inside."

He doesn't respond immediately. "You're right, but I want to be with you right now, to hold you in my arms and take in your scent."

The cum induced high crashes and now I'm depressed. My chest tightens, and I don't know how to get us out of this. I sob, releasing weeks of pent up loneliness and private heartache, and for a second, just a second, I think I hear him crying. For his sake, I hope he's too drunk to remember this in the morning, but I won't forget. I can't. I won't be able to sleep again tonight.

Chapter 9

If There Ever Was an Excuse to Drink

April 7, 2006

Traditional, colorless and boring. That's my brother's personality, so I wasn't expecting Katrina to be incredibly interesting. We have nothing in common that I've been able to discover, but I only met her yesterday. Yesterday! I finally meet this chick after hearing about her since January of last year and, well, is there a word stronger than "unimpressed"?

Like Greg, Katrina is fanatical about traditional. She doesn't listen to music composed before 1900. She dresses modestly. She doesn't question anything, curse, drink – not even a toast at New Year's. She's still living at home, like a good Greek girl should, which means she's probably a virgin. I'm guessing Greg is, too, although I never asked him. I'm not going to either.

Oh, God, can you picture the wedding night? The 29- and 34-year-old virgins. The awkwardness. The consulting sex manuals for tips. Only fucking after dark with the lights off.

I'm pretty sure Katrina doesn't like me. She judges me based on who knows what? The fact I moved away from home and, gasp, lived alone? The fact I listen to metal? The fact I married a musician who performs the aforementioned metal? The fact he's not a nice Greek boy? The fact I was pregnant when I got married? The fact I refuse to drive my daughter 45 minutes to attend Greek school? Okay, she has lots of things to judge me by.

Thank God, it won't be a dry wedding. I'm going to need a shot or six of ouzo after this and maybe a stiff whiskey. And a stiff cock wouldn't hurt either.

Greg doesn't have friends. He's allergic to them. And Katrina may not either. Chris will be best man, Vanessa and I will be bridesmaids, and Megan and Kendra will be flower girls. Because what can go wrong entrusting two, two-year-olds with a basketful of stuff they're supposed to throw around?

Tonight is the rehearsal dinner. People giving speeches. Won't we get enough speeches tomorrow? With a far-off expression, Mr. Franopoulos, Katrina's father, reminisces about his baby girl. Everyone's eyes are on him, except mine.

I lean toward Nat, placing my hand on his thigh. "I'll bring my bikini and we can use the hotel hot tub," I say as low as possible.

We drove to Naperville today – it's two counties from home – but tomorrow we're staying in a hotel.

"We should get our own hot tub," he says. "Imagine the possibilities."

"I already have, but the HOA won't allow one. I checked."

"Damn. I'd love to see you naked in a hot tub."

I move my hand up his thigh. "I love to be naked. Doesn't matter where. Just so long as I'm with you."

We're about to kiss when Dad clears his throat. His expression tells me to quit it or else.

Megan bangs her sippy cup three times against the tray of her highchair.

"Owww," I say louder than intended when, on her fourth attempt, Megan bangs my elbow.

Mr. Franopoulos stops talking, and the audience turns its attention to me, the interrupter of this wistful speech about the perfect child.

I smile. "Sorry. She hit my funny bone. Continue please. It is such a lovely tribute to your dear daughter."

Greg shoots daggers with his eyes. What? A bit much?

Mr. Franopoulos continues speaking, and Megan continues banging until Nat picks her up.

"Daddy, juice," she says, holding her cup.

"Yes." He smiles. "Let's go look at the lobsters in the tank."

Nat carries her out of the restaurant's private room, leaving me to hear a boring tribute to a dull girl.

Mr. Franopoulos finally finishes and is awarded with polite applause.

Before anyone else can make a toast, dinner is served. Oh, thank God. I don't think I could take much more of this. We didn't have any of this shit at our formal wedding. We had a party, but Greg and Katrina don't party. They complain.

EYES WEARY, I CAN'T wait to get the hell out of here and get a good night's sleep. I stand, flush the toilet and exit the restroom stall.

"Oh," I say, laughing when I realize I nearly hit Katrina with the door, "I didn't know you were there."

She says nothing, doesn't laugh, doesn't do anything.

"Are you excited about tomorrow?" I say.

Her expression doesn't change. "It'll be good to get everything over with after a year of planning. You know what that's like. Oh, no, you don't. Sorry. Las Vegas, was it?"

I smile. "Yes, that's right. We eloped, had a great time."

"From what Gregorio tells me, you had a good time seven months before, too."

It takes every fiber of my being to keep the smile on my face. "Yes, well, Nathaniel and I are very much in love. Did Gregorio tell you that?"

She purses her lips. "I hope you and Vanessa teach your daughters not to make the same mistakes you did."

My temperature rises. "Megan can have as many unplanned pregnancies as she wants."

No, wait. That came out wrong. Really, really wrong. What I meant to imply was that she won't be judged for her choices.

Katrina squints. "Greg was right about you. You are a smart alec."

I clench the stall's handle. "I prefer the title 'smart ass.'"

"That's not something to be proud of."

What the hell has my brother been telling her about me? Jesus, he's more judgmental than I thought. If I get him alone, he better hope I control my temper because right now I have my doubts.

"Well, hello," Penny says, entering the restroom all smiles. "What a great time we're all going to have tomorrow. It's so exciting."

She's delusional.

I give Katrina one final glance then, avoiding eye contact with Penny, walk to the sink.

"Oh, yes," I say, turning on the water, "tomorrow is going to be great."

Katrina and Penny enter stalls, and I wash my hands.

"Oh, Cassandra," Katrina says, "I wasn't with you for the dress fitting, but I hope your rear won't be protruding too much tomorrow. I don't want men staring at it during the ceremony."

My rear protruding too much? What about Vanessa's or Maroula's or Persephone's? I turn to the side and examine the reflection of my ass. Round and high per usual. But so are theirs.

"Well, the Economos family is accustomed to my protruding rear. It's looked this way since I was 14 or so, so you must be worried about *your* side of the church. Your cousins maybe, or your brother. Does he love a nice piece of ass?"

I hear something other than urine coming from one of the stalls. Someone gasped.

"You leave my brother out of it," Katrina says. "He's a nice, upstanding gentleman like Greg, not a sex fiend like you, Vanessa, Chris and Phil."

Oh, holy shit. A toilet flushes. Penny emerges, face red when she joins me at the sink. Well, I see she is no longer delusional.

"You can love sex and still be a gentleman," she says.

A second toilet flushes.

"I don't see how," Katrina says. "That's not how I was raised. I don't believe that's how you were raised either."

She emerges from her stall, expression reminding me of a teacher about to reprimand her class.

I smile. "If you excuse me, my sex fiend gentleman husband and I have a toddler we need to get to bed or else she might throw a temper tantrum during the ceremony tomorrow."

Katrina shoots me a displeased glance, and I get my high, round protruding rear the hell out of here. Oh, yeah, tomorrow is going to be really fun.

APRIL 8, 2006

What can I say about the wedding? Let's start with the fact I was disappointed neither Megan nor Kendra threw a fit. I understand how terrible that sounds. Why would I want my brother's wedding ruined or interrupted? Three words: Greg and Katrina. After last night's comment, I changed the shoes I planned to wear with my bridesmaid's dress to ensure my ass looks as high and round as possible. I even changed my posture during the ceremony. Suck that tummy in and push that booty out. Nat'll thank me later.

The ceremony itself was traditional Greek Orthodox. Why would Greg and Katrina do anything else? I wonder what BS Greg told the Franopouloses, considering our family doesn't go to church. The closest ones are in Peoria or East Moline. I've been to maybe a handful of services my entire life. I bet he memorized the Lord's Prayer in Greek and told them he drives two hours, one way, every Sunday.

God forbid someone should get married in the afternoon. Otherwise, there wouldn't have been a lull of a few hours between the ceremony and the reception. My parents and aunts and uncles watched the grandkids, and we went to a bar for appetizers and drinks with Chris, Penny, Vanessa, Brandon, Maroula, Steve, Phil, Jennifer, and my other cousins who live in Illinois. We range in age from 25 to 39, and I don't hang out with them much anymore.

Mr. Franopoulos must have big bucks is all I can say. He rented out what must be the most prestigious restaurant in the city for the entire night, for as long as guests want to stay, for the reception. The joint's chic and fancy with huge, crystal chandeliers hanging from a 14 foot ceiling and foods on the menu that I've never even heard of. It puts Costas' Place to shame. It aggravates me when my old life in Sterling is put to shame. I'm not working class trash.

I'm feeling pretty good. That's what three – or is it four? – mixed drinks made with vodka will do. Nat drank I don't know how many beers imported from, from, I don't know, some damn place along with a shot or six of Jägermeister with Phil. I had some, too. It's, it's different. Megan is— Shit, where the hell is Megan? Nat, where the fuck is Megan? Oh, yeah, she's with the other kids in an area designated for them.

At least the happy couple hired a half way decent DJ who must be in charge of the music because neither Greg nor Katrina would select anything fun.

I clench Nat while we dance, stepping on his foot and laughing so hard I can barely see. He responds by spinning me in a circle like a fucking top. Oh, no, no, why did he have to do that? After a couple of twirls, my body stops but my head continues spinning. I fall, my hand in his, and nearly trip the couple dancing next to us with my foot.

He laughs and attempts to help me up, but he's so off balance I pull him to the floor.

"You're trying to fucking kill me," Nat says, grinning.

"You started it," I say, mumbling.

He stumbles a couple of times before getting up. He offers me both hands, which I take, and I try to stand, my feet slipping on the floor. Nat stumbles, bumping into another couple. I have no clue who they are. Someone from Katrina's side. Oops. I'm on my feet again. Phew. Heels can be tricky.

We lock eyes and dance. His hand moves to my ass and squeezes, and I press my body firmly into his. Uh, huh, knew he'd like it in this dress.

Someone clears their throat. Loudly. Oh, the bride and groom are beside us. Wow, I didn't know Greg dances. You have to be uninhibited to dance, and Greg's not uninhibited. So I guess that makes him inhibited. Hibited? Inhibitated?

Except they aren't dancing. They're scowling. Katrina's hand wraps around Greg's arm. They look so formal, like there's been no such thing as women's lib and it's 1900.

"Katrina's grandparents are here," Greg says. "So I have to ask you to fondle each other somewhere else."

"Fondle," I say to Greg. "That's a silly word. Fon-dle." I laugh then turn to Nat. "Honey, you should write a song called Fondle about a brother with a stick up his ass."

Nat laughs and squeezes both ass cheeks. I yelp and, feeling a bit tipsy, grab a fistful of his jacket and hold on.

Katrina's face reddens. "Please. They are in their 80s. They don't like public displays of affection. So either stop or go somewhere else. And I'm telling the bar you've both had too much."

I cross my eyes and stick out my tongue.

Greg's nostrils flare. "Don't make me call security on my own sister and brother-in-law."

I shake my head. "Okay, okay, you're no fun."

Nat and I leave the dance floor, arms around each other.

"He couldn't even bother to cut his hair," Katrina says to Greg behind our backs.

"Goddamn rock star," Greg says, but I can't hear the rest over the music and crowd.

Where the fuck are we supposed to go? We head toward the front door, although our table is on the opposite side of the venue, and exit the restaurant into the cold night. The air feels like a slap in the face. Plus, the sun already set, and the sky is nearly dark.

"Let's go sit in the car for a while," Nat says, struggling to retrieve the keys from his pocket. "They'll forget we exist by the time we go back in."

I haven't seen any of these cars before in my life. They all have Illinois license plates. How the fuck are we supposed to know which one is ours?

"Where is the car?" I say.

"Under a light?" he says pointing to a random parking lot light.

"Which one?"

There's, like, six of them, and the lights look even more alike than the cars. At least the cars come in different colors.

"Fuck if I know."

"Every wonder why Illinois is spelt so funny? Like why do we need two Ls and all those letters we don't pronounce?"

"Nope." He fishes the keys out of his pocket and stumbles, me stumbling with him. "But why the land of Lincoln? Lincolns are made in Michigan. The remote has a whatchamacallit, a radio signal in it, to find the car."

He outstretches his arm, and we stumble in the opposite direction of the building. A little red light comes on every time he presses a button on the remote.

I wrinkle my nose. "Don't ya have to point it away from yourself?"

He turns the remote and points it at the first car we see even though it isn't under a parking light. "Nope. Not ours."

After checking every car under every parking light, which is saying a lot because sometimes there are, like, 12 of them instead of six, we finally find our motor vehicle. Why do they call it motor vehicle? Are there non-motor vehicles? Whoa. Is that what a horse and buggy is?

When Nat unlocks the car, we let go of each other and quickly get inside, him on the driver's side, me the passenger. I shiver. I don't know how it's possible, but it's no warmer in here. In fact, it might be colder.

Nat reaches over, puts his hand on the back of my head and pulls my face toward his, sticking his tongue in my mouth. Woah, that made me dizzy, but if you think that's going to stop me from making out with my favorite man, then you don't know me very well. I grab the back of his jacket.

We move closer to each other. My knee bumps the gear shift. Shit, that hurts. His elbow hits the horn.

Beep!

Our lips part, and we're overcome by giggles.

He tugs on my floor length dress, and it seems as if he's been tugging for days yet only reaches my knees.

"In the battle between man and dress, dress wins," I say, pretending I'm a sports announcer.

"Jesus Christ, who designed this thing? Prudes of America? That's the union for the sexually repressed, ya know. Katrina's on the board of directors." He rubs my calf. "Help me out here."

I pull my skirt to my waist.

His hand moves up my leg. "Why the fuck did you wear underwear?"

"You don't want my pussy getting cold, do you?"

He tugs at the waistband, but my underwear doesn't budge because I'm sitting on it. Jesus, do I need to help him out with everything? Can he take his underwear off while sitting on it? I lift my hips and put him out of his misery by removing my thong and shoving it in his face. He grabs it and throws it on the dashboard.

I part my legs for him to finger fuck me, my knee pressing against the emergency brake, but he wants none of it.

"I need to fuck you," he says. "Get in the backseat."

I squeeze between the bucket seats, my ass briefly in his face. He slaps it with a laugh. I get in the back and move to the side, allowing him to follow.

"Well, come fuck me," I say, playing with myself.

Oooh, that feels good.

He pulls me to him, tongue once again in my mouth. I fumble with his belt and fly. Why do men guard their junk like it's gonna go somewhere without them like in King Missile's "Detachable Penis"? After some trouble, I get the belt unbuckled and unzip his fly, pushing down his pants.

"And why the fuck did *you* wear underwear?" I say, pushing it down to his knees and releasing hard cock.

I look down too quickly and, oh, fuck, my head spins. But what a beautiful sight. Actually, dicks are ugly as sin, but I love them. Nat's in particular.

I push and straddle him, my knees sandwiched between the car door and Megan's car seat, and slip my wet pussy on top of that lovely cock. The car seat won't budge.

He gasps. I pump with my hands on his shoulders. We lock eyes, although sometimes, if I focus too hard, he's got more of them than usual.

He clenches my ass like NBA players clench basketballs. I love it when his hands are all over my ass. I pump harder, and he groans. Once, twice, thrice, four times. I pump as quickly as I can, my moans echoing his groans. Megan's car seat digs into my skin. Oww. That's going to leave a mark.

It's a good thing the car windows fogged up, considering every once in a while someone walks past the back of the car. They can't see us, but they probably hear us.

After 15 or 20 minutes, I feel like I'm on an amusement park ride without Dramamine. Nat

slouches. This unpinches skin, but squishes his body between the front passenger seat and the back seat.

"Cum already," I say between moans. "Before we both leave this car stiff."

"You make me stiff."

He makes a weird half laugh, half groan and contorts his face before cumming. I continue pumping as the muscle contractions build before collapsing, out of breath, on him when they subside.

"Want to cum?" he says, fingering my clit.

Oh, I'd love to cum, but not here, not where I can't lie flat and spread my legs.

"At the hotel. I need to piss."

Nat caresses my hair. "I still want to see you in the hotel hot tub."

"And I want you to bend me over and fuck me from behind."

Shit, why didn't I think of that before? I could have sat on his dick instead of straddling him. I pull off. I think my bladder is about to explode.

He moans. "I like that image. How about fucking you from behind in the hot tub?"

I laugh. Not because what he said was funny, but because I bet Greg and Katrina would never have this conversation and they definitely wouldn't approve of quickies.

AFTER A BATHROOM PIT stop, we return to the reception and find wedding cake waiting at our seats. It's some weird white and chocolate combo thing that Persephone says is called a marble cake. I'm not sure marble cake exists in Sterling because I never heard of it.

Nat attempts to feed me a piece of cake off his fork and misses, smashing it against my cheek. We didn't even do the cake in the face thing at our own reception – it's fucking disgusting – so I should be pissed he smeared my makeup with icing. Or at least I would be pissed if I hadn't those four – or is it five? – vodka drinks. I laugh and try to dab some icing on his nose with my finger, but he grabs my wrist and kisses me.

"There you are?" Maroula says, approaching our table without me noticing. "Yiayia wants to take a picture of all the grandkids."

Mom wasn't kidding when she said Maroula planned to have her kids close together She's got 10-month-old Lucas, and she's six months pregnant with the next one. Not the next Lucas. This one's Atlas. I stare at her belly as if expecting the creature from *Alien* to pop out. She'll never fit back into a bikini, not that Maroula wears bikinis. She's a tankini gal.

"Greg and Katrina kicked us out for enjoying ourselves too much or something," I say.

Oh, look, I still have some cocktail left in my glass. I finish it.

"Well, if it makes you feel any better, almost everyone is drunk. This picture should only take a minute. You guys probably want to leave so you can go to bed."

Nat bursts out laughing, but I don't feel good. Drank that last bit too fast maybe. Oh, I really don't feel good. I think I'm going to— I cup my mouth, but it's too late. The contents of my stomach expel. Maroula shrieks, jumping back to save her shoes surprisingly quick for a pregnant woman.

Still laughing, Nat rubs my back. I can imagine Greg and Katrina looking down their noses. If they know what's happening, that is.

The puke stops. I take some deep breaths, then a swig of lukewarm water. Taking a couple more deep breaths, I wipe my cheek and mouth on a napkin.

Feeling a lot better, I stand and slap my palms on my thighs. "Okay, where is Yiayia?"

Maroula wrinkles her nose. "Don't you want to fix your makeup or anything?"

"Nope. If we're all drunk, we're all drunk."

Nat stands, too, his foot catching on the chair and nearly tripping him.

Maroula extends her arms. "How about Steve drives your car back to the hotel, and I drive ours? I wouldn't want you to end up arrested. Or dead."

"Did you know," Nat says, "Katrina is on the board of directors for Prudes of America?"

"No." My dumbfounded cousin shakes her head. "Come on. Yiayia is this way. Then we drive you back to the hotel, all right? Megan's probably cranky."

"Hot tub." Nat points at Maroula. "Can you watch Megan, so we can go to the hot tub?"

She nods. "Sure."

She'd say anything at this point to shut him up and get this picture out of the goddamn way.

Nat goes in the direction of the designated kid area to get Megan – I hope he can find it – while Maroula leads me to where the cousins wait. Yiayia waves a disposable cameras in her hand, posing everyone.

"Oh, Cassie, *koukla*," Yiayia says, kissing me on the cheeks.

Maroula stands nearby with a fake smile.

"You go stand by your brother," Yiayia says.

Christopher looks like he's two socks to the wind or whatever that fucking saying is. Please tell me she means Chris. Please.

"Chris?"

"No, no, Greg. Go on. We've been waiting for you."

I don't answer and squeeze through everyone.

"Jesus," Phil says, "you smell like vodka and puke. This is either the worst night of your life or it was totally awesome."

"About as totally awesome as when you porked Jennifer for the first time."

Vanessa shakes her head, briefly hiding her face with her hands. Persephone groans, also briefly hiding her face. Oh, maybe she doesn't know that story, about how her brother fucked my close friend one drunken night before they even had a first date. Oh, and judging from his expression Phil doesn't know that I know what I know.

I reluctantly take my place beside Greg and Katrina, purposefully ignoring them.

"You were gone long enough," Greg says. "I hope you and Nat took a long walk and sobered up a bit."

"We consummated your marriage for you."

Katrina, who had been focused on Yiayia, slowly turns her head. Greg eyes me, too, and I can't tell whether he thinks I'm serious or being a smart ass.

"That's disgusting," she says, "I wish the Naperville police found you and arrested you for lewd acts, and both you and your precious husband would need to register as sex offenders for the rest of your lives. See what that does for his career. Maybe he'd be home more often and get a real job."

Yiayia is too far away to hear, but everyone else can. I have two options: either start a cat fight, but she's bigger than me and would probably win, or lie. I already have enough wounds from the car and I don't want hot tub time ruined so...

I laugh. "You're so fucking gullible. Do you believe everything? You probably believe Elvis is still alive. Well, actually, he is still alive. He married us. Well, not you and me, but Nat and me. And it was aliens that crashed in Roswell. Or was it a weather balloon? We'll never know."

"Leave her alone," Greg says. "She's drunk, and you're letting her upset you. It's not worth it."

Yiayia claps her hands to get our attention, snapping the picture on three.

I see Nat walk toward us, Megan on his hip and her sleepy head on his shoulder. Oh, my God, it turns me on when he's being daddy.

"Are you jealous or something?" I say to Katrina before I can stop myself. "I mean, you just married my brother. You have a husband, yet you seem obsessed with mine."

She opens her mouth, shuts it, repeats. "What? Why would I be jealous of a man who's away from home so much, that looks like that – all scrawny with messy hair that needs cut – and who admires you with passion in his eyes?"

Nat flashes me a smile, his hair plastered from sweat to a section of his forehead.

"You just answered your own question. Because he admires me with passion in his eyes. Does Greg do that with you?"

I walk away before she can answer.

Chapter 10

Setting Them Straight

August 19, 2006

Megan bobs her head, curls bouncing, while jerking her fingers.

"What is she doing?" Mom says in a way that makes me think she's worried her granddaughter may be having an epileptic fit.

"She's imitating Nat when he sings. Or making fun of him. I'm not sure which."

"She needs a playmate. When are you having another baby?"

I exhale. Why don't people mind their own damn business? Men never get asked that question, but women do all the time. First it's "Do you have a boyfriend?" then it's "When are you getting married?" then it's "When are you having a baby?" and finally it's "When are you having another one?" Men never, <u>ever</u> get asked these questions. Irks the hell out of me.

Of course, Vanessa and I only had to endure the first question. After that it was "What are you thinking? He doesn't have a degree. He doesn't have a stable career. He doesn't... You're ruining your life." If that little girl in her Cookie Monster t-shirt ruined my life, I must be doing something right.

We congregate, along with Yiayia, Vanessa and Katrina, in Chris' backyard under a shady tree. Chris and Penny live outside Sterling city limits, so they have a decently sized yard that the kids run around in. The house even has air conditioning. Penny and Chris are inside cooking while Dad, Greg and Brandon drink Greek beers and discuss politics on the patio.

"We're neither planning nor preventing," I say, watching my daughter run off with Kendra.

"What does that mean?" Yiayia says. "If you're going to give me another great-grandchild, better do it before I die."

Vanessa answers for me. "It means that she's not using birth control and whatever happens happens."

"Why should I pump artificial hormones into my body when Nat isn't home that much?" I say, not wanting to get into how we came to our decision. "Waste of money, too."

Mom frowns. "That's the problem. He's barely home. He's cheating on you. I can guarantee it. Probably has a woman in every city."

"Jesus Christ, not this again." My cheeks grow hot as my temper rises. "Why do you think *he's* cheating? I could have a man coming in every night of the week for all you know."

She shakes her head. "No. You have Megan. And you're a woman."

"So let me get this straight. A man is expected to cheat when he's away from home, but a woman would never so much as think about cheating when she's home alone for weeks?"

"He has a penis, doesn't he?"

I refuse to answer. Mom's constant assertions that I'm being cheated on makes me wonder what Dad has been doing all these years on his business trips, and I really don't want those thoughts in my head.

I glance briefly at Katrina, who sits beside me, because I could have swore I saw her smirk. What does she care? I'm Greg's sister. She's not getting rid of me even if I would get a divorce, which I'm not. Mom has an overactive imagination. She says these things with no proof whatsoever other than Nat is a man. Double standard.

"Shawna had a girl," I say, trying to change the course of the conversation. "They named her Alyssa. She's larger than Megan was. More than eight pounds."

"What's her skin tone look like?" Yiayia says.

I think Shawna has a beautiful complexion. If it was anyone other than my 89-year-old grandmother, I'd call her racist, but I've heard all the comments before. The bullies in school called Shawna chocolate swirl. I've also overheard ignorant, cruel comments made about other biracial people. Sadly, asking about the baby's skin tone is a pretty benign, although she's at least three-quarters Caucasian. Why would she be darker than her mother?

"She looks white."

"That'll make it easier for her later in life."

Ugh, I think I just replaced one can of worms with another one.

My text message alert dings, and I take my phone out of my shorts pocket.

"What is it?" Mom says as if the message is intended for her.

"Nat texted me a picture of a car."

"Why?"

"Because he's at a car museum."

"Why?"

"Because that's where the whores hang out. Why do you think? Because he likes cars."

My phone dings again. Another photo. Him making a goofy face and giving a thumbs up.

"Let's see it," Katrina says, speaking to me for the first time since I stepped through the door earlier today.

Remember when I told her she was obsessed with my husband? Yeah. She isn't debunking that statement, now is she? More likely, she probably believes I'm lying about my message and thinks she's slyly calling me out on it.

I pass my phone around. I'm the only person in my family with a smartphone, and I resist the urge to giggle at how everyone holds the device as if it's made of thin ice.

"He needs a haircut," Yiayia says.

"I like it. I hope he grows it down to here," I say, putting my hand to the base of my neck.

"He'll look like a hippy. He looks young. How old is he?"

"Thirty," Mom says.

Why can't she ever remember how old Nat is?

I correct her. "Twenty-nine."

"No, he's three years older than you."

Unbelievable. My mother actually believes I don't know my own husband's age. I purse my lips. "No. I was born near the beginning of the year, and he was born near the end. For four and a half months, we're three years apart. The rest of the time, we're two."

She wrinkles her brow. "Are you sure? So what is it now?"

"Yesssss. Oh, my God." I briefly cup my forehead in my hand. "It's two. If I'm 27 and he's 29, then it's two."

I get my phone back as another text message comes through. It reads: *What r u doing?*

"Nessa, can you snap a picture of me with Megan, so I can send it to Nat?"

Vanessa smiles. "Sure, but you'll have to show me how."

I stand and walk away from the other women. Vanessa follows. Megan and Kendra play near the garden, pushing over rocks and poking rollie pollies with a stick.

"Megan, Sweetie, let's take a picture for Daddy."

I squat to Megan's level, and Vanessa takes the photo.

"Thank you," I say, taking the phone back. "I need to use the bathroom. Be back in a bit."

I make a beeline for the house. I don't really need to use the bathroom. I need an excuse no one will question to get away for a while. According to my family, I swear too much, drink too much, my skirts are too short, black nail polish is disgusting, and I'm going to poison myself putting blue highlights in my hair. I'm tired of their opinions.

When I approach the patio, I say hello to Brandon. The family softened their opinion of him since the move to Minneapolis and the gallery show. He's home every night with Vanessa and the kids. That's what matters most to them, I think.

Dad and Greg sit at the picnic table, so engrossed in their conversation that they don't acknowledge me. I enter the kitchen through the sliding glass door, and something delicious assaults my nostrils.

"Dinner's nearly done," Penny says with a smile.

"That is," Chris says, "if you still like souvlaki and pilaf. Nowadays, I know you prefer bratwurst and sauerkraut."

A bottle of ouzo sits on the counter. I pour myself a shot and drink it.

My brother's face reddens. "Whoa, whoa. Take it easy. I was just razzing you. I don't care what nationality he is. I really don't. He could be a Martian for all I care. Mom giving you a hard time again? She'll get over it."

"It's been four years. When is she going to get over it?"

"It's been 13 years with Vanessa and Brandon, and Mom and Dad still hope he'll find a real job."

"Great. That's really encouraging."

This entire situation reminds me why I don't return often to Sterling.

I'm tempted to take another shot when my phone dings. The text reads: *My hottie & her mini me. Miss u. XO*

"Where is your hubby?" Penny says as if she knows who the message is from.

"They play Nashville tonight. He's at the National Corvette Museum in Kentucky right now."

"You've always been strong willed," Chris says, ignoring what's just been said. "I never knew our parents' opinions bother you."

I return my phone to my pocket. "They can think what they want. I just don't know why I have to hear about it all the time."

"Well, then you have to find a way to make them stop. Hey, I like the guy. He enjoys food, even if he is all of 100 pounds."

"Ha, ha."

Like I haven't heard all the skinny *and* short jokes before. Dumb joke aside, my brother does have a point. But what can I say to my parents that Vanessa hasn't already said about Brandon?

"What's Mom been saying this time?" Chris says, moving the liquor bottles to a different counter.

"She keeps insisting Nat's cheating on me. She's been saying this for years."

Penny grimaces. "That's awful. Why would she do that, Chris?"

My brother shrugs. "I don't know. Paranoia. If you haven't noticed, our mother worries and over the years it's gotten worse, and I think she says these things as if they're perfectly normal."

It's true. Mom has gotten worse. It started years ago when she shared caregiver duties of their parents with Thea Ilena (Persephone, Phil and Maroula's mother). It only intensified after my grandparents passed away. Maybe she needs therapy or something.

"Has Dad?" I say to Chris. "Has he done something to make Mom distrustful?"

Chris thinks for a minute. "Not that I know of it, but it isn't like they'd share something like that with me. Ask her. But you might not want to know once you do."

I shake my head. "No, that's okay. I wondered because she doesn't insist Brandon is cheating. Anyway, I said I was going to the bathroom, so I better get out there."

I leave the house, casting a suspicious glance at Dad when I pass the picnic table. Brandon says hello, but Dad and Greg still don't notice me, absorbed in their insistence that the country wouldn't be in Iraq now had Dukakis won in '88.

MIDWAY THOUGH DINNER, my phone dings three times. *At the venue. It's a nice dressing room. Wish u were here.* A selfie Nat took in a mirror accompanies the third text. It is definitely not family friendly, and I feel a twinge between my legs. Damn, I miss him.

"I feel sorry for you," Mom says because I must not look happy enough or something. "You deserve a man who is with you every day."

Now that's ironic, isn't it, considering Dad was on business trips for most of their marriage? Would she like it better if Nat worked in a warehouse picking orders like he did before he was able to support himself with music? I don't think so.

I give her a steely glare. "I support him in his career and he supports me in mine. That was in our wedding vows, remember?"

Dad laughs. "What career? You gave it up the moment you got married. The career you had been harping about and planning for for years. Makes no sense."

I direct my steely glare to him. "HR was a means to an end. It got me to Chicago – sort of. I've been writing. I wrote a novel. It came out last month."

There's an expression of surprise on most of the faces at the picnic table. Vanessa knew I wrote short stories when I was a teenager, but she didn't know I continued.

"You wrote a book?" Dad says slowly. "Can I read it?"

"No."

Dad laughs again. "Then how do I know you wrote a book if you don't let me read it?"

"It's erotica." I wag my finger. "You're not reading it. No one in this family is reading it."

All the adults, except for maybe Yiayia, know what that means. There are a variety of reactions. Katrina covers her face with her hand as if she can't bear looking at me. Greg looks like he's going to shit his pants. Hilarious.

I ignore them. "When Nat comes home next month, we're going to celebrate. Do you know why? Because he's proud of me and my accomplishments, and I'm proud of his. And you know what else? I started working on a second book. I enjoy it, and I'm going to keep on writing them."

Mom says, "We only want what is best for you."

"The type of man you aspire for me to have, I don't want. The type of man I wanted when I was younger, I don't need. I have the man I both want and need. The sooner you accept that and get over it, the better. Without complaint or judgement."

No one says anything for a moment.

"That's exactly what I want," Vanessa said. "Only I've wanted it for nearly a decade longer than you have."

"You got pregnant at 19," I say. "At least I waited."

"I was with Brandon for two years when Noah was born. You and Nat were shacking up after four months. You call that waiting? What were you waiting for? The next sunrise?"

Greg shakes his head and sighs. "You both fell in love with creative guys, okay. Bravo. Move on. You realize you're competing to see who is the bigger disappointment?"

"Shut up, Greg," Nessa and I say in unison.

"I have to say," Chris says, "that it's you, Cassie. You're the winner. Erotica. Holy shit."

I feel something tug on my arm.

"Mommy, I have to go potty," Megan says.

"Okay, Sweetie," I say, smiling. "Let's go to the bathroom."

I stand, take her hand and go inside. The moment I close the sliding glass door, debate erupts at the table. Who knows what the fuck they are discussing? Something I said no doubt, but what? The book or my instance they accept Nat as he is?

"Think Cookie Monster likes baklava," I say when we pass the dessert sitting on the kitchen counter.

Megan smiles. "Uh, huh. He eats yummy stuff."

"So does Daddy," I say, trying to figure out how I can take a pussy pic and text it to him.

We enter the downstairs half bath, and I help Megan sit on the toilet. It's so nice having a potty trained child, made my life so much easier. I briefly wonder what's being said behind my back, but focusing on "no more diapers" gives me less of a headache.

"All done," she says.

"Good job, Sweetie."

I lift Megan off the seat, and she flushes. I pick her up so she can wash her hands and look at myself in the mirror. There's a fiery expression in my eyes.

"Mommy needs to do something," I say, setting her down. "Wait outside the bathroom for me. Don't move. Wait for me before you go back outside. Can you do that?"

She nods. "Yes."

"Good."

I open the door, locking it behind Megan after she leaves the bathroom. If I can figure out how to make myself tall enough, I can use the mirror above the sink for my pussy pic.

I take off my shorts and thong and kneel on the counter. If I take the picture this way, it'll only capture my pussy lips. Not a bad shot, but not a great one either. If I sit on the counter, there won't be any pussy in the photo. There is a third option: a squat. Oooh, perfect. I squat, separate my pussy lips with my free hand and snap the photo.

Send. Yes, Nat will enjoy that. I look at the photo he sent me, a dick shot, and wish I had time to jack off. Yeah, I know. You're probably wondering how I can be horny on a day like today. Let me put it this way. Nat went back on tour two days after Greg's wedding, so it's been ages since I had a fuck.

I carry Megan when I go outside. Maybe this will remind everyone that when they critique, say terrible things about her father, she can not only understand but remember.

No one says anything for a second.

"Hey," Chris says, "Katrina would love to read your book."

She gasps, putting her hand on her chest and looking as if she's about to leap over the table and strangle him.

"Yes, by all means," I say. "You might learn something."

"How dare you?" Katrina says, standing. "You're both perverts. Degenerates."

She stalks off into the house.

"Jesus, Greg," Chris says, "what have you been doing with her? Maybe you need to learn something, too."

I start singing, "Greg and Katrina sitting in a tree. K-I-S-S-I-N-G."

"I hate you both," Greg says before following his wife into the house.

Chris and I laugh.

"Mommy," Megan says. "What's K-I-S-S-I-N-G and why do you do it in a tree?"

We laugh even harder. Others join in this time, and we even get a smirk out of Yiayia.

Chapter 11

Published Author

S eptember 27, 2006

Nat beams at our waiter. "My wife wrote a book."

The waiter says something before leaving with our order, but I'm so focused on the man across the table that I don't comprehend a word.

"You don't need to keep telling people that," I say, smiling and taking Nat's hand.

He squeezes mine. "Why not? I'm proud of you."

"That's very sweet of you, but not everyone would agree."

He shakes his head. "I don't care what ignorant people have to say. I hear it all the time in the music industry, too. People think it's easy, that anyone can do it. They fail to see all the work that goes into it behind the scenes."

"I know. I've learned so much about the industry because of you. I suppose I wasn't thinking about people in general. Specifically, I was thinking about my family. Me publishing this book exposes the fact that I have tons of sexual experience."

He chuckles. "Who cares? They say to write about what you know."

Well, that's true, but there are two ways to know things: through your own experiences and through someone else's. My own experiences are pretty limited. I had a strict upbringing, went to school, got a job, fell in love and had a kid. Those aren't very interesting topics to write about. All that remains is my high sex drive.

"I'll go months, maybe even years, without thinking about how rigid the rules were growing up then, bam, I'll feel ashamed about something. It's weird. I guess that stuff's always in my subconscious."

"You can't let it bother you. You're not writing for your family. You're writing for you and for people who like reading erotica. That's it and that's all. I'm going to keep telling people you wrote a book. I want people to know it exists so they'll buy it."

I straighten my back. "That makes two of us. A $7,000 advance is great as a chunk of change, but it won't pay off the mortgage."

Nat's eyes widen. "You want to pay the house off?"

"That is a goal, yes."

He laughs. "Patience. You gotta have it in the creative fields. Look at Brandon. Took him 15 years or something like that to really start to make money off his art."

"1 know." I squeeze his hand. "I really wish you were home more, but I know that can't happen unless I make a significant contribution to the family finances."

"No pressure, right?" He smiles. "I'm going to focus on the here and now. I won't be home again for six months, but you and Megan will come see me for Thanksgiving and Christmas. Nadine and Blake will come, too, and Kaleb and Jerome's wives and kids. And you're coming out to California for the video shoot. That'll be fun."

He thinks these things make up for him being away, but he actually proves my point. But I really don't want to think about that on date night. My in-laws have Megan overnight, and I want to have a good time tonight.

Nat looks a bit scruffy, hair covering his ears. It's a different look but I'm digging it, even if Yiayia says he looks like a hippie.

"Let's not talk about work anymore," I say, gazing into his eyes. "I like the new hairstyle. Gives me a bit more to run my fingers through when you're on top."

He averts his eyes for a second or two, as if I somehow embarrassed him, then grins. "I'm just going through an early mid-life crisis."

"Come on. Be serious. It really looks good. Believe me, hair is a physical quality in a man that I always notice, and I appreciate great hair."

"You really like it?"

"I really, really like it."

He seems extremely flattered by this. I have no idea why. It's not as if I've never paid him a compliment.

Okay, maybe I don't always notice a man's hair. Our waiter returns with our drinks, and I realize the young man is blond. I hadn't noticed until this moment. Remember when blonds were my type? I've turned to the dark side, as least as far as hair goes, and I have Nat to thank for that.

He unlaces his fingers from mine and raises his glass. "To your success, Honey. And I really am very proud of you."

It's my turn to avert my eyes in embarrassment, and I glance at the tablecloth before we clink glasses.

For one night we're a dating couple again. When we actually were dating, we came into Chicago to go to clubs, not fancy restaurants. At the time, all I could think about was him. Okay, that part hasn't changed over the past four years.

"Are you glad you married me?" I blurt out without thinking.

He wrinkles his brow. "Of course, I'm glad. Why? Are you unhappy?"

"No." I shake my head. "Just reminiscing is all. Remember, on one of our first dates we went clubbing? You saved me from that guy who wouldn't take 'no' for an answer."

He nods. "I wasn't about to let him have you. You were mine."

I raise an eyebrow. I was his? It was our second date, I think. How did he know? I mean, obviously, he felt the same sparks between us that I did, but the statement sounds a little possessive. Is it anti-feminist to admit I want to be possessed?

"I liked it whenever a slow dance came so I could be close to you. That was the most sensual thing we had done together at that point."

My heart races when we lock eyes. I still enjoy being close to him. Shawna and I listened to Papa Roach's new album *The Paramour Sessions* the other day, and I have the chorus from "Forever" stuck in my head.

"Do you want to go clubbing tonight," he says, "for old time's sake?"

I'm tempted, but we aren't dressed for it. I mean, I suppose it doesn't really matter. My dark purple, formfitting dress wouldn't be too out of place and if he ditches the sports jacket, he'd be fine. He's wearing black wash denim, so he's dress-casual, I suppose.

"I would," I say, "but not tonight. I don't want to have to share you with anyone. Let's go somewhere more romantic."

He smiles. "More romantic? I know where we can go."

The waiter returns with our appetizer.

"So is any of your book based on reality?" Nat says, passing me a plate.

I swallow. Why is he asking me that? We haven't talked about past lovers since before we were married. We once said that it didn't matter if we had one past lover or 100, we were with each other now, rendering all previous relationships meaningless. They were practice.

"Not directly. I based it on my old short stories which were mostly fantasies."

"Oh. Because I was gonna say, you were with some buff dudes. I wondered if you like that sort of thing."

I shove a piece of mozzarella stick into my mouth. I was with a lot of buff dudes, and I did like it, and Nat's skinny as a rail. Why is he asking me this? He knows I crave him.

"You read the book?"

He smiles. "Of course, I read it. You wrote it."

"Did any of it turn you on?"

"You had a lot of exciting scenes, but I didn't like the buff dudes."

I smile. "Well, usually women read those. Generally, women go for beefcake. But not me. I go for musicians who know their way around a guitar head."

We laugh.

NAT AND I WALK HAND in hand. Chicago is the city of dreams. Or at least it was for me. Who knew I would end up in a small suburb where the most interesting thing that happens is someone gets into an argument in the supermarket checkout line?

It's chilly, so we practically have the entire riverwalk to ourselves. The Chicago River is a bit creepy at night, but the city, illuminating either side, twinkles. This is exactly where I once imagined I would live. Well, not at the riverwalk, but where there's tall buildings and plenty of activity.

The lights flicker on the water and the dancing colors, combined with the strings of overhead lights, exude magic. He bumps into me accidently, as I gawk at our surroundings like a child, and smiles shyly.

We sit on the first park bench we find, Nat wraps his arm around me, and I lay my head on his shoulder. For a few minutes, we sit in silence, enjoying the view and being together.

"Want to go back to the hotel," he says, "so you can run your fingers through my hair?"

I smile. "Yeah. I'd like that."

We stand and walk back the way we came.

BY THE TIME WE GET back to the hotel room, I'm ready for bed. I toss my leather jacket onto one of the beds, while I wait for Nat to drop his keys and wallet on the TV stand, and place my hands on my hips.

"You're beautiful," he says. "I love that dress."

My dress, with slight ruching at the hips, hugs every curve. The hemline falls mid-thigh with a neckline giving a peekaboo of cleavage and long formfitting sleeves.

I take the few steps necessary to reach him and caress his cheek with my palm. "Thank you. I feel sexy in it."

I move closer to him, my hand still on his cheek, and press my lips to his. Gently, I suck on his bottom lip before his velvety tongue dances with mine.

He grabs hold of my arms and throws us onto the bed where we land with a thud. Why are hotel mattresses always so firm? I don't like firm mattresses, but there's one thing I do prefer firm.

"You have a beautiful smile," he says.

Now isn't that a coincidence? *His* smile is a trait I found attractive from the beginning.

I thank him not with words but with a kiss, my hand pressed between his shoulder blades.

His hand runs down to my upper thigh then reverses direction. He repeats this several times and, even though it is over clothing, it sends a shiver of anticipation up my spine.

I unbutton his sports jacket and stick my hands inside. Hey, I said it was chilly tonight. I need a hot body to warm up against. I drape my leg over his hip and attempt, unsuccessfully, to kick off my heels.

This time when his hand reverses direction, it runs under my hem and tugs on my thong.

I untuck his shirt, and he breaks the kiss to toss his jacket onto the adjacent bed near to my coat.

"Would you do a striptease for me?" he says, a mischievous glint in his eyes.

"I can do that," I say, tweaking his nipple before hopping off the bed.

A striptease would be better if I had some music to dance to. Humming Buckcherry's "Crazy Bitch" under my breath, I twirl my hips a few times before slowly raising my dress's hem. When it reaches my waist, I pull my dress over my head. I swing my hips a few more times then throw the dress on the bed with the coats.

Watching me the entire time with eager eyes, Nat undresses himself.

I don't do anything sexy with my slip-on heels. Toes pointed like a ballerina, I place my left leg on the bed and run my hand over my hosiery. Unsnapping my thigh-highs from their garter belt, I push the stocking slowly to my ankle then pull it off. Nat might cum just watching. Repeat with right leg. I unlatch my bra and throw it on the bed, followed by my thong.

Naked, I climb onto the bed and sit on Nat's face. He grabs my hips and sticks his tongue between my pussy lips. Ooooh. Oh shit, that's nice. My body jerks uncontrollably with every tongue tickle of the clit. I can't cum this way, but I'll let him eat me for as long as he wants pussy juices flowing down his chin. Reaching back, I stroke his hard cock and make him groan.

"I can't take it anymore," he says. "Lie down."

I climb off him and spread my legs. He situates his body between them, and we lock eyes. He has beautiful eyes. I could gaze into them for hours.

"I love you," he says, hard cock entering sticky pussy.

I smile. "I love you, too."

He drops to his forearms and thrusts, giving me the opportunity to run my fingers through his hair. My breath hot in Nat's ear, I squeeze his ass with my free hand.

I moan, quietly at first but growing in volume with each thrust.

We flip over. I move my hips in circles before pushing his cock as deep as it'll go. He clenches the headboard, knuckles white, and lets out a series of groans. I ride him like a cowgirl on a bull until my thighs burn and my knees hurt.

He takes over, but I can tell he isn't going to last long. A minute or two later, he twitches, thrusts faster and cums. My thighs and knees hurt so bad it's a relief when he pulls out to focus his attention on my button.

My partially outstretched legs bend and spread when an orgasm overcomes me.

"I really am proud of you," he says, fingers brushing my temple as we lay in each other's arms. "Encouraging you to write full time is probably one the best things I could have done. Look at what you accomplished."

"Thank you. I'm grateful I have your support." I smile. "Just imagine the fucking you'll get if my book becomes a best seller."

"I always have a good time with you." He laughs. "But now I suppose you can considering fucking me research for your next book."

I rub his chest. "Oh, well, then, I have a ton of research I need to do."

He kisses me, and I whimper.

Chapter 12

Birthday Wish

October 2, 2006

Sound waves vibrating against our chest walls, we watch Dramatic Sneezer perform. Megan has seen more concerts in her in two years and nine months than I did in my first 23 years. It's silly to admit I'm jealous, but I am in a way. Just think how many she'll see by the time she's my age. Of course, it is her dad and aunt's band, and Megan wears noise-cancelling headphones to protect her tender hearing, but still.

If I didn't wear the same sort of earplugs they wear onstage, I'd be deaf. I still can make out the lyrics and sing along. I know every word. Megan can't hear the music, but she feels the beat and dances to it. I have to be careful, though, because she'll run on stage if I let her or turn my back.

Nat and I always make it a point to see one another on our birthdays, even if it means I must travel. That's what brings us to Houston. His 30th birthday.

The song ends, the arena goes dark and the band leaves the stage. I pick up Megan to prevent her little toes from being accidently stepped on.

Nat smiles when he sees us, bending to kiss Megan on the forehead and me on the lips. Sweat plasters hair to his forehead. Damn, I wish he were sweaty for a reason other than stage lights and guitar playing.

"We have to go back for the encore soon." He removes Megan's headphones. "Are you enjoying the show, Sweetie?"

She points to herself. "Daddy, I like it. I like to dance."

"Great, Sweetie." He smiles and rubs her back. "Mommy, are you enjoying the show?"

"I always enjoy the show," I say. "And the after show."

He knows what I mean. Megan wouldn't be here without the after show.

He leans close. "I'm especially looking forward to tonight's after show. Although, technically, by the time it gets started it might be after midnight, and it won't be my birthday anymore."

"It'll be your birthday until we go to bed no matter what time the clock says."

He looks pleased. "That sounds really awesome."

"It's time for the encore," a staffer says to Nat.

Kaleb returns to the stage. Two more songs, and it'll be over.

I push Nat's sweaty hair off his temple and give him a good-luck kiss. He follows Nicole and Jerome back on stage, and I replace Megan's headphones. She has some concept of birthdays, I think, knows it's a person's special day. When I told her a few days ago that Daddy is as old as all her fingers and all her toes plus all my fingers, her eyes went wide.

The first encore song begins, and Megan points to the floor. I set her down, and she dances. She helped me wrap gifts – I know she understands the concept of presents – although the only gift we brought with us is the one tucked in my suitcase, the one that's for Nat's eyes only.

THIS EXCUSE FOR A BIRTHDAY party consists of ourselves, Nicole, Kaleb, Jerome and Terry. Members of the road crew periodically drift in and out, but I suppose it's the company you keep that matters. Dinner, takeout from a local restaurant, was served with room temperature beer. No birthday cake, only a super cupcake the airport gave me a hard time about because I had it in Megan's carryon along with a tube of icing in a resealable bag.

Megan doesn't know the words to "Happy Birthday" but sings anyway, waving her arms like a conductor.

We finish singing, giving Nat and Nicole a brief round of applause. They lean forward to blow out the candles on the cupcake and nearly bump heads. Yeah, the airport questioned me about the candles, too. You'd think they never saw a wife traveling to celebrate her husband and sister-in-law's 30th birthday before.

"What did you wish for?" Terry says with a straight face. "To grow two inches?"

"There wasn't a lot of room to grow in there with this one around," Kaleb says, pointing to Nicole's head.

Nat accepts all the jokes with grace. In his place, I'd have flipped out by now. His entire family is on the shorter side. Mine is, too, I suppose, although no one was teased about it.

"No," Jerome says, "I'm sure he wished for a tropical vacation at the beach."

"Well, that would be awesome," Nat says, shaking his head. "But I can't tell you or my wish won't come true."

"Since when have you been superstitious?" Nicole says, taking a bite of her half of cupcake.

He takes a sip of his beer. "I just don't want to tell is all."

She wiggles her fingers in his face. "Ooh, so mysterious."

Nat takes another sip. "What did you wish for, Nic? A bucket of eyeliner pencils?"

Nicole applies an over-the-top smoky eye for her stage makeup.

"Ha, ha," she says with a grimace.

Megan leaves the table and pulls a sheet of paper out of my purse, a drawing she made of lines and circles in various colors. She drew it specifically for Nat, and I think she's proud of it.

Face brightening, she hands it to Nat. "Daddy, this is for you."

He smiles and runs his hand over her hair. "Oh, Sweetie, it's beautiful. Thank you. I'm going to hang this in my bunk on the bus. You want to help me pick out just the right spot?"

"Yes," she says, jumping and clapping her hands.

"Okay. We'll do that first thing after we leave here."

He picks her up and sets her on his lap before sharing his half of the cupcake with her. She shoves her piece into her mouth, and crumbs rain on her shirt.

"You have gifts waiting for you at home," I say. "Except for one. It's in my suitcase. You'll get it later."

"I'm sure it's fantastic," he says, grinning. "How could it not be?"

"I hope you feel that way when you see it."

He takes a taste of beer and says nothing. Megan reaches for her travel cup and washes down cupcake with lukewarm apple juice.

"Can we go to the bus now?" she says, looking up at him with wide eyes.

"Uh, yeah. We can go back to the bus and find a special place for your drawing." Nat stands. "Plus, we need to get to the hotel, so you can go to bed."

I gather our stuff.

MEGAN REMAINED REMARKABLY pleasant, considering she stayed awake hours past her bedtime, and conked out almost immediately after I tucked her in. She enjoyed dancing at the concert, but I think the highlight of her evening was helping Nat find a special place to hang her drawing. Afterward, they laid in his bunk for bedtime stories.

"Is she sleeping?" Nat says over my shoulder. "I'd like to get my birthday gift."

"I think so," I say, peering at our daughter. "We'll just have to leave the lights dimmed and the volume down."

"About that birthday gift."

"Well, someone is impatient, isn't he?" I leave Megan's bedside and remove a large cosmetic bag out of my carryon. "I'll be right back with that gift."

I emerge from the bathroom a few minutes later wearing an orange crotchless teddy made of a shimmery satin material. It squeezes my boobs so tightly they nearly spill over the top of the bra cups. The leg holes reach to my hipbones, providing a cheeky view in back. I completed the ensemble with the orange heels I wore to Shawna's wedding.

"Happy birthday," I say, leaning against the doorframe. "I hope you like it."

His eyes widen. "I was expecting something great, but this exceeds expectation. Come here."

I strut to the bed, pretending I'm a model on a runway.

Nat runs his hands over my curves. "Holy fuck. Where did you find this?"

"At the mall. I'll tell you the story later." I rub his crotch. "But for now, a little birdy told me the birthday boy needs a long, hard fucking for his big day. It would be a huge shame if he didn't get one. But he has too many clothes on."

I push his t-shirt to his armpits, pulling it over his head when he lifts his arms. I also unbutton and unzip his pants, pull them down, and sink to my knees. His eyes upon me, I stroke his dick before sticking it in my mouth and sucking.

He stumbles backward. I continue sucking, moving my head back and forth and sometimes in a circle while my tongue licks his dickhead as if it's a melting popsicle. I stop before he cums, because, well, I didn't buy this teddy not to be fucked in it. I stand, push him onto the bed with a smile, and straddle him.

"Wait," he says, looking at the adjacent bed. "Megan hasn't been in bed long. What if she isn't sleeping soundly?"

I follow his gaze. Megan dozes with her lips slightly parted and hugging a stuffed animal to her chest.

"She was pretty tired. Looks like she's sleeping soundly to me."

"How would we explain what we're doing and why part of me is in part of you?"

"Being a bit paranoid, aren't you? But if it bothers you, we can go into the bathroom."

I get up and wait for him to pull his pants off before offering my hand. He takes it, and I lead him into the bathroom, closing the door after us. I hop on the counter and spread my legs.

"I'm not going to last long," he says, entering me.

"Thanks for the warning," I say, wrapping my legs around his waist the moment he thrusts.

I sucked him to the brink of cumming, so I anticipated a quickie.

Somehow my ass ends up in a cold puddle, feels like I pissed myself, but I grin and bear it for the sake of Nat's birthday.

With every thrust, I moan in his ear, my arms wrapped around his neck. His hot skin makes up for my cold ass. Well, almost. Shit, I really hate air conditioning right now. What the hell is on this counter? A melted ice cube? I'm relieved when he cums. Normally, I want him inside me as long as possible, but damn I'd really like to get my ass out of this puddle.

"How do you get this thing on and off?" he says, catching his breath.

"I can show you."

"I mean you look fantastic in it, but you'll look even better out of it."

He pulls out, and I slide off the counter, hoping the wet spot on my teddy isn't noticeable. I show him how the crotch snaps on either side of my pussy lips then shimmy out of the rest of the teddy. Red marks line my skin in places where seams and boning squeezed. What we women won't do to keep our men happy.

"So," I say, standing in a way that I hope is provocative. I can never tell with that sort of thing. "Is there going to be a round two?"

"Fuck yeah," he says, grabbing me and slamming his lips into mine.

This is the first real kiss he's given me since we got here. I rub my body against his, his cock slippery with pussy juices.

I don't want to fuck again in this bathroom, so I take a step or two toward the door while tugging on his neck. After a few times, he gets the hint and we leave the bathroom.

Megan sleeps with her Elmo doll. She slept through the entire thing. I knew she would.

I straddle Nat same as I did 15 minutes ago, although this time he doesn't stop me. I kiss his lips followed by his neck. Lips parted and slightly licking his skin, I kiss his chest. When I reach where bare flesh gives way to pubic hair, I suck his skin, wondering if it's possible to give someone a hickey somewhere other than the neck.

I slip my pussy on his rock hard cock. I wish I had the ability to pump as quickly as a man can thrust because he deserves a good fucking. I interlace my fingers with his and shift my legs to a squat. He watches his dick disappear in and out. I wish I could watch, but we would need to fuck in front of a mirror for that to be possible. Note to self: Fuck in front of a mirror. Make that happen.

He groans loudly. While it flatters my ego to know he enjoys the fucking, he was the one paranoid about waking Megan.

"Shush," I say and lower to my forearms, shutting him up by sticking my tongue down his throat.

We roll on our sides, and I expect him to flip me onto my back but he doesn't. Scissoring works, I guess. It's a good position for cutting down on noise, but this position reminds me of two things: fucking while half asleep or fucking while pregnant and big as a whale.

He maintains a steady pace that rubs his cock against my clitoris. I run my fingers through his hair, kissing him with increased intensity. Fuck, I think I can cum simply thinking about his hair.

Speaking of cumming, that's exactly what Nat does while I'm daydreaming about cumming.

He continues thrusting and I squeeze my pussy muscles, milking his cock for every drop of cum.

"My birthday wish came true," he says with a grin. "I was hoping you brought something sexy to tempt me with tonight."

"Surprise," I say. "I hope you had a wonderful birthday."

"I did," he says, kissing me. "I fucking did."

Chapter 13

The Video Shoot

January 4, 2007

A few months ago, when Nat suggested I come watch the music video for "No Bullets in My Gun" (from the new album *Golf and Other Silly Games*) be filmed, I jumped at the chance. Who wouldn't want to be in sunny California in early January? Remember that white shit called snow? Yeah, I don't either.

"Nat, Honey, you and Megan have the same hairstyle."

I hold my phone to his cheek and compare his likeness to the photo of Megan I'm using as my wallpaper. Sure enough, her dark hair is nearly down to her shoulders and curling on the ends like his.

He pushes the phone away. "Don't you need to go sit down so the director can do his job?"

Have I embarrassed him in front of his bandmates? Sure thing. I mean, what guy would want to be compared to his nearly three-year-old daughter?

I laugh and take my seat.

"Action!" the director says, and they begin.

I arrived, exhausted, at the airport early this morning. We dropped my luggage off at the hotel, I changed clothes, then almost immediately we left to drive to the set. I expected to be fascinated by the filming process, but I must confess one person occupies my attention. Transfixed, I watch Nat, noting his mannerisms. I watch his lips, wishing I kissed him instead of teasing him. Oh God, I want to kiss him. I suck my bottom lip.

Playing his guitar, he moves around the set, shaking his body, and I am reminded of all those times I wrapped my legs around those hips. I cross my legs and shove my hands in my hoodie's pockets. I try touching myself, but my pockets aren't deep enough to reach. Damn! I want to go into the ladies room and jack off, but I also want to watch him. I stay put, fidgeting.

They say absence makes the heart grow fonder. It also makes the pussy grow wetter. Or at least that's always been the case for me.

My torture isn't broken until the crew takes a mid-morning break. Maybe I can get my mind off the fact my thong is damp and I desperately want to remove it.

Nat tugs on my hood's strings. "You cold?"

This coming from a man dressed in layers indoors. I nod.

"The air conditioning is a bit chilly," I say, although I'm hot.

He smiles. "Let's go somewhere more comfortable."

Nat takes my hand, and we wander through the building, looking for someplace private. I try acting causal, as if we do this sort of thing all the time, but my heart races. We stop when we reach a women's restroom. The kind for one person. I go in and he follows, locking the door behind us.

"I missed you," he says, pushing my hair behind the ear.

All I've wanted to do since filming began is rip his clothes off.

We make eye contact. "I, I, I'm so fucking horny."

He smiles. "Good because—"

He doesn't finish his sentence and darts his tongue into my mouth. Sandwiched between the wall and his body, I grab the back of his jacket and hold on. You know what else absence does? It makes the dick grow harder.

His hand runs under my sundress and up my inner thigh until it reaches my V. He finger fucks and kisses me as if releasing years of pent up passion. I break the kiss and look at him with large eyes.

"Take off your underwear," he says, breathing heavily.

I obey, propping a foot on the edge of the sink. He knows what that means without me saying a word and quickly drops his pants. Amazed by the affect I have on him, I stare at his hard cock.

Adjusting his posture and leaning into me, he slides in without effort. The first few slow and steady strokes are replaced by a quickened pace. I could cum now, but I control myself by tightening my pussy muscles around his cock. There's only time for a quickie, but I wish this could go on for hours.

His breath hot against my temple, I run my hands through his hair – his gorgeous hair.

After several minutes, my leg smarts. His thrusts intensify. I know what that means. He's going to cum and will pull out at any moment. He should pull out. I told him twice, reminded him this morning, that I'm mid-cycle and he needs to pull out. But he doesn't pull out. His dick muscles vibrate, and he pushes into me. Pushes in! I specifically instructed him to pull out. How the hell could he forget? He stops thrusting, and I relax my grip on his clothing. His thumb plays with my button. I should stop him. I really should stop him, but I'm so fucking sensitive right now. I can't. I just can't. My body starts to twitch, and I cum easily, back arching.

We make eye contact.

"That's just a preview of what you're going to get later," he says, pulling out.

"Horny as I was, were you?" I say, cum running down my shaky inner thighs.

Goddamn it, he was supposed to pull out.

"How could I resist you in that short dress?"

The door handle jingles. We exchange a glance.

"One moment," I say to the door.

The door handle jingles again. We've been caught.

"One moment!"

We quickly make ourselves presentable. I open the door and am happy to see it isn't someone from the film crew. It's an older, overweight woman, her annoyance at having to wait replaced by shock when she realizes there's a man in the restroom with me.

"Our apologies for the wait," Nat says to the woman.

She stares, mouth agape. We exit the bathroom, push past her, and walk hand and hand down the hallway. When we round the corner, we burst out laughing.

"DON'T THINK, NATHANIEL, that just because I'm smiling that I'm not pissed at you."

His back toward me, he fiddles with our hotel room keycard.

"What?" he says as the door unlocks. "What did I do?"

"I told you twice," I say, holding up two fingers and brushing past him to enter the room, "twice, that today is my fertile day and you were supposed to pull out. Yet what did you do? Push it in as far as it goes. If you got me pregnant again, it's your fault."

The door slams followed by the lock's click.

"That's stupid," he says, staring daggers. "If I did it, then of course it's my fault."

Damn, that was redundant. Figures he'd catch that.

"That's not the point," I say, setting my purse the TV stand. "It could have been prevented."

"I'm sorry." He shakes his head. "I'll pull out the rest of the time you're here. Would that make you happy?"

"No. It's too late for that. Your sperm count was the highest in that, in that bathroom!"

"Considering where we were," he says gesturing, "it seemed like the thing to do. What? What did you want me to do? Cum on the floor? Maybe I could've jerked off in the sink. I fucked up. I'm sorry."

"If we have another tax write off in nine months—"

"All right. Enough. I already admitted I fucked up. Just because it's possible doesn't mean it's a done deal. We'll know in two weeks. Either way, I suppose it'll be my fault. Whether I knocked you up or not, it'll end up being some commentary on my manhood."

We stare each other down. Since when I have ever questioned his manhood? Did he miss the point? There is no "either way." I don't want to be pregnant.

My nostrils flare. "How long are you going to keep your hair that way? You're 30 fucking years old, not a teenager."

"I don't know. For someone who hates it so much, you've been running your fingers through it all day."

"Have I?"

"You have."

He takes a few steps toward me. I take off my hoodie and catch a glimpse of myself in the mirror. My black sundress *is* short and low cut, but that's no excuse for violating our family planning rules.

When I turn, he's taken off his jacket and he's giving me *that* look, the combo of admiration and lust.

He sits on the king-sized bed, waiting for whatever I'm going to do. I purse my lips, slowly taking the few steps needed to reach him.

"I'm sorry," he says, rubbing my arms. "Let's not let this ruin your time here. It's going to go by fast, and I don't want to argue with you the entire time. I fucked up, but I can't go back and undo it."

His eyes drift to my stomach. Not long ago he said the possibility didn't mean it had happened, but he's talking as if there's something in there other than dinner. I'll know in two weeks.

I nod. "I'm sorry, too, for how I told you you forgot."

He smiles and pulls me down with him. I kick off my sandals when we kiss, place a leg on his thigh and somehow manage to roll us over.

"I have you exactly where I want you," I say, smiling.

Yeah, I'm pissed at him, but horniness is like hunger. You can satisfy it for a while, but it always comes back. And besides, I'm only here for four days. I have no desire to spend it arguing. I came to enjoy myself.

"How long have you been walking around with no underwear on?" he says, reaches up my dress to squeeze my ass. "I saw you put it back on after we had our fun."

"I took it off when I used the bathroom at the restaurant. It was wet. You forgot to pull out."

"Oh, not this again," he says, slapping my ass cheek so hard it hurts.

Oww, that really stings.

"I'm stating a fact."

My lips graze his skin, kissing his temple, check, ear, neck. I lift his t-shirt and kiss his chest from collarbone to waistband, stopping to tweak each nipple with my tongue.

He watches as I unbutton and unzip his pants, reaching in to discover his cock predictably hard. I massage its most sensitive spot for no other reason than to drive him fucking crazy. I stop after a minute or two to take off my dress and bra. Fully naked, I turn my attention back to him, pulling off his pants and underwear to reveal a cock standing at attention.

I place my body between his legs and kiss his inner thighs, balls, penis. My tongue darts in and out like a snake, licking his cock's sensitive part. He moans, eyes rolling back. Excellent! I have him on the brink. I want him to want me, to need me, to crave me.

Sticking his cock in my mouth, I taste dried pussy juice from earlier. Eww, okay, I've had enough. I lift my head, smile as if I enjoy the taste of my own bodily fluids, and help him remove his t-shirt.

His hands on my ass, I guide him inside me and pump as quickly as I can. I can only keep up this pace for a few minutes, so I pleasure him by moving my hips in a circular motion, grinding my body down then pumping again. This triggers a string of moans.

Eventually my thighs hurt, and, pace slowing, I lower myself to my elbows, boobs pressing into his bare chest. It's been too long since my lips touched his, and I kiss him, my fingers in his hair. I moan loudly when he takes over thrusting and couldn't care less if the entire hotel hears me.

Firmly holding my hips, Nat cums after about half an hour. When the muscle contractions stop, I pump a few more times before collapsing, thighs burning, at his side.

"I'm glad you were able to come watch the video being made," he says, wrapping his arm around me.

I swallow. "So am I."

Although I might be regretting this entire trip later.

"You're beautiful and sexy."

He kisses me before I can respond, hand moving up my thigh, and fingers penetrating a still wet pussy. I expect those fingers to touch my clitoris at any moment, but they don't. Our lips part, and I open my eyes. His cock is hard again. So soon? Jesus, he's going to kill me.

I should resist him. I should tell him "no," but holy shit, his fat cock. I roll onto my back and spread my legs. He plunges in, and I'm so sensitive I feel every inch of girth with each thrust. I run my fingers through his hair, wrapping my legs around his hips exactly as I daydreamed.

A few minutes later, my knees on my shoulders, I try to keep my eyes open, but the sensation is so intense that I can't. He eases up enough I can place my feet on the bed. When he kisses me, our tongues doing a well choreographed dance, I hug him with one arm while running the palm of my free hand down his back to squeeze an ass cheek.

We stare deeply into each other's eyes for a moment, and then he pulls out. What? Now he pulls out? After I'm dripping in cum? What's the point?

"Get on your hands and knees," he says.

Okay, so he isn't ready to cum. I assume the position - head low and ass high – and we moan in unison when cock reunites with pussy.

Our colliding bodies make a slapping sound, and my juices coat my ass cheeks and upper thighs. While he fucks the shit out of me, I watch his cock disappear, reappear, disappear, reappear.... He reaches forward slightly and touches my button. I squirm, thinking I might cum, but his fingers keep slipping and the motion isn't constant enough.

His thrusts slow, and he pulls out. I lay back and spread my legs, and he re-enters with a smile.

After a minute we're back where we started, on our sides with my leg over his hip, with him thrusting slowly, every thrust rubbing my clitoris.

Soon I recognize the familiar body shakes, and he cums. I'm playing with fire now, I know, but there can't be many swimmers left at this point.

He withdrawals, and we collapse side by side.

Adjusting his body, he finger fucks me with one hand while rubbing my button with the other. I moan, clenching the covers. My eyes snap shut. His tongue replaces his finger on my clitoris. My body grows hot. My pussy muscles tighten. I shake. I partially sit when I cum, his tongue still on my button, and collapse, out of breath.

"Did I do a good job?" he says, lifting his head.

He's teasing. He already knows the answer.

"Any time you want to do that, feel free," I say.

"I learned long time ago anytime I want to slip my dick inside you, I just have to ask."

I run my fingers through his disheveled hair. "You just have to be near me and I get wet. I've wanted to rip your clothes off all fucking day."

He smiles. "What should we do now?"

I should sleep, but it's only evening.

"How about the hot tub?"

His smile widens.

IT SEEMED LIKE A GOOD idea, but we've been soaking in the hot tub with an older couple since we entered the poolroom. You'd think we were from the fucking moon, judging from all the annoying questions they keep asking. It's as if they never heard of Chicago before today.

"It must be hard to be separated so often?" the wife says after finding out what Nat does for a living.

"Oh, it is very, very hard," I say.

Nat instantly grasps the double meaning and smiles. She contorts into a strange expression, making me think she thinks the smile means he never misses me at all. Her husband, however, understands the double entendre. His foot brushes my leg.

The dude looks like he walked out of a bad '70s porn flick. He probably hasn't changed his look in 30 years. He's beefy, hairy to the point it looks like he's wearing a rug, gold chain around the neck with fake orange tan to match. The nerve of the guy when his wife sits right beside him. And what indication did I give that I would welcome *his* touch?

The bubbles conceal what's happening, and Nat doesn't know this stranger tried to play footsie. I pull my knees close to my body, turn slightly and place my legs across his lap. I am no one's piece of meat, except for one man, and that's because he's my piece of meat in return.

The dude frowns and turns to his wife. "We should go up to our room. It's getting late."

When they leave the hot tub, I exhale.

"You can't get enough, can you?" Nat says once we're alone. "You're lucky I can keep up with you."

He's right, so I don't bother to tell him the real reason why my legs are across his lap.

"I need to find an excuse to get you to wear this bikini more often," he says.

I put my arm around his neck, snuggling closer. We kiss. My temperature rises and not from the heat of the water.

You'd think that after fucking three times today that it would take longer to become aroused, but today is just one of those days. We're revved and ready to go. I don't know why we have this affect on each other, but it's been this way since we met at Nadine and Terry's party.

He gropes my breast, and I slide my hand down the front of his swim trucks. Of course, he's hard. It's one of those days. I gently squeeze his dick.

He pays me back by moving aside the crotch of my bikini bottom and finger fucking me. A moan breaks the kiss.

I have an idea, and if the look in his eyes is any indication, he has the same one.

"Can you take your bottom off without getting out of the water?" he says.

Yep, same idea.

"I can if you help me."

Honestly, I don't need help, but it's more fun this way. Together we remove my bikini bottom. A jet of water sprays my sensitive spot, and I've discovered a new way to get off.

I free his dick from his shorts and run my hand up and down the shaft several times.

"You're torturing me," he says.

"Not torturing. Teasing. It turns me on."

"Here all this time I thought *I* turned you on."

"Oh, you do," I say, straddling him and sitting on his hard cock. "Oh, you do."

His hands on my hips, I move my body. The pace is slower than earlier, but I don't have much energy left.

I lick his lips before passionately kissing him. He runs his hands up my back, accidently loosening my bikini top between the shoulder blades.

Jets of water shoot up around us. And there goes my top. My suddenly bare boobs collide with his chest. I'd laugh but my tongue is otherwise occupied.

Someone might walk in. Eh, who cares? I want to scream and cum all over his dick.

The pace slows even further, and I release my lips from his. My bikini top, still attached around the neck, floats on the water. I giggle, and he smiles. I remember the first time he smiled at me and insert my tongue back into his mouth.

Pace slow and steady, cock and pussy please each other. I run my fingers through Nat's hair.

He gazes into my eyes. "So you were saying I turn you on."

I pretend to be exasperated. "Not just anyone can make my pussy wet, you know."

He smiles. "Glad to hear it."

The pace quickens, and he cums. We linger for a moment, out of breath, water swirling around us. Eventually, I pull my body off his, putting my swimsuit back on and settling onto his lap.

"CASSIE."

I open my eyes, my head on Nat's shoulder. I didn't even know I nodded off until he startled me awake.

"Come on," he says. "Let's go to bed. To sleep this time."

I nod. I'm so exhausted, it's a struggle to force myself to get out of the hot tub. That's what lack of sleep, jet lag and a fuck marathon will do.

"I forgot to tell you," he says while we towel dry, "Nicole's in the room next to us."

I quit drying for a second, feeling pins and needles. When I said I couldn't care less if the entire hotel hears me moan, I failed to consider someone I know hearing me. Breakfast tomorrow will be awkward. Oh, well. I finish drying. It's not the first time, nor will it be the last.

Chapter 14

He Didn't Pull Out

February 5, 2007

I have been this late one other time, and Megan was the end result. But stress can also cause periods to be late, and it's safe to say I have been incredibly stressed since leaving California, constantly worrying Nat neglected to pull out when he should have. It hasn't helped matters either that he keeps asking me if my monthly visitor has arrived or whether it's on a nine month delay.

It's possible it's a weird month and I'm causing my period to be late by stressing over it. It can happen. There's such a thing as a phantom pregnancy. Clearly, I am no Fertile Myrtle because Megan is three and it's not as if I've been celibate since her birth. It could be that Megan is actually the fluke, that her existence was meant to be for some reason. No, that's ridiculous.

Yep, probably a weird month. I'll laugh about it someday, about how I got so stressed I made the situation worse.

I purposefully went to the store when most people are at work. Remember the days when I had a 9-5? I certain don't miss nosy coworkers. I swallow and turn down the feminine hygiene aisle, Megan riding in the supermarket shopping cart. Another woman stands where I need to go. She has three small children with her, all close in age. Jesus, does she really need a fourth kid in as many years? Speaking of Jesus, I imagine, based on her loose ankle-length skirt and her hairstyle, that she is highly religious. She probably has sex with her eyes closed, always in the dark, always missionary and like a cold fish, whereas I have one child that is the result of a quickie in a locker room and another who is the result of a quickie in a restroom.

My mouth is dry. No. I don't know that I have a child as a result of my trip to California. Last time I bought one of these tests, I brought Shawna along for moral support. I should have done that today. Why didn't I? To make matters worse, I have Bloodhound Gang's "Bad Touch" in my head.

"That doggie is stilly," Megan says, pointing to the dog food bag in the cart next to her.

I smile. "Yes, Sweetie, very silly. Our Scooter is silly. He likes to smell everything."

Wrinkling her nose, Megan makes a sniffing sound and laughs.

A second child means dividing my love, doesn't it? Newborns are stressful. Toddlers aren't easy, but at least Megan can walk, talk, feed herself, dress herself and use the toilet. If another one is on the way, we're back to square one. Plus, I'll be outnumbered when Nat's away.

Woman-who-screws-with-her-eyes-closed is taking forever, it seems. I could elbow my way over there and grab what I want, but I would like some semblance of privacy, even if I am in a public place and Megan is with me.

Green Day's "Wake Me Up When September Ends" starts playing on the store's sound system, and Megan makes herself comfortable against the dog chow and sings along. I bet Woman-who-screws-with-her-eyes-closed's kids only know gospel spirituals. I'm not saying that's a bad thing. Who am I to judge?

Oh, but apparently she can judge me. She finally makes a selection and gives me a sour look as she passes a singing Megan and me in my leather jacket that's too light for a day like today. Ugh.

I am not looking forward to the multitude of doctor's appointments or losing my figure. But I could be getting ahead of myself. That's why we are here.

I sure as shit hope Megan doesn't ask questions about what I'm looking for or why we're here, but at the moment she seems preoccupied looking at the cats on the cat food cans. Good. I rub her head and place my body between the cart and the packages on the shelves. I'd like to say that I know what I'm looking for, but I was so nervous last time that I can't even remember the brands I purchased. I only know one cost more than the other.

Some are digital. Most use the one or two line method. Oh, yes, I remember the thin blue lines. I pick up a box and read the back. "Results accurate as soon as four days before a missed period," the box says. Oh, wonderful. I'm about two weeks past sooo...... Yeah, I know, I wait way too long, but every month isn't exactly 28 days. I don't know any woman's whose is.

I pick one and put it in the cart, hiding it between a bag of potatoes and a box of rice.

"You ready to go home, Sweetie?"

Megan claps her hands. "Scooter and Maisie will be happy to see us."

"They will, yes."

I smile. What the fuck am I going to do with two pets and two kids? When will I have time to write? Even if Nat were home every night, it still doesn't seem like I'd have much free time. Sigh. A promising career stopped short before it really even began. Just call me Mommy Extraordinaire. Actually, no, don't. I'm terrible at it. I'm selfishly thinking about my figure and my career when I should be thinking about my children.

Children is plural. I don't know that yet. My hormones could be out of whack. There's been a lot in the news about estrogen in our environment from pollutants. I grew up in an industrial town. We can't rule out the possibility that I've been poisoned.

I put items on the checkout conveyor belt, beginning with the dog food bag and working my way to the smaller items. Megan helps as best she can, standing in the cart and putting the cat food cans on the belt.

"Cassie? Cassandra Hardwick?" I hear a woman's voice say, and it takes me a moment to figure out it's coming from the woman in line behind us.

I force myself to look up. Oh shit. A former nosy coworker. It's Sheila, the office gossip from when I worked at Jordan Dairy Farms.

"Sheila Bronowski?" I say.

I guess I could have played dumb, denied who I am, but too late. I said her name aloud.

She looks pleased as peaches. (Can peaches be pleased?) "Yes. Oh my God, imagine seeing you here. I haven't seen you since your going away party. Oh, my, is this your little one?"

No, I just borrowed a kid to take to the store. What the fuck does she think? Who else would it be?

"What are you doing here? I mean, shouldn't you be at work?"

"Personal day. I got my hair and nails done." Sheila holds her hand up to show off her manicure before turning her attention to Megan. "She really is a precious little one, isn't she?"

Megan eyes Sheila suspiciously. *Please start throwing a tantrum. Please start throwing a tantrum. Please start throwing a tantrum.* But Megan stays calm and quiet.

I reach the last item in my cart – the pregnancy test. My cheeks burning, I place it on the conveyor belt while avoiding eye contact with both the cashier and Sheila.

"Did it again, did you?" Sheila says. "Still with that musician husband of yours?"

"Of course, I am," I say, tone betraying annoyance.

I focus on the register, pretending I'm watching the items tally, and find myself playing with my engagement and wedding rings with my thumb.

"I was wondering," Sheila says, placing her wine bottle, cheese and crackers on the belt behind my order. "Today is my wedding anniversary. Thirty-two years."

Wow. Imagine a man staying with Sheila for 32 years. It gives me a headache thinking about it.

"Congratulations. That's longer than my husband and I have been alive. We hear 1975 was a really great year. Did you wear disco shoes down the aisle?"

She laughs. "Oh, no, but if we had eloped like you did, that would have been appropriate."

The cashier tells me my total is $69.69. I take out my wallet to pay. Soon, I'll be able to make my getaway. Unless Sheila's car is parked near mine. What a terrible thought.

"I've always thought your engagement ring was very unusual," Sheila says as I hand the cashier my credit card.

Unique, yes. Unusual, no. That's a dig whether she thinks I realize it or not.

"It's mine and my husband's birthstones," I say, putting my swiped card back in my wallet.

"Oh." Sheila fakes a smile. "There's an actual story behind it? I always thought he couldn't afford a diamond."

Couldn't afford a diamond? I could punch this woman in the face?

"Diamonds are boring. My man put thought into my ring. It was nice running into you, Sheila. Hopefully, we can both go grocery shopping at the same time again in three more years."

I take my receipt and push the shopping cart out of the checkout lane as quickly as possible.

"Good luck," Sheila says to my back. "Maybe the morning sickness won't be so bad this time."

Holy shit. I always suspected, and she just confirmed without overtly saying so, that she started the rumor I was coming into work hungover when I really had morning sickness. I knew it. The woman's skilled at both spreading gossip and creating it.

"I'M GOING TO USE THE potty upstairs." I say, hands shaking, after I finish putting the groceries away.

My heart thumps against my chest as if I'm doing something I shouldn't, as if I'm being sneaky about something. Megan barely acknowledges I've said anything. She's engrossed in her PBS Kids show, and that's exactly what I need right now.

I enter the master bathroom, put the toiletries away and open the pregnancy test. Okay, I remember how this is done. The instructions make it seem like it's easy to mess up, but it really isn't. I gotta pee on the stick and wait to see if there is one line or two. Results in two minutes, it says, but last time it took two seconds.

I sit on the toilet, hold my breath and let 'er rip. I refuse to look at the stick until I'm finished. I'll clean up, wash my hands and take it downstairs. If it's negative, then I really am being poisoned by toxic chemicals dumped into our environment by unscrupulous manufacturers. If it's positive, I'm losing my office, and my computer is going into storage because there is no place else to put it.

I accidently catch a glimpse of the test when I move it out of the way to wipe. Fuck. Two blue lines.

What good did it do to figure out my fertile days if Nat wasn't going to pull out? I should be outraged. I sorta am still pissed at him. But right now I'm mostly numb. After worrying about it for a month, losing sleep over it, test results seems anticlimactic.

I sit seemingly unable to move. I have confirmation now, finally have an answer when he bugs me about my visitor. You know, I already knew. I knew in that bathroom when he didn't pull out. It felt different somehow, like intuition or something was telling me, warning me, what had happened. He knows, too. Why else would he kept asking? And there's nothing I can do about it. Well, yes, I'm still prochoice, so there *is* something, but I could never do that to his baby.

I inhale, hearing my breath pass through my nostrils. I need to get up. Megan is downstairs alone. I should exercise, feed Scooter and Maisie, plan dinner. I should write, too, but what's the point?

I stand, flush and pull up my pants. I can't look at myself in the mirror when I wash my hands as if I'm ashamed. I'm married this time, so I'm not sure where the inner guilt comes from.

Downstairs, I observe Megan for a moment singing along to a counting song on her TV show. I suck on my thumbnail. Life's going to change, and she's not going to understand. She's not going to have my full attention, and I'm very, very sorry.

Maisie jumps onto the back of the couch, and when Megan turns to watch her, she spots me and waves.

"Hi, Mommy. Go potty?"

I smile and come closer, grabbing my phone from the kitchen counter. "Yes, Sweetie. I'm going to text Daddy. Maybe call him. Then we can play a game."

"Okay."

Megan stands on the couch and talks to Maisie, a cute one-side conversation about tails.

I text Nat: *Do you enjoy being a dad?*

My phone dings as Megan resumes singing.

I love Megan. You know that. Why?

I swallow. He knows. He's gotta know. He didn't pull out. I'm two weeks late.

I take a photo of the test stick, a close-up of the blue lines, and send it to him.

A response comes almost immediately: *Does that mean what I think it does?*

A second later, the phone rings.

"Hi," I say, voice low.

"Does that mean what I think it does?" Nat says.

"It does."

"I'm to blame. I've been thinking about that. I'm sorry. You're probably still pissed. What's done is done. I can't change it. But, hey, another mini-you or maybe a mini-me."

Don't tell me he's happy about this. I know he loves kids and all. But does he love them so much he'd—

"Nat, you didn't do it on purpose, did you?" I say, a pit forming in my stomach. "I mean, we said we were neither planning nor preventing, but we were preventing. I kept track of my fertile days for a reason and, and you didn't pull out. If you had, we wouldn't be having this conversation."

"I love being a dad but I would never get you pregnant on purpose. Wait. That came out wrong. What I mean to say is I wouldn't without us both agreeing to it."

I glance at Megan. "Twice now, and neither one of us agreed to it. First time, we got caught up in the moment. Second time, you didn't pull out."

"I know. I was there, remember? It's like I told you with Megan. Unplanned doesn't mean unwanted. This could be a good thing. It is a good thing."

"Are you happy?"

He chuckles. "Yes, I'm happy. I said it was a good thing, didn't I? You know, I've had a whole month to think about it. I was worried about it at first, but then I got used to the idea."

He got used to the idea? Didn't he say that with Megan, too? How does he get used to the idea of babies? Is it because he grew up in a ridiculously large family?

"Are you happy?" he says.

I swallow. "I don't know what to think. We have a lot to consider. This house is prefect for the three of us, but we're running out of room, and I don't know if you'll be here when the baby comes and I hated the hospital experience and—"

"I'll worry about the scheduling, and we can discuss the rest. Take a deep breath. This is great. Really. Two kids'll be fun."

Fun? Maybe eventually, but I have to be a human incubator for nine months. That's not my idea of fun.

Megan jumps on her couch cushion, frightening Maisie and causing Scooter to howl.

I laugh nervously. "I love you."

"I love you, too, and I love Megan, and I'll love this latest addition just the same."

That is so sweet. I tear up. Goddamn hormones.

"You always say the right things."

"I say them because they are true. I fucked up, and now we're going from a trio to a quartet."

I rub my temple. We're going to be Mommy and Daddy all over again. I knew I left California pregnant. I knew it, yet this doesn't feel real. I give Megan a bear hug.

Chapter 15

A Better Option

February 28, 2007

It's no secret that I didn't enjoy the experience of being treated like a piece of meat during my first pregnancy. (See, I actually can say the word this time. That's progress.) So I haven't made a doctor's appointment. If something bad is going to happen, it's going to happen. No doctor's appointment can stop that.

A few nights ago, the evening news reported on 10 Fingers & 10 Toes Birthing Center opening in Lake County. It's run by a staff of midwives. Midwives! I didn't even know those existed, except in the 1800s, but it gave me an option. So I made a phone call, and here I am.

"So tell me," Connie Schmidt, one of the midwives says while we sit in her office, "why have you opted for a birthing center?"

"Well, I'm more than a set of reproductive organs, and I didn't feel like I was seen that way last time."

"Last time? You have other children?"

"One more. She's three."

Connie writes this down on the form the front desk asked me to partially fill out. She's in her 40s, I would guess, and has been smiling nearly the entire time I've known her, which, in all fairness, has only been three minutes.

"Hum," she says, nodding, "there are two things you need to know. First, we do conduct prenatal exams and testing here. You won't be able to escape that. However, we never do anything without first explaining what we will do and why. You have the right to refuse any test. You have that right in a traditional doctor's office as well, but I'm guessing they never told you that, did they? We are accredited through the state, but we are only licensed to treat low risk pregnancies. Any complications or emergencies would need to be referred to a physician or hospital. Do you understand?"

I nod, all hopes of avoiding being prodded by medical instruments dashed. Connie asks me a series of questions, medical history stuff. I answer "no" to all of them, and she jots this on the form, too.

"Wonderful," she says. "Now, to address what else you said. We do treat the whole person. We assist our patients with diet and exercise plans, birth plans, pain management, and breastfeeding techniques. We also focus on our patients' emotional health because emotional health and physical health are connected and vital for a healthy baby. How does all this sound?"

I suppose this is the closest I'm going to get to feeling comfortable with the medical portion of the process. I force a smile. "It sounds good."

"Wonderful." She stands. "Let's go on a tour."

Connie leads me out of the office and down the hall, explaining that each midwife has her own office that she uses for consultations, instruction and planning. They look like ordinary offices except for the couches and armchairs. This puts midwife and patient on equal footing, she says.

The exam rooms have windows, bringing in natural light. Frosted glass and sheer curtains provide the patients with privacy. Connie says, should I decide to go with them, we'll do the first prenatal exam today. I swallow. I'm not mentally prepared for that. I'm never prepared for that.

"And here's one of our birthing suites," she says, outstretching an arm.

I follow her into a room that resembles a bedroom down to the lamps on the end tables. Huh, I wasn't expecting something nice. I saw the birth suites on the news, but figured the crew hide the clinical, medical stuff.

"Queen-sized bed," she says, "so the father or anyone else you choose to witness the happy event can join you at your side."

"There is a father," I say as if she somehow thought I could reproduce asexually like an amoeba. "He's on tour. He's a musician."

"Ah." That smile hasn't left her face. "Music is important to a child's development. In the bathroom, you'll find a shower and a birthing tub. You can use the tub, the bed, or both during labor and delivery."

I check out the bathroom. It's larger than the one at home.

"So, what do you think?" Connie says. "Will we be assisting you on your journey to motherhood? The second time around."

I'd like to fast forward about a year, but whatever.

"Yeah," I say, "let's get this show on the road."

THE MOMENT I GET BACK into the car, I take out my phone. Shit, it's a lot later than I thought it would be. Now, I have a decision to make. I either call Nat like I promised because he's no doubt waiting, or I drive to Shawna's and pick up Megan because they are waiting.

Damn it. I shiver and toss off my gloves. I'll give it a minute. One minute. I dial.

"Hello, beautiful," Nat says when he answers, "did you have your consultation at the place?"

"The birth center, you mean. Yeah. I talked to one of the midwives, toured the place and had my first prenatal. Everything's good. I'm due late September. So no birthday fuck for you this year."

Why the hell did I say that? That's what's concerning me the most at the moment?

"Your mouth still works, doesn't it?"

Now why the fuck did he say that?

The car is freezing, but my cheeks burn. "You know, I have to go pick up Megan. I'm not going to have time to suck you off. I'll have a newborn in the house. And I won't get much sleep. And, and, you should have pulled out."

"Okay, chill. I was just joking. I'm going to be sleepless right there with you, remember? I wasn't expecting anything for my birthday. You brought it up. I was playing along."

I exhale. "I did. I don't know why. A comment on the timing, I suppose. Last year I wore that orange, crotchless teddy for you and this year— I don't want to think about it."

"You'll get your body back. I mean, technically, you haven't lost it yet, but you'll get it back."

My figure? I wasn't even thinking about my figure. I was thinking about the bleeding and the stretched tissues and the recovery time.

"I wish you were home."

"I'll be back in July for a week, and we'll go house hunting."

That's not until my third trimester. I meant now so he can be here for the journey like a normal husband, but this isn't a normal marriage, not by traditional standards, and it never will be.

"Yeah, house hunting," I say. "It'll be great. I'll get an office. I'll be able to continue writing."

"See, that solves one thing you were worried about, and now that you have a due date, I'll be sure to be home. It'll be fine. We're making it work."

We sure are. We're making this life we have together work. But there are times, times like this, when I wish he could make money off of recording alone.

"I gotta go get Megan. I'll call you later," I say and hang up before he notices I'm crying.

"THEY HAVE A WHIRLPOOL tub?" Shawna says, bouncing Alyssa on her hip. "That sounds soothing."

Megan tugs on my sleeve. "Mommy, Mommy, I won *Chutes and Ladders* three times."

She holds up three fingers, proud either that she won or that she knows how many fingers equal three.

I pretend to be impressed. "Oh, wow, Sweetie, how many times did you play?"

"Three."

I really owe Shawna for watching Megan for longer than expected. After all, she has her own baby to worry about. She doesn't look annoyed, though. No, that's been me lately.

Megan runs after Cosmo, the Wrights' dog, and I turn my attention back to Shawna.

"I'm not going to say the place is great because, you know," I make a motion with my fingers near my crotch, so she knows I'm referring to the exam, "but I did feel respected and it does seem like more individualized care."

Shawna nods to indicate she understood my meaning. "When will you tell Megan?"

Good question. I have no idea. I'm hoping Nat will be with me when I do, but he won't be home until July. We have plans to go see him in March for my birthday, but that seems too soon.

"I'm not sure. We won't tell anyone else until after 12 weeks."

Alyssa tugs on her mother's neckline. Shawna switches the baby to the other hip, grabs a bottle off the end table and starts feeding her.

"Is that when Nat'll be home?"

"Nope." I sit on the couch and fold my hands in my lap. "I've turned into my mother."

Her eyes widen. "What? No, you haven't. When he's away, you text, send picture messages and talk throughout the day. Yeah, I know your parents didn't have cell phones, but they could have set up a time each day for your dad to call, but they didn't. Their dysfunction is on them."

Dysfunction is a good word for it.

"That's true. We have found ways to stay connected emotionally. It's physically that's the issue. I suppose I'm just depressed because kids grow so fast, and he misses so much."

"Mommy, Daddy lives on a bus," Megan says from across the room, proving my point.

Shawna and I exchange a glance.

"No, Sweetie," I say, "Daddy lives with us. He goes to work using a bus. There's a difference."

"If it's any consolation," Shawna says, sitting next to me and adjusting the baby on her lap, "Megan did great with Alyssa. I think you'll have a little helper on your hands."

I pat the couch beside us. "Come here, Sweetie."

Megan skips over and plops down on the cushion.

"So tell me," I say, "what do you think of little Alyssa?"

"Um," Megan sucks on her bottom lip, "she's cute."

Shawna and I briefly laugh.

"Yes, she is cute," I say.

"And stinky," Megan says.

Stinky? Shawna and I laugh harder.

"She went poopies in her pants," Megan says.

Ah, I guess at some point I'll need to explain how diapers work. Damn, and it was so nice having a child who is potty trained.

MARCH 10, 2007

First trimester exhaustion might be worse this time. Sometimes I can barely keep my eyes open. Yeah, I was working a 9-5 in 2003, but other than my job all I had to worry about was Scooter. Now I have a toddler and two pets, and a constantly messy house because of the aforementioned child and pets, plus I'm trying to finish my second novel.

I gave Megan crayons and a stack of coloring books and told her I was going to take a nap. I suppose I should open my eyes, but it feels so nice lying here with my face squished in my pillow.

I open my eyes and look at the clock. What? I've been asleep for an hour and a half? I intended to lie down for 10 minutes. And it's been an hour and a half! I bolt upright. I don't smell smoke. The house doesn't appear to be on fire. Can Megan unlock doors? Did she eat something and choke? Hurt herself? Fuck. We're going to end up on the evening news.

I run for the bedroom door and throw it open.

"Hi, Mommy," Megan says from the hallway.

Phew. She's alive and unharmed, but why is she outside my door? I glance up and down the hall. Every available wall space from baseboard to as high as she can reach is covered in scribbles. Oh, no, no, no. What a mess, and I don't have a drop of energy to clean.

"What are you doing?" I say, keeping my tone calm.

"Coloring. Scooter went poopies in the kitchen."

Wonderful. A second mess. I hope he didn't track it throughout the house.

"We don't color on the walls, Megan. That's what coloring books are for."

She looks up, eyes welling. "You don't like it?"

"It's, um, beautiful, Sweetie. But drawing on the walls is a no-no."

She starts crying. Oh, God, I didn't want to make her cry. But what am I supposed to do? I can't leave crayon all over the walls.

"Tell you what?" I say, picking her up. "I'll take pictures of your drawings, so you can remember them forever, then clean the wall. You can help me. I'll give you a sponge."

Megan nods, tears streaming down her cheeks, and sets her head on my shoulder.

"Tell me about your drawings," I say, hoping to cheer her up.

She wipes her tears on her sleeve. I set her down and she points at a drawing on the wall between her room and the office.

"That's Scooter," she says, regarding an oval with stick legs and tail, an oval head and triangle ears.

Beside it, a similar figure is Maisie. Between the master bedroom and the bathroom are a bunch of sticks and ovals and what I'm guessing is hair.

"That's you, me and Daddy."

I squint. Sure enough, those are three stick people. I wonder how Megan will take news of an upcoming sibling. I want her to know, but Nat and I will need to decide what to say. But how do we explain it in a way a three year old will understand?

"Very nice. Megan, Sweetie, what would you think if Daddy and I had another kid besides you?"

She shrugs. Probably thinks I mean someone her age.

"Some mommies and daddies have more than one. Like Grandma and Grandpa or Yiayia and Papou."

Her eyes are wide. I don't think she gets it. I'll try one more thing before letting it go.

"A baby like Alyssa only smaller."

She wrinkles her nose. "Babies are stinky. Like Scooter. He went poopies in the kitchen."

Oh, shit, literally. I'll worry about how to tell Megan about the baby later. There's a mess to clean before dinner. I glance at the walls on either side of us. And a mess to clean up after dinner.

Chapter 16

Mini Me Two

May 24, 2007

We told Megan earlier this month. She doesn't get it. How could she understand at her age? I mean, it doesn't feel real to me either. With Megan, it wasn't until the ultrasound that reality set in. That was when the "it" became a "she." Today, another "it" takes on an identity.

"Set the scene for me," Nat says via speaker phone.

"The scene?" I say, laughing. "What do you think this is? A play?"

"Come on. I don't know how these things go."

Sad, but true. He missed Megan's ultrasound, and he's missing this one. That's what happens when you're a rock star's wife. I take a deep breath. I'll focus on the positive instead. He loves us and he's involved, even if it is remotely.

"Well," I say, "I'm on the exam table and there's a machine. The ultrasound tech is going to use that to see the baby."

"That's right," the technician says, speaking as if Nat's half deaf. "We're going to start once I get the gel on Cassie's stomach."

Ah! I resist the urge to yelp. It's cold. It's cold. It's cold!

The technician puts the wand on my belly. "So where is your daughter today?" she says, adjusting the picture.

"With my mother-in-law," I say.

"Oh, nice. Time with grandma. I bet your mother-in-law is excited about another grandbaby."

"Oh, she's just as excited as we are," Nat says, "to learn if it's a boy or girl."

"We'll know shortly," the tech says.

She starts with the medical stuff. Heart strong. Measurements where they should be.

"First babies tend to be smaller than their siblings," the tech says when I tell her this one is a bit larger than Megan at this stage.

That's her way of saying I'm going to need to push out an even bigger human. I sit up slightly.

"It's fine," she says. "Nothing abnormal."

Easy for her to say. She's not petite. Big potentially leads to complications, jeopardizing my ability to stay with the birth center, and I don't want to go back to the hospital.

"Ready for the gender reveal?"

Nat and I answer in the affirmative. I wonder how this experience is for him, waiting on the other end of the phone line, practically eavesdropping on our conversation here at the center, connected to the situation yet still not.

"All right. I see it. Ready? See this here." She points to the screen. "That is a penis. You know what that means?"

No. What does it mean? Of course, I know what it means. I know what a penis is. I got into this situation because of a penis.

"You got your mini-me," I say to Nat.

"Yeah, that's cool. Call me back when you get back in the car."

He hangs up. Um, okay. That was a bit abrupt. I press my lips together.

"Congratulations," the tech says. "Now, you'll have one of each."

I LOCK THE CAR DOOR and insert the key in the ignition before digging my phone out of my purse and calling Nat.

"Why did you hang up like that?" I say without a hello.

"Uh, yeah, about that. Well, I had to go the bathroom. I had to get up earlier than usual this morning to make it in time, so to speak, and so I drank a lot of coffee. Full caffeine. Now, I'm jittery and I have to take a piss every five minutes."

I try not to laugh, but I can't help it. "It's, like, a 15 minute appointment. You couldn't stay awake for 15 minutes?"

"We had a show last night, you know. You try going to bed at 2 a.m. then getting up at eight. I'm in Pacific Time, so it was really 6 a.m., so that's four hours of sleep."

"What?" I say, laughing again. "You just said you got up at eight. Now it was six?"

"Eight Central. These time zone changes drive me crazy sometimes. So I need caffeine. And a calculator, apparently. But never mind that. If we don't hurry up, I'll need to go again."

I finish laughing at his expense. The time zone changes drive me crazy, too. It gets confusing. When you say what time it is, do you use Central Standard Time or the other time zone? And I'm not too proud to admit that I use four fingers to figure out time differences. Each finger represents a time zone. Lord help me when he's outside continental North America.

"We have one of each," I say, repeating the tech's sentiments. "Does this mean I'll get pissed on whenever I change a diaper?"

"Yeah, you will," he says as if it's the greatest thing in the world. "Maybe there's some trick to it. Talk to Mom whenever you go back to the house to pick up Megan. She did it five times."

Yeah, I'm not doing that. I'm not asking my mother-in-law how she handled – eww, bad choice of words – my husband and brothers-in-law's penises when they were babies. There's something really perverted about that. Mom, Penny and Vanessa did it, too, and if you've seen one baby penis, you've seen them all, right? No, scratch that. I can't ask my mother either because I'm not inquiring about my brothers' penises. Chris was born the same year as Woodstock. He was probably naked most of the time. And Greg behaves as if he was born in 1872, so he probably doesn't even like to touch himself to use the bathroom. No, I definitely need to ask someone whose sons haven't remotely reached puberty yet.

"Maybe she has some of those naked baby pictures of you," I say as a diversionary tactic. "You know the kind people used to take. Naked baby on a rug. I'd really love to see what your baby butt looked like. I bet it was so cute."

"Um, yeah. Maybe don't ask Mom. Megan will be with you. She doesn't need to see my baby pictures."

Oh, so there really are naked baby pictures? Now that we're having a son, I have an excuse to ask to see them. For comparison purposes, you know.

"Aww, but I'd love to see the little baby who is now making his own little babies."

"Have you thought of any names?"

Have I thought of any names? Smooth. Diversionary tactic of his own. I place my hand on my stomach. Honestly, I had been hoping for a second girl so Megan could bond with a sibling like Vanessa and I did. And also for practical reasons, like hand-me-downs.

"No, not one. You?"

"I dunno. We could name him after the city he was conceived in, but Los Angeles is an awfully weird name for a kid."

I laugh at his dumb joke, although there are parents who do name their kids after where they were conceived. It's as if they're proud of it or something. I would consider it for Austin, since that is also a real name, but that's it.

"Then Megan should be named Milwaukee. I wonder if it's too late to change it."

"I kinda like Josh. Joshua, I suppose. Eh, think about it. I gotta go to the bathroom. Love you and Baby Boy."

"Love you."

I hang up and laugh.

I SIT ON THE COUCH and pat the cushion beside me. "Come sit with me, Sweetie. I want to show you something."

Megan bounds over, wearing Maisie as a fashion accessory. The moment Megan sits, the cat meows and makes a quick escape. I should chastise her for that, but I let it go, focusing on what I'm about to do instead. I take a string of six photos off the coffee table.

"You stayed with Grandma today because I went to use a very special machine. Remember how Daddy and I told you Mommy has a baby in her belly?"

Megan nods, mouth slightly agape. "Uh, huh."

"Well, I used the very special machine to take pictures of the baby." I show her the photos. "You're going to have a baby brother. Do you know what a brother is?"

She shakes her head, never once removing her eyes from the ultrasound photos.

"Well, let me put it this way. Theos Chris and Theos Greg are my brothers, and Uncle Aaron, Uncle Julian, Uncle Adrian and Uncle Gabe are Daddy's brothers. Do you understand?"

I'm not sure she does. I know she still struggles with the entire concept of a sibling. All right. I'll try something else.

I point to one of the photos. "See, here's his head from the side. See the shape of his face. He's probably going to have a nose like yours and Daddy's. I can see it."

I can't. But I'm not telling her that.

Megan stares, but she ain't saying anything.

"You can see it, too, right?" I say. "That's clearly a nose. And here's his little chin. And in this picture, you can see a little hand. His hand is probably smaller than Maisie's paw right now. His entire body is only 11 inches tall."

Well, that was a dumb thing to tell her. She doesn't know how large 11 inches is because she doesn't know how to measure.

Baby Boy's swimming around. I can feel it. Unless it's bad gas.

I scowl for second. How can I get Megan to understand? I'm certainly not going to point out a baby penis. That'll confuse her even more.

"What I'm trying to tell you is that the baby is a boy. He'll be your little brother, and you'll be his big sister. Thea Vanessa is my sister, and Aunts Amy, Nadine, Nicole and Deanna are Daddy's sisters."

Out of ideas, I set the photos back on the coffee table and wait.

"Babies are stinky," Megan finally says.

"Oh." I raise my chin and lower it, not quite nodding. "Well, not all the time. Only when they need a diaper change."

"Why don't they go poopies in the potty?"

"Only big kids can do that, and you're a big kid."

Connie suggested I buy Megan a washable baby doll that can be pretend fed and have its diapers changed, so she can learn before the real thing arrives. I think a trip to the toy store is in our future.

"That's why babies are stinky." She slides off the cushion. "Mommy, I'm hungry."

"Okay, Sweetie, I'll get you a snack."

I take her hand, and we move to the kitchen peninsula. I guess progress was made. I can't tell. I hope by the time the baby comes, she understands he's coming to live with us.

Chapter 17

The Old Gang's Back Together Again

June 16, 2007

"You're the designated driver by default," Shawna says, pulling into the Sterling High School parking lot for our 10-year high school reunion.

"I'm jealous. You know that," I say, butterflies building in my stomach. "I may need a drink after all of this."

She laughs. "I doubt it. It'll be fun to see most people."

"Yeah, most people."

I curl my lip at the thought of our old nemeses, Karen King, the boyfriend stealing slut, and my ex-boyfriends Keith Cook, Travis White and Jason Brookes. Todd Miller, my only high school ex who doesn't make me cringe, won't be here because he was two classes ahead of us. Last I heard, he married a fellow attorney and is partner at his father's law firm.

Shawna parks the car and turns off the engine. "We don't even know who's going to be here."

"That's the problem," I say, regretting I let my friends talk me into this.

I thought it would be a fun. That must have been the morning sickness talking. Almost anything seems fun compared to morning sickness.

I exit the car and check my reflection in the passenger window. I did my makeup an hour ago, and it looks great, but there's nothing I can do about this belly. Can't suck in six months worth of baby. I've tried. Joshua kicks as if he can read my thoughts. People keep telling us it's everyone's dream to have both a girl and a boy. I think it's the latest in a list of stupid shit people say when you're expecting a baby.

"I have to go pee," I say. "Let's go find a public restroom and come back."

"What?" Shawna says, tossing her keys in her purse. "There's bathrooms in the school. You'll be running to them all night."

Damn. She caught my attempt to delay. I really do have to go to the bathroom, although I think it's more from nerves than baby.

When I was pregnant with Megan, I was thin during the hottest months of the year, but this time it's the opposite. I tug on my dress, adjusting it. Does it look ridiculous to have a short hem, engorged boobs and this roundness? I say it does. Nat claims I'm the sexiness pregnant woman he's ever seen, but I think, since he gets laid either way, he only wants to boost my fragile ego.

I nod. "Let's go."

Maroula and Jennifer, currently in their own states of roundness, wait for us outside the main entrance. Maroula's working on baby number three, Damian. She says this'll be the last kid. She and Steve hoped for a girl, but after three kids in three years, she really doesn't want to try again. I can't blame her. Holy shit.

Jennifer's working on number two. Her and Phil's daughter, Grace, was born the same year as Megan and their son, Ethan, will be born the same year as Joshua. Chris had a field day with that one, making all kinds of crude comments about Phil and I coordinating our love making efforts to see which couple's sperm hit its target first. Nat and I both times. We won. Not that there actually was a competition.

"You're late," Jennifer says.

She married someone of Mediterranean decent. She should know that scheduled start times are merely guidelines.

"Potty breaks," Shawna says, pointing to me with her thumb.

I shake my head. "It couldn't be helped. It's a hot day. I drank a lot of water."

"Yeah. That was why," she says, tilting her head, probably rolling her eyes beneath those sunglasses.

Maroula rubs my belly. I allow her only because she is family. No one else better try tonight, or I'm slapping their hand away. I should rub her belly back, but I'm larger than she is and how would that look?

"So exciting." She almost bounces on her feet. "The others are inside."

What a quartet we must make – three pregnant (and related) chicks and Shawna who's curvy in all the right places.

We enter the school gymnasium. The set up reminds me of a wedding reception, round tables throughout the room along with a couple rectangular tables containing a buffet. A DJ plays Live's "Lightning Crashes." I remember all the lyrics and sing along under my breath.

Maroula parts ways to find her group of friends. The nerds basically.

"Everyone else is this way," Jennifer says, leading us to a table near the center of the room where Jen, Jenny and Tiffany sit chatting.

Jen jumps up the moment she sees us. "Cassie," she says taking my arm, "do you see that guy there? The one in the red polo shirt."

My eyes follow her gaze to a group of four guys talking not too far from us. The guy in the red polo shirt is bald and fat and looks a least a decade older than the rest of us. I squint, but I don't recognize him.

"No, who is he?"

"That's Keith Cook."

Holy shit. I considered losing my virginity to *him*? Thank God I didn't. I've said that multiple times for multiple reasons, and I'm saying it again for another one. If he tries to talk to me, I am going to conveniently not know who he is.

"What happened to him?"

Jen shrugs. "I don't know specifically, but I do know this. Jenny was the first person in our class to get married, but Keith was the first to divorce. He's got four ex-wives."

"Four?"

That must have been before he lost his looks. So how long did he stay married? Like, two months? Cheated on all of them, I'm sure.

"Tell her what else," Jenny, who finally found a boyfriend and got over Derek, says.

Jen leans forward as if she has something awfully juicy to share. "Travis is in prison. Drug possession. Three strikes, you're out."

Travis did steroids in high school, told me getting a football scholarship was his only means of attending college. Only Shawna knows. I didn't tell the rest of my friends because the steroids gave him sexual problems, and I always protect my lovers' privacy. So he moved on to other drugs? Maybe his college football career plans didn't work out and he took it hard. Bad choice of words. Hard. I feel guilty now that I made up an excuse to break up with him. I should have been truthful and told him it was the drug use. It could have made a difference. You don't know.

"It's so weird seeing you this way," Tiffany says, eyeing my stomach. "I thought we were both in agreement on women's reproductive rights."

Unlike me, Tiffany stuck to her feminist rantings. But it's been years since we both were in agreement on much of anything.

"Well," I say, "I've come to a new understanding of prochoice. Choice means choice. Whether it means the legal right to an abortion or whether it means deciding to become a baby machine."

She looks pissed. "And are you a baby machine?"

I shake my head. "No. I wouldn't go through this for just anybody. Only Nat."

We had this very conversation the night of my formal wedding. I thought she understood my perspective. Then again, catch a whiff of her breath. She's been drinking. Jen and Jenny also have two kids. Harass them.

"I'm gonna use the bathroom," I say, pointing toward the exit, "and when I get back we can gossip some more about our ex-boyfriends."

I kept up with my friends over the years, so I know what's happening when it comes to love, marriage, kids and career, but I have a feeling I'm going to spend the rest of the night answering people's nosy questions. There's a rumor going around that I married a rock star. Makes me laugh. I say "rumor," because everyone, other than my friends, thinks it isn't true, that it's a story someone fabricated. After all, I had a reputation back in the day for being a music fan.

I leave the gym, amazed I still know my way around the building's halls, and spot a familiar face. Kelly Williams Schneckly. We were co-captains of the majorette team senior year and roommates at U of I. I haven't seen her since my wedding. A month or two later, she moved to Indianapolis, and I didn't expect to see her tonight.

"Shane's back at the hotel," she says after small talk. "I was hoping you'd come catch a drink with us later, but," her eyes scan down and back again, "there's no point dragging you to a bar when you can't drink. Where's Nat tonight?"

"Calgary."

"Calgary? I don't know how you two do it."

"Dedication and determination. Hey, I was on my way to the restroom, but I promise I'll catch up with you later."

I do my business and return to my friends' table. A woman lingers near Tiffany's elbow. What the fuck does Karen want? I join the group, hoping to find out why everyone listens intently to whatever she's saying.

"I'm glad you're here," she says when I sit. "I wanted to apologize for my behavior when we were in school. I shouldn't have started the feud between us."

Um, wow, I never expected that. Not that it matters much after all these years. She tried to steal Derek and she did steal Keith. In hindsight, she did me a favor.

"Well," Tiffany says, "you know I don't believe women should have different sexual standards than men, but you caused a lot of people a lot of heartache."

Karen drops her eyes. "I know. I've done a lot of soul searching over the years. My mom wasn't the best of role models, but that's no excuse. I've gone through therapy. The psychologist encouraged me to reach out and make amends. Otherwise, I wouldn't have come today. But I needed to face my reputation."

"I was one of those people who went through hell," Jenny says, "but I don't hold grudges."

I whip my head in her direction. She doesn't hold grudges? She held a grudge against Derek for five years. No one else sees the irony in this, and everyone but me agrees to let bygones be bygones.

"Yes," I say, when my silence makes me the center of attention. "Why shouldn't we do that? We're adults now. There are more important things to worry about."

Karen smiles. "Great. I won't keep you any longer. Have a great night."

THE REUNION ENDED NOT being bad after all. It gave my friends and me an opportunity to hang out that didn't revolve around a wedding, baby shower or anything else where our attention would be divided. I heard songs from the '90s that I haven't heard, or even thought about, in ages. Plus, who doesn't want to learn who got fat, ugly, divorced, successful, etc.?

I already said my goodbyes, but I need to use the bathroom one more time before Shawna and I leave. I'm half way to the gym exit when Jason stops me. He looks older but otherwise the same.

"I wanted to see how you were doing?" he says.

Oh, he did, did he?

"I'm doing okay. Thanks."

I glance at Shawna, mentally sending her the signal to come rescue me.

"So the rumors are true?" he says, face serious.

"That I'm okay?"

"That you married a rock musician."

I feel a kick and rub my belly. "Uh, yeah."

"I would have thought you would have done better with your life than that. You were the salutatorian. You could have had anyone, and that's who you pick?" he says, shaking his head in disgust.

Whoa, that's harsher than anything my parents ever said.

My heart races. "I don't identify my spouse by his profession. He is a person, not a label."

Jason looks like he smelt a steaming pile of shit. "I would have expected better, but then again, maybe not. He probably thinks with his private parts, same as you."

I narrow my eyes. "Wow, Jason, you once were a great guy and then something happened – I don't know what – to turn you into a judgmental prick. Looks like you haven't changed a bit since senior year. Even slutty Karen matured enough to apologize. I guess you'll forever be 18, placing value in things like private schools and low sex drives. I am a truly ashamed I ever let you fuck me. Now, if you excuse me, I have my life to get back to."

Shawna receives the subliminal message and takes me by the arm, ushering me toward the door as quickly as possible.

"What did he say to you?" she says, handing me my purse.

"Judgmental shit about how I could have done so much better than Nat."

I want to leave. I'll hold it in until I get back to Mom and Dad's.

She rises her eyebrows. "What? But he isn't here. Why would Jason even think to bring him up?"

"To be a snob. I told him I was ashamed I ever let him stick it in me."

She laughs. "Bet he didn't take that well."

I put my hand on her elbow. "Come on. I don't want to talk about Jason anymore."

We step out into the warm night, and it feels good to realize I'm an adult and I never need to see these people again unless I want to.

Chapter 18

House Hunters

July 3, 2007

"This'll be the 15th house we've looked at," I say, running my fingers through Nat's hair while we wait at a stop light. "I had been hoping to do something fun while you're home."

"The 17th and, yeah, I know. I'd like that, too, but at the same time we need to pick the right house. I don't want to move again in a few years because we're unhappy with it."

The light changes, and he drives on.

"I get it. I don't either. But it's summer and it's hot, and I'm carrying 15 extra pounds around. I'd love to do something relaxing after this."

"The only thing that's hot is you in that dress." He reaches over and briefly puts his hand on my thigh. "But I promise you something relaxing after this."

He turns, and the houses get larger and farther apart. These properties appear to be above budget by thousands, maybe tens of thousands.

"Did you get lost?" I say.

"No. This is the road."

"These houses look like they're $400,000. We can't afford a house that's worth double the townhouse."

Nat doesn't answer. I'm aware he doesn't know any more than I do, but these houses look fancier than the others we toured. A few minutes later, we pull into the driveway of the house where Donna, the same realtor we used when we bought the townhouse, told us to meet her. She stands on the porch, holding the MLS sheet.

"See," he says. "This has gotta be it if she's here."

We exit the car. The sun beats down, and I wish I were sunning in the backyard watching Megan run around instead of house hunting. Or better yet, lounging by Shawna and Jason's pool. They live only a few miles from here. The bean-shaped pool is gorgeous and, because it's heated, can be used April through October.

I take Nat's hand, and we amble to the porch.

Donna smiles. "I'm glad you found it. Now, I know this house is different than the rest."

Yeah, because it's over budget.

"This is a lot of house, Donna," Nat says, "and property."

"It's an acre, 3,300 square feet, $299,999."

She hands Nat the MLS sheet. He smiles. I can tell he likes the price.

I fold my arms. "Why so cheap? What's wrong with it? Haunted? Murder scene?"

"Foreclosure. The previous owners had a financial setback, sadly. But the house has been on the market for less than 24 hours. I thought of you immediately because it meets all your needs."

Nat hands me the MLS sheet. I glance over it. It looks good on paper, but I've heard horror stories about foreclosures. Some people go a bit nutty and destroy their properties, or the houses have been vacant for so long they are in disrepair. The porch looks good, glass intact in the windows and door, but that could be misleading.

Donna unlocks the door and steps aside so we can enter first. Prepared for the worst, I take off my sunglasses only to be met with a large great room that's the same layout as our current one. The only difference is the wall we share with the neighbor. Here, it's a wall of windows.

"Well," Donna says, "as you can see, similar layout to your current home. Behind the garage, there's a bonus room, however. I'll take you there in a minute. Hardwood floors throughout. Granite countertops in the kitchen and bathrooms. The fireplace is gas. I'll give you a minute."

The room is vacant, so the only thing to explore is the French Provincial kitchen. It's not my taste but beautiful nonetheless with black countertops providing a nice counterbalance. I open and close some of the cabinets and drawers. There's maybe double our storage space.

"Oh, look," Nat says, opening a door. "I can picture the kids hiding in here."

I have no clue what Joshua will look like so I have a tough time picturing anyone but Megan, but clearly Nat has an image in his mind.

I glance up from the cabinets under the island to see a walk-in pantry larger than my parents' master bedroom closet. How would we ever fill a pantry that large? Maybe if we fed the entire extended family.

"Come on," Donna says. "I'll show you the bonus room."

She leads us through the great room and down a short hall to the left.

"Cassie, this is where your office could go," Donna says.

It's decently sized, built-in bookcases on one side, lots of natural light with windows on two walls, and a view of the yard. This would be fantastic. I merely nod.

Donna leads us back down the hall, through a sliding glass door and onto a covered patio.

"Fenced-in yard is perfect for young children or your dog," she says.

Most of the houses we looked at weren't fenced-in. Scooter could be let out without fear of him scampering away, and the kids would be safe, too. This house has no swimming pool, but the patio might be as large as our current backyard.

Donna takes us back through the great room and shows us a laundry room, a bathroom and the door to the garage before going downstairs to the basement.

"It's semi-finished," she says. "Completely waterproofed and insulated but no internal walls other than the ones hiding the furnace and hot water heater. But that might be a good thing. Allows you to customize it as you choose."

Nat turns in a circle, eyes wide. "Honey, I could have a studio down here, and we could have a playroom for the kids."

He's mentioned a home studio before, but I thought he was daydreaming. Guess not.

"It's ours to customize like Donna says," I say, not wanting to start a debate in front of her.

"I'll wait in the kitchen while you check out the bedrooms," Donna says. "There's five of them."

Five of them? Why do we need five bedrooms?

Nat starts up the two flights of stairs, and I follow, watching his ass.

"Honey," I say when we reach the top floor, "why do we need five bedrooms?"

He turns and smiles. "We don't, but better to have more space than we need than less. Look how quickly we outgrew the townhouse, and that was more house than we needed in the beginning, too."

He takes my hand, and we examine the bedrooms. The spare bedrooms are the same size and layout and share a bathroom with double sinks. The master bedroom, complete with his and hers closets, and the bathroom are larger than our current ones.

"So what do you think?" he says. "You said you were tired of house hunting. This place gets us the most for our money."

I am tired of house hunting. But making a decision on the spot after we saw 16 other houses seems silly. When we picked the townhouse, I had already narrowed down to three.

I bite my lip. "You want to make a decision right now?"

"We don't really have much choice. I'm only home a few more days, and I don't want to get into a bidding war over this place. Donna said it recently went on the market. If we're the first ones, we just might get it."

It is a beautiful house with room to spare. Maybe too much room to spare.

"Who'll take care of the lawn when you're gone?"

"We'll hire a service. Unless there's an HOA." He checks the MLS, and his face brightens. "There isn't. We could get that hot tub we've been talking about."

"All right. Full price offer then. They either accept it or they don't. If they don't, we pick from one of the three-bedroom houses we looked at."

"Agreed." He squeezes my hand. "Let's go tell Donna."

THE MOSQUITOS ARE STAYING away tonight, which is nice. Even nicer is the dark, almost moonless, night enveloping us like black velvet punctuated by sequins. The crickets serenade.

Nat wraps his arm around me and pulls me close. One reclining lounge chair for two is a tight squeeze, but we can't snuggle with armrests between us, now can we? My belly isn't even that big yet. When he next returns home, I'll be ready to pop. What a terrible thought.

"I felt the baby kick," he says placing his palm on my dress. "I find it fascinating that there's a little boy in there floating around."

"Very little. He's still smaller than Scooter or Maisie length-wise."

"We created him."

I want to say "You created him when you didn't pull out," but I don't. I've forgiven even if I haven't forgotten.

We interlace fingers, again failing silent as the crickets sing around us, our attention skyward.

"Think aliens exist?" Nat says after a shooting star appears overhead.

"I think it's mathematically impossible that they don't. Especially now that we know exoplanets exist."

"Of course, they exist. It's so stupid to think our sun is the only one in existence with planets orbiting around it. How would ours somehow be special?"

"Tell the religious people that."

"I'll tell them to read some Carl Sagan. *Pale Blue Dot* specifically."

I laugh. "You do that."

I close my eyes. This afternoon I told him that I wanted to do something relaxing after house hunting. Seeing as I'm about ready to fall asleep, this is it.

Nat's phone rings, jarring me to attention and silencing the crickets.

"It's Donna," he says, pulling the phone out of his pocket.

He answers, and I hear bits and pieces of her end of the conversation, catching apology, bank and something about paperwork.

"We got the house," he says after he hangs up. "She wants us to meet her in the morning.at the real estate office to sign something."

"Your mom and dad's cookout is tomorrow."

"She says it won't take long."

"That's good," I say, again shutting my eyes.

"You know." His hand moves to my breast. "We'll need to christen every room of that house."

"And buy a hot tub."

"And buy a hot tub."

He squeezes my boob, and I move my leg across his lap.

Chapter 19

Five Years Ago This Week

July 4, 2007

Nat and I arrive late to his parents' cookout. Life with a toddler. Megan threw a fit because she wanted to bring her favorite stuffed animal along. We said no, that she risked losing it or getting it dirty. She cried, pounded her feet. We didn't leave until she calmed. Now that she's three and a half, the meltdowns are farther and farther apart, but I'm glad Nat got to witness one. Why am I glad? I dunno. Maybe because he misses these parenting moments when he's away.

Nat holds Megan when we enter his parents' backyard, and she's happy as a clam. (What a weird saying. Are clams happy?) She has cousins to play with, and I guess that made her forget all about a stuffed animal that's losing its stuffing.

"Daddy, put me down," she says when she sees Josie, Aaron's daughter and the closest girl cousin in age.

Nat holds a finger in front of her nose. "If I put you down, you must do something for me."

Megan's eyes widen. "What?"

"You must promise to stay in the backyard and don't go anywhere an adult can't see you."

"I promise."

He makes her pinkie swear before allowing her to run away with Josie. My in-laws have an elaborate play area for the grandkids. They rarely stray far.

Nat smiles. "You should move away from me, so we can recreate when we met."

I smile back, confused. "Recreate it?"

"Well, as best as we can." He clears his throat. "So what do you know about cars?"

Oh, well, okay. I guess either we're going to recreate it or I'm going to be a stick in the mud. Who pokes sticks in mud?

I push my hair behind my ear. "I had Matchbox cars as a kid."

"I got a new car. Honda CR-V. It's got room for *two* car seats."

I almost laugh. That's certainly not how the original conversation went. The Honda is my new car. What am I supposed to say next? In 2002, he bought a Mazda Miata.

"I have a 1990 Volkswagen Jetta."

That was the car I drove when we met. When I got pregnant with Megan, we traded it for a 2003 Toyota Matrix. Our new house has a three-car garage, so Nat's sports car is safe and he can drive the Matrix during winter, or whenever taking a sports car wouldn't be appropriate, and I'll use the Honda to haul the kids' little asses around.

"That's almost a classic. I love classic cars. Did Nadine tell you I love music and cars?"

I shake my head. "No. Not at all."

He starts talking about cars, telling me things I already know, and I pretend I'm clueless.

"We should get back the party. We haven't had a chance yet to talk to anyone else."

We part ways. I was drinking at the original party. Can't drink now. I grab some lemonade and intermingle with my sisters-in-law. Nat heads off toward the men, flashing me a smile whenever our eyes meet.

"How are you feeling?" Amy says.

And here comes the belly rub. I brace myself.

"I'm as good as I can be. We bought a new house yesterday."

It's a great diversion from belly rubbing, considering it's true. I tell them about the house and how we're waiting for an inspection, but if all goes well, we'll be moved in well before the baby comes.

"A big yard will be nice," Nadine says. "You should get a swing set. We had a blast with ours as kids."

"We haven't talked about it."

I feel sorry for Nadine. She's been trying for a baby for years. She made a comment, years ago when I was pregnant with Megan, that some people have happy accidents. She didn't sound bitter when she said it, but she might very well have felt that way. I haven't told her Joshua also is a happy accident. I reminded her that we were neither planning nor preventing, but we were preventing. Natural family planning is a form of birth control.

The sisters tell me about games they used to play as child. I interject here and there, sharing bits and pieces about Vanessa's and my girlhood. Eventually, though, pregnancy bladder necessitates a trip to the bathroom.

When I reach the house, I find my mother-in-law sitting on the porch with Deanna's fiancé, Hayes, who she met when studying graphic design at Northern Illinois University. He's a handsome guy with strawberry blonde hair and a contagious laugh.

"Have you met Hayes?" my mother-in-law says.

I smile. "A handful of times."

She turns to him. "She and my Nat met at an outdoor gathering like this five years ago. Then they went for a car ride and came back in love."

"Oh, I wouldn't say it happened that quickly," I say.

"Yes, it did, dear. Everyone could see it."

Well, okay, then. I have no intention of arguing with her. But how are we going to replicate that part of the evening? On the other hand, how long are we going to keep this fit of make-believe going?

I use the bathroom and check on Megan, reminding her of her promise. She hasn't budged from the play area, but I felt it best to remind her anyhow.

"Want to go for a ride?" Nat he says, coming over.

"Excuse me?" I say, trying to pretend I'm incredibly shocked.

"On my hard cock. What did you think I meant?"

I smile. "Sorry. I heard you wrong. Let's go."

He takes my hand, and we move away from the group. Wait a minute. Are we actually going to have a quickie instead of a car ride?

We pass a perplexed Nadine who outstretches her arm. "Hey, where are you going?"

"Relax," Nat says, "we'll be back."

"I have something important to say. I want you to hear it."

"Can everyone be quiet for a minute?" Terry says. "We have something to say."

His voice startles me, and I flinch. Nat and I stop short. What the hell is going on?

Blushing, Nadine beams at Terry and clasps his arm. "I'll be quick, I promise," she says when the crowd quiets. "This just seemed the easiest way. Well, you know we've been wanting a baby for a while."

Have they decided to adopt? I'm surprised they didn't think of that years ago. Or hire a surrogate. Not me, of course. I have a tough enough time carrying my own children.

"It's finally happened." She jumps. "We kept it secret because we're superstitious. The baby is due in December. Josh'll have a little cousin to beat up on."

She smirks at us, and Nat and I exchange a glance. I can tell from his expression that he was clueless. So was I. How did I not notice the bump before this, yet there it is?

My mother-in-law comes running from the porch and throws her arms around her daughter's neck. My father-in-law appears from somewhere to shake Terry's hand.

"I'm so happy for you," I say in Nadine's ear. "We'll go shopping. It'll be fun."

"That's the first thing we do once Dramatic Sneezer goes back on tour," she says.

I congratulate Terry, too, but it's impossible to say much with other people vying for the couple's attention.

Nat again takes my hand, but this time instead of heading away from the house we head toward it.

THIS IS WHY I HAVEN'T fucked in a twin bed since college. It's, shall we say, limiting. I've entered the portion of my pregnancy where sexual positions become difficult, and this damn bed isn't helping.

I open my eyes and notice a beam of sunlight highlighting a Black Sabbath poster on the wall. Nat's teenage bedroom is virtually unchanged, I'm told, preserved for one grandson or another to use during sleepovers.

Since he can't lay on me, Nat leans over me propped on his hands, which must be uncomfortable considering how long he's been doing it. I shift my focus from the wall to his face. He gets this expression when he's fucking me as hard as he can, which often happens during quickies, that's almost a grin, almost like he's crying from pleasure. He's got it now, although with his hair flopping over his cheeks.

My dress pushed over my belly, I can't see his cock anymore. Such a shame. I'd love to watch it sliding in and out of my slippery tunnel. But I feel him. Oh, do I feel him. I clench the comforter and try to keep my feet from vibrating off the edge of the bed.

Really, though, shouldn't I be on top? He asked me to ride his cock, not for him to ride my pussy. I should say something, but I'm trying too hard to control the volume of my moaning. Later. I'll say something later. We can fuck again tonight.

While daydreaming about later, I moan louder than I intend. He stops thrusting, and we look at the door, straining to hear if any relatives are within earshot. I hear nothing and neither must he because after a few seconds he resumes thrusting.

I squeeze my eyes shut and suck my bottom lip. I'll be quiet. I can do this. He's bound to cum soon. I want him to cum and I don't at the same time. Has anyone noticed we're gone? What if Megan needs us for something?

His body starts to shake with growing intensity. He pushes his hips toward mine, and I feel him cum. Usually he lingers for a bit, but today he pulls out almost immediately. His arms and wrists must be killing him by now.

"Scoot over," he says.

The hem of his t-shirt ends where his cock's shaft meets pubic hair. Speaking of pubic hair, who knows what sort of terrible shaving job I've been doing lately. After I gave birth to Megan, I discovered unshaven patches. I grimace.

"Or don't scoot over," he says.

"Oh, sorry," I say, moving toward the wall. "I was thinking about shaving."

He grins. "I could shave you."

"Don't joke about that. I might take you up on it."

He climbs onto the bed beside me, pushes the hair off of my face and kisses me.

"I would have killed to have done that while I was still living at home," he says.

"Fucked a pregnant woman?"

He laughs. "Fucked in my bed."

It's my turn to push hair from his face. "So tell me something. Five years ago, when you asked me to go for a ride in your car, did you really mean a ride on your cock?"

He doesn't say anything for a minute. "Well, you gotta realize that men are visual creatures, and you're incredibly hot. So, yeah, I was hoping. But I wasn't going to come out and say it. I was willing to work for it. I wanted you to like me."

"If all you wanted was a lay, why did it matter if I liked you?"

Gazing into my eyes, he caresses my cheek. "Because there was something about you that snagged me from the start. I wanted you to like me because I wanted you. Not just a lay. I wanted you."

"So, if we're recreating how we met, you owe me a date tomorrow."

"Anywhere you want to go," he says, smiling, "so long as I'm with you."

I'd go to the ends of the earth for him. I kiss him.

Chapter 20

Big Days Ahead

September 3, 2007

I open Megan's closet door and pick out two outfits for tomorrow. "Which one?" I say, holding them up.

Megan points. "That one."

I hang it on a hook on the back of her new bedroom's door.

We heard some children regress when they have a new sibling, so we enrolled Megan in preschool in the hopes exposing her to kids her own age will counterbalance any urge to regress. We're also hoping this will give me opportunity to write. I'm not so confident about that second one.

"Are you excited for school?" I say, sitting on the bed.

She nods. "Yeah. We'll do crafts and stuff."

"You'll like that. You understand that I won't be with you while you're there?"

"It's okay, Mommy."

Not gonna lie. I'm nervous, but I don't want Megan to know and become anxious. She's been away from me before, of course, but always with family. This will be my first experience entrusting my daughter with strangers. Well, actually the second. A few years ago when we were in Minneapolis, Vanessa and Brandon hired a babysitter, but Megan was with her cousins so I still don't think it's comparable.

"I will always come pick you up, but if one afternoon Grandma comes to get you, it means your brother has left my belly and come to live with us."

Megan picks up the baby doll I bought her after my ultrasound and cradles it. We've been using it to try and teach her about bottles, diaper changes and the like. I wonder if she realizes a real baby won't lie quietly for hours until she decides to pay attention to him.

"You understand, Megan, he will only live in my tummy for a short while, but he'll live with our family forever?"

She nods again, setting her doll in its toy crib and running to place her hands on my abdomen.

"'ello, Joshua," she says, pronouncing his name Jos-who-a.

I smile, hoping she'll feel this enthusiastic when Joshua is born. "I'm sure he's looking forward to meeting you. We have all this month to wait."

A month is a long time for a three and a half year old. It might as well be a year from her perspective. Nat'll be home in two weeks, but I'm impatient. I want him here now. It's impossible to have an intelligent conversation with a preschooler. But is that what I really yearn for? Intelligent conversation? Sure. But there's more to it than that. I'm frightened to give birth again, so I need moral support.

And I really, really, really need laid. No, not just laid. A long, hard fuck, even if it'll be awkward as hell.

"Can we go look at Jos-who-a's room?" Megan says, tugging on my hand.

"Okay." I stand. "You know, being the oldest you got to pick your room. Joshua didn't get to choose. Mommy and Daddy did it for him."

"I'm lucky," she says, tugging my hand harder.

I open the door to her room and in bounds Scooter. I don't think he's stopped sniffing since we moved in a week ago.

Megan giggles. "He's looking for Daddy."

I swallow Geez, I hope not. That's sad. Nat hasn't been home since we closed on the house. His father and brothers, along with Amy and Nicole's husbands, helped us move.

I take Megan's hand and we cross the hall to the nursery, a room decorated in smiling cartoon dinosaurs. Megan plops on the rocking chair and swings her legs.

"I like my room." Hers is decorated in pastels and flowers. "But this chair's fun."

"Would you like a swing set?"

The moment I say it I know I shouldn't have. Nat and I never discussed it. I never even thought about one until Nadine mentioned it on the Fourth of July. But I can see merits in having one. It'd be a good way for kids to burn off energy. The only problem is Nat might not agree. After all, a really nice swing set doesn't come cheap and with car payments and a bigger mortgage plus a new mouth to feed he might not want to shell out more money.

Megan springs off the chair and jumps. "Yes, yes, yes, yes."

"Okay, well, maybe in the spring. We already bought enough big and expensive things this year. And I need to talk to Daddy."

The baby pushes his foot into my belly button, and I'm reminded I'm about to be outnumbered. Holy shit. How am I going to handle that?

SEPTEMBER 29, 2007

Nat enjoys himself, judging from the groaning. I pretty much have to lie here and take it. Spooning's a position I can do when I'm as large as a whale, but only my pussy participates. The rest of me is redundant.

Don't get me wrong. I enjoy the feel of his hard cock. But I yearn for his lips. I want to kiss him and rub my hands all over his body. I can't wait until I can fuck like a normal person again.

He reaches forward and squeezes a boob. Well, I guess my boob is participating. Good for it.

He thrusts, and I groan, partially from pleasure and partially because I've been having abdominal pains on and off. Contractions. If you recall with Megan, I didn't even know what these pains were until some stranger in Denny's restroom told me. I give myself kudos for knowing what they are this time, although knowing doesn't make them any less annoying. I haven't told Nat I'm in labor. Should I have, even if contractions are too far apart and inconsistent to inform the birth center?

I grip the fitted sheet and squint, trying to get a glimpse of Nat in the dresser mirror, but all I see is myself and only my hip and thigh at that.

He drapes his leg over my thigh, and the sensation changes. If I were thinner, I would put my leg over his, allowing him to reach forward and play with my button while he fucks me. Sigh. I haven't had a mind-blowing orgasm in months.

Thrusting becomes more intense, prompting a series of moans to tumble uncontrollably out of my mouth, before Nat cums. I feel the muscle vibrations – I miss his face – as he pushes his body into mine.

He withdraws after a minute or two, and I roll over to finally look at him. I say roll over, but it's more like a walrus flipping over.

"Do you want me to help you cum?" he says.

"I dunno. Cumming is weird nowadays, and I'm tired. I should probably rest while I still can."

Nat yawns and pulls up the covers. "I'll get up with Megan on Monday."

"I'm going to go get ready for bed."

I kiss him and after three tries maneuver off the bed. I feel another pain, a mild one. I hope I can sleep tonight. I slowly walk to the bathroom to brush my teeth.

While I put my toothbrush away, something rolls down my leg. At first I think it's cum, but there's too much of it. I touch it, smell it. It's clear. Reminds me of water. Water? Water!

I look between my legs with my hand mirror. I'm not pissing myself. Phew. I throw the mirror back in the vanity drawer and slam it.

I hurry out of our en-suite bathroom. Nat's eyes are closed. Oh, please, don't let him be asleep.

"You broke my water," I say, hoping I don't sound hysterical.

He bolts upright, eyes wide. "What? How did I break your water? A cock can't reach that high. It—"

"Nathaniel, it's rolling down my leg. It—"

"Maybe it's cum."

"It isn't. It's different. I can tell. Water breaking speeds up labor. It speeds up labor!"

His eyes grow wider. "Since when have you been in labor?"

"Since this morning. The pains started this morning."

"Okay, okay, chill." He pats the bed. "You're in the early stages. Come lay with me."

I nod. How he expects me to relax, I have no idea. I get into bed, and he pulls up the covers before putting his arm around me.

"We'll meet our little boy in a few hours," he says. "What do you suppose he'll look like?"

"A baby," I say, rubbing my sides.

"Smart ass. *Who* do you suppose he'll look like?"

"You someday. For now, he'll look like Megan did."

Nat rests his head on my stomach but lifts it not long after, shaking it slightly. "Little dude kicked me."

"Little dude barely has any room in there. I'm about to evict him."

SEPTEMBER 30, 2007

When I arrived, Connie was attentive, asking questions, giving pep talks, fluffing the multitude of pillows that will cushion my head and back, but I haven't seen her in more than hour and I'm starting to wonder if she forgot me.

"How are you feeling?" Nat says, rubbing my head when I reach forward on the green athletic ball I'm balancing myself on to grab him.

I can't answer until my pain passes. "Just peachy."

"Maybe you should lie down. I'll give you a backrub."

Yeah, because that'll help. With my head pressed against his stomach, I can't see his expression. I suppose he feels bad that I'm in such pain because of him. At least I hope he feels bad. It'll remind him to pull out next time.

Connie enters the room, all smiles, per usual. "Joshua will be the second baby born tonight. A girl was born down the hall. You have me all to yourself now. Let's check and see how dilated you are."

I was at seven last time she checked before she disappeared to deliver that other baby. Nat and Connie help me to my feet, and I waddle to the bed, the pain so intense I want to cry. Since the bed has no scary medical instruments or attachments, I lie on the edge.

She inserts two gloved fingers, and I squint at Nat who watches. This sure as shit better not be turning him on or I'm going to fucking kill him.

"You're at 10," she says. "You remember what we talked about regarding pushing?"

I nod as I'm overcome by the next contraction. Unlike at the hospital, where I was told when to push and for how long, Connie taught me to listen to my body and push whenever I feel it's necessary.

She helps me stand. "Good. Let's make you as comfortable as we can."

Nat smiles. "We're going to meet our son soon. Focus on that instead of how much it hurts."

I nod. It's almost over. Second babies come faster, on average anyhow.

Connie fluffs the pillows one more time, and Nat and I get on the bed near them.

"Now remember," Connie says, getting on the bed at the foot. "You're the one delivering the baby. I'm simply here to assist. Listen to your body."

Feeling the urge to bear down, I open my legs, grab my knees and push, collapsing into the pillows when I'm finished.

"Very good," she says. "Keep listening to your body. Breathe through your pain."

When the urge returns, Nat wraps an arm around my shoulders and clasps my hand. I take comfort in the fact he is allowed to be this close. I need his emotional support. And besides, I wouldn't be in this situation without him.

"You're doing great, Honey," he says.

I think he means it, but women have been doing this for millennia. It's not easy to mess up. In fact, I bet the contractions can do all the work themselves. Oh, no, here comes another one.

"Every woman and every pregnancy is different, of course," Connie says to Nat, "but considering your wife pushed for around an hour with Megan, and taking into account the baby's size, I'm predicting a fast delivery."

I hope she's right.

In-between pushes, I breathe as deeply as I can. Nat said to focus on the fact we will be meeting Joshua soon. I try, but shit, it hurts.

For half an hour – I know because of the huge clock on the wall – I push and sure enough Connie's prediction comes true. The baby crowns.

"Full head of hair," Nat says. "You were right. So far, he looks like Megan."

If he's trying to make me laugh, now is not the time. I grimace.

"You can touch it if you want," Connie says.

Nat touches the top of the baby's head. I'm not sure I would touch it if you paid me money. I'm not good with newborns, even my own.

The rest of the head emerges. Nat smiles, not once taking his eyes off the baby. I don't know how he can watch a person come out of the same pussy he fucked a few hours ago without finding it, and me, forever repulsive.

The hardest part is done. I can do this. I can do it. One more time. That's all I need. The urge comes again, and I push.

"Welcome to the world, Baby Boy," Connie says, and the shriek of young lungs fills the room.

Joshua Nathaniel officially arrives at 1:11 a.m.

Connie grabs a pair of surgical scissors off a tray on the nightstand and hands them to Nat. "Here you go, Papa. I think you've done this before."

Nat cuts the cord, and after clamping the stump Connie places a still screaming Joshua on my chest. His little eyes are open but squinting. It must be awfully bright out in the world. And cold. I put my hand on his back, and it covers both shoulders. He actually does look like newborn Megan with his red, wrinkly skin and matted hair. And that white stuff. He hasn't been cleaned yet. This nightgown is ruined, but I knew that going in.

"You did it, Honey," Nat says, kissing the top of my head and placing his hand on our son's hip.

"Okay," Connie says. "I need you to deliver the placenta. One push should do it."

One more push and out it comes. We opted to store the cord blood, so she needs to do something special to store it. Cord blood can be used to help treat serious illnesses. We're hoping we never need it for either child, but it's a nice safety net to have.

Connie opens a previously hidden cabinet and pulls out various instruments.

"He's 21 inches long and 7 pounds, 2 ounces," she says, examining Joshua to be certain we don't need to call a pediatrician.

She writes his stats down, presumably for the birth certificate, then returns the baby to us washed and swaddled in a blanket. I'll need to feed him in a bit, but right now he's warm and quiet.

"He's the best souvenir you could have brought back from California," Nat says, admiring the baby.

"And I brought Megan back from Milwaukee. I should stop fucking you when we're out of town if this is going to keep happening."

He grins. "You can't keep your hands off of me and you know it."

"I could accuse you of the same thing."

"True. I'd like to hold him."

I hand the baby over. Nat kisses Joshua's forehead and rocks him. I always love watching Nat be dad. I relax into my pile of pillows and smile.

WE LEFT THE BIRTH CENTER slightly after 7 a.m. and promptly went to sleep after we got home, Joshua in a bassinette beside our bed. It's hard to believe I had sex in this bed a few hours ago. Now I won't have sex for six weeks, at least.

"Mom and Dad brought Megan home," Nat says, gently waking me. "Should I have them come up or do you want to come down?"

I'm relaxed and tired. I don't feel like moving.

"Bring them up."

He leaves, returning with his parents and Megan.

"Oh, my, he's precious," my mother-in-law says, her bobbed gray hair concealing her face when she stoops to see the baby.

Megan climbs on the bed and peers at her brother with a mixture of curiosity and disappointment.

"This is Joshua," I say. "He came out of Mommy's belly because he was getting too big to stay in there, and now he lives with us."

"Baby," she says, and I wonder if she's trying to comprehend what I said.

We discussed my pregnancy several times, with Nat there and without him, and I thought Megan was as prepared as a preschooler can be for a new sibling. Was I wrong?

She smacks Joshua's forehead, making him cry. "Baby!"

"Megan!" every adult in the room says in unison.

"Not so rough, Sweetie," Nat says taking her hand while I comfort the screaming newborn. "You can hurt him."

"I'm sorry," she says and kisses her brother.

Oh, boy, a love-hate relationship already.

After Joshua calms, my mother-in-law takes our first family portrait. It'll go on the wall in the back hallway next to the photo of Nat and me with Megan on her birthday.

My mother- and father-in-law take turns holding their grandson. Megan snuggles on the bed between Nat. and me Maybe she's overwhelmed or establishing her territory. I don't know. All I know is life will never be the same. We're a quartet.

Chapter 21

Mr. and Mrs. Prude

March 22, 2008

I have *two* new nieces, Kaylee Bergstrom and Korina Economos. Funny, I didn't know Greg had sex until he invited me to Sterling to meet Korina, six months younger than Josh, and make friends with Katrina. I'm all for meeting my niece, but friendship with Katrina ain't gonna happen. He thinks we will bond as moms. I guess he doesn't realize it takes much more than that for two women to give a shit about each other.

I wish Mom would stop by or one of my aunts. Why is it when I need them to interfere with my life, they don't? Nat's on tour, and Greg's doing whatever chemical engineers who work for paint companies do, so that leaves me with Katrina and the kids.

We already discussed the weather. Okay, need a new topic. Um.....

"How do you like Sterling?" I say.

Katrina shifts Korina in her arms. "It's not much smaller than Addison, so it's fine. How did you like growing up here?"

That's all she has to say? It's fine? Nothing about missing her family or making the move for love, or whether the community is nice or isn't? No explanation or details at all?

"I moved away," I say.

More than one of us can give a vague answer.

"Greg says that's all you used to talk about when you were a teenager."

As if Greg would know. He was away for six years earning his degrees. He returned when I was 17.

I shake my head. "Not true. I used to talk a lot about Nirvana."

She fidgets with her crucifix. "The Buddhist end of suffering?"

I could laugh but control myself. Yes, that's right. I was a spiritual teenager who explored Eastern religions to piss off her parents. All I needed to do was turn on MTV to do that.

"The band."

Katrina wrinkles her nose. "You are a music fanatic."

She doesn't mean that in a positive way. I know it, and she knows it.

Megan plays on the floor with some of the toys I brought along in a tote bag. Josh, beside her on his blanket, practices pushing himself up from his belly.

I pat the diaper bag at my feet. "Who knew such little people can't travel light?"

Katrina wrinkles her nose again. "Everyone knows that."

I smile. "If everyone knew that, there wouldn't exist baby advice books."

Katrina finally puts Korina in the bassinet beside the couch. It's almost as if she's afraid the baby will disappear if left alone. I thought babies were the ones who didn't grasp the concept of object permanence.

Katrina probably could use help. She had a C-section and an emergency one at that. Every woman's worst nightmare. If she were Vanessa, Penny or one of my cousins, I'd help, but I'm not going to offer assistance to someone who won't appreciate it.

"Breast or bottle?" Katrina says.

Hum. I squint. Them's fightin' words in the mom community. There are people on both sides of the issue. Pick the wrong side and the other women will rip you apart. I have a good notion what side of the coin my sister-in-law is on.

"I breastfeed them both until they were a month or so old, so they could get the antibodies they need, then switched to bottle."

"Because you're lazy."

"Because with a bottle my husband gets to share in the bonding experience that occurs while feeding a baby."

"He can bond in other ways. Being home more often, for instance."

I exhale. This is going to be one hell of a visit. I'm going to ask her to change Josh's diaper later in the hopes he'll pisses all over her. I mastered diaper changes without being peed on the hard way.

I wonder if Maroula is home or any of my other female cousins. I haven't seen Anastasia in ages. It's hard to believe my baby cousin turns 26 this year. How would she react if I showed up on her porch unannounced with two kids?

We descend into silence, except for the children. Megan talks to herself as part of her game while the babies make sounds.

Five minutes go by. Katrina and I say nothing. Damn, I wish Nat would call. Or Vanessa. Why didn't Greg invite her here, too? He's no longer my favorite brother. No, wait, he never was.

"So, what's your favorite sexual position?" I say, partially joking and partially because I know Katrina won't like it.

"I'm not going to be research for your smut," she says, voice rising.

Smut? Whoa. She went for it right away.

"My next book comes out later this year. But I don't interview people for my books. They are fictional-ish."

"What do you mean 'ish'?"

"If it's smut, why do you care?"

She sits forward. "I don't care about the smut. I'm curious about the writing process."

"The writing process?"

"Yes, the writing process."

I sense some bullshit.

"Well, some things are pulled from reality and some are fantasy. That's why people read erotica, to escape from the drudgery of real life. Very few people have mind-blowing sex lives. Only certain people who really click."

I think of Nat and smile.

"That's very interesting. Yes, fantasy can be good. People need escapism."

"So will you tell me your favorite position?"

"No. Never."

I shrug. I didn't think she would tell me. We again descend into silence.

I pull my phone out of the diaper bag's outer pocket and shamelessly send a bulk text message to all my female cousins: *I'm in town w/ the kids. Let's get together.*

I send the same message to Jennifer, Jen and Jenny. I skip Tiffany. She doesn't associate voluntarily with baby machines.

I should text Penny, too, but she and Chris know I'm here. They will reach out, I'm sure of it. Maybe Chris will invite us to dinner at Costas' Place.

Finally, I text Nat: *This was a fucking stupid idea*

"Who are you texting?" Katrina says.

Why does she care? Am I not allowed to text in her house?

"Nat. He's working."

"Yes, I know. Did he finally cut his hair?"

He did, much to my chagrin, said it was becoming too high maintenance and he didn't feel the look flattered him. He'd been saying this for months, but I persuaded him to keep it long until after Josh was born so his hair would be in the family photo. Then he graciously kept it a while longer so I could run my fingers through it when he's on top.

"He cut it after New Year's."

"Because of what I said to him at Christmas?"

I shake my head. "You said something to him at Christmas?"

Katrina looks proud of herself. "I told him he looks like white trash."

Nearly dropping my phone, I straighten my back. "You told him he looked liked white trash?"

"Well, yeah. If he was a teenager going through a phase, that's one thing, but he's 31. Now I have no idea what sort of home he grew up in. Is he white trash?"

Holy shit. Nat's father was a professional cellist who retired from the Chicago Symphony. His mother is a retired music teacher who does charity work. All the children play instruments.

"No! My children are listening."

Katrina glances at Megan and Josh. "If he isn't white trash then you have nothing to worry about because they won't know what that means."

They wouldn't know what it means either way, but that's not the point, is it?

"What did he say to you?"

"He said he'd take it into consideration."

I'm pretty sure he didn't say that. I'm pretty sure he laughed in her face and then forgot completely about it.

"What hairstyle do you think a 31 year old should have?"

"A buzz cut."

"A buzz cut? Oh, no, no, no. There's nothing to run your fingers through. What is your favorite sexual position?"

She curls her lip. "I'm still not answering your question."

I shrug and put my phone back in the diaper bag. "Suit yourself."

I TICKLE JOSH'S BELLY. He giggles as if it's the funniest thing in the world and continues to giggle when I lift him off the dresser to throw away his soiled diaper.

I turn and find Greg standing in the threshold, watching us.

"Hi. How was work?"

His face reminds me of a boiled lobster. "Why have you been talking to my wife about sex?"

"Well, how-do-you-do to you, too. I'm allowed to talk about what I do for a living. She asked me about writing."

"You brought it up from what I hear."

I throw the diaper in the trashcan. "So what?"

"So what? I asked you to make friends with Katrina and talk to her about motherhood since Korina and Joshua are so close in age. How is sex an appropriate topic?"

Josh lies his head on my chest and makes himself comfortable despite my rising voice and temperature.

"Appropriate, Greg? Appropriate? She's a grown ass woman, not a child. If I want to ask her a question, I'll ask her a fucking question."

"Do what you want in your own home, but when you are here—"

"What, Greg? I will follow your rules? You sound like Dad."

"It's disrespectful," Greg says, pacing. "Your mind is always in the gutter. Always. Who knows what you do with your time? Nat should demand a DNA test for those kids."

My eyes widen. Nat should demand a DNA test? Thank God Megan is downstairs. She has no idea what DNA is, but she knows her father's name and would interpret her uncle's tone.

"My children are his. You should be able to tell that by looking at them."

"They could have gotten the hair and eyes from you. Maybe you have a thing for slight men. Cover your tracks that way. He'd know the difference otherwise when 'his,'" Greg makes air quotes, "kids grow up to be big boned and six foot six."

I take a step forward. "I'm loyal to the people I love!"

"You either follow the rules or you—"

"I'm not a fucking child. But you." I point at Greg. "You have officially lost your mind."

I place Josh in the middle of the bed, grab the suitcase I'm sharing with the kids, and randomly throw our belongings into it.

Greg stops pacing. "What do you suppose you're doing?"

"What do I suppose I'm doing? I don't suppose anything. I'm leaving. That's what I'm doing. It's too late to drive home. I'll go to Yiayia's or Mom's or Maroula's or Chris' or any number of other relatives' houses, but I'm not staying here. You talk about disrespect. Apparently you can say whatever you want to me, and that's okay."

Greg says nothing, simply watches me gather my things like a madwoman.

"What's going on here?" a female voice says.

Great. The tattletale makes an appearance.

I stop what I'm doing only long enough to look at Katrina. "Your husband has suggested I repeatedly cheated on mine. He went so far as to say Nat should seek a DNA test."

"Gregory," she says from the doorway, "why would you suggest such a thing?"

Greg looks mortified, and I wonder if this is the first time she's disagreed with him.

"She says and does disrespectful things." He stamps his foot. "I'm tired of it."

"She's your sister. Apologize at once."

All the blood rushes from Greg's face – and believe me he was beet red – and I think he might faint. "But—"

"I'm lonely," I hear Megan say. "Mommy, what's going on?"

Megan appears behind Katrina. Why not join the party? Everyone crowded into this tiny room is going to make me hyperventilate.

"Well, Sweetie," I say. "Theos Gregory, um."

Katrina and I turn to Greg, putting the pressure on him to answer.

He ignores his niece and turns to his wife. "Katrina, you're fine with all of this?"

She nods. "Your sister and I will never have anything in common other than you, but I do believe she means well, and I don't for an instant believe she cheated."

"What? She asked you an indecent question. How is that meaning well?"

Katrina sticks her perfect nose – why was she blessed genetically with a perfect nose? – in the air and says to Megan, "Come on, *koukla*, let's go check on your cousin."

She takes Megan's hand, and their footsteps recede down the hall.

Greg promptly returns his attention to me. "I am not done with you!" he says, sounding as if he's trying to scare a stray dog off his property.

Josh cries. I pick him up, his tears wetting my shoulder, and bounce him on my hip.

"I will not forgive you for making my son cry. All this over unfounded accusations. And because I asked one question. One question that was meant partially in jest."

"I'm, I'm sorry," Greg says. "Are you going to leave?"

My nostrils flare. "Don't you think Yiayia would like to see her great-grandchildren?"

"She's 90. You'll give her a heart attack if you ask her her favorite sexual position."

"Is that the only reason I shouldn't go? There are other relatives who would gladly take us in."

Greg looks absolutely defeated. "No, not the only reason."

"You need to loosen up," I say as Josh's snot joins his tears on my shoulder. "Life is too short not to enjoy it."

Greg takes a step backward. "I enjoy life."

"Bullshit. Leave us alone." I rub Josh's head. "I want to be left alone!"

He takes another step backward. "Are you staying?"

"I don't know."

He hangs his head and leaves.

A FEW MINUTES LATER, I descend the creaky stairs to Greg and Katrina's living room. They sit on the couch while Megan builds something out of Duplo blocks on the coffee table. I sit opposite them and set Josh on my lap. He babbles, sticking his hand in his mouth.

Dinner burns in the kitchen, and the odor of charred chicken fills the air. If Katrina wants to burn down her house, so be it. Everyone in the Economos family can cook. Leave it to Greg to marry someone who can't.

"What are you building, Sweetie?" I say to Megan.

"A house."

"A house. Well, I'm sure it'll be a great house. I'll take a picture and send it to Daddy when you're done."

"Well, are you staying or not?" Greg blurts out like a person holding his breath lets out a huge exhale.

Well now, the way I see it, the ball's in my court. Katrina took my side, sort of.

"I don't feel comfortable here," I say, shaking my head. "I want to stay with Phillipos and Jennifer."

Greg sits forward. "You want to stay with Phil?"

Katrina holds her hand in front of Greg's chest like a parent would a child's after stepping hard on a car's brakes. "They're closer in age. He married her friend. I'm sure they have much to talk about."

His face reddens. "We invited her here, not Phil."

"She can come back in the morning."

As much as I enjoy them debating about me as if I'm not here, I must say something.

"He's more of a brother to me than you are," I say.

Greg's mouth opens and closes. He sits back. "You are my sister and I love you, but I don't understand how we could possibly have the same parents. We're so different."

"Maybe you're the one who needs the DNA test, Gregory."

He shakes his head. "That's not funny."

"Did I say it was?" I exhale sharply. "We do not get along. We really never did. I'm not sure what you expected when you invited me here."

Josh giggles. Greg narrows his eyes. If he yells at a six-month-old, I'm out of here. End of discussion.

Katrina pats Greg on the knee and stands. "I'm going to check on dinner."

Well, it's about time. I have a feeling we're going to Costas' Place tonight. Well, at least the kids and I are. We might be going home with Chris. I actually don't know where we're going, but some relative will take us.

"I, um, thought it would be helpful to Katrina," Greg says. "She has no family nearby."

"If you haven't noticed, I'm not nearby either. I live in the same part of the state as her family. This isn't about her. It's about you. Maybe you wanted to make a fool out of me."

"No."

"What then?"

Greg adverts his eyes. "I, I, don't understand you. Goddamn it. I don't understand you."

He stands and stomps out of the room.

Megan looks up from her house. "Are we going to Theos Phil's?"

"We might. I'll call him. Let's go see Theos Chris and Thea Penny first."

She nods.

I fish my phone out of the diaper bag and discover I have responses to some of my text messages. I tap on Nat's response. It's one word: *Run!*

Chapter 22

Lord, Help Me

October 7, 2008

"Hello," Nat says over the phone. "What's going on over there?"

Josh screams inches from my ear, his skin a color I haven't seen since he was born, and I can barely hear. Who knew the littlest people can scream the loudest?

"Joshie is feverish."

I should call my mother-in-law, any of my sisters-in-law, Shawna, but, no. I call the person who is 900 miles away. I don't know what I expect him to do.

"What's the matter?"

"Megan brought something home from preschool, I'm sure of it. Other than the fever, I don't know. Is he in pain? Why is he screaming?"

I ask Nat as if he'll somehow know. The person who is 900 miles away. Again, why did I call?

"Maybe he's uncomfortable." Nat's voice is quiet, or maybe I can't hear him over the ringing in my ears. "Can you give him something for it?"

My gaze drops to the floor. "The only thing we have is the chewable kind."

"Well, that's not good," he says in a way that makes me think it's a judgement.

I'm the parent who is here fulltime. I should know that a baby and a preschooler have different needs. I should have been prepared.

I lie Josh in his crib. He sits and pulls himself into a stand, outstretching a hand toward me while clenching the crib rail with the other.

"I'm scared. I wish he could talk and tell me what's happening."

"Don't hesitate to take him to the ER if you have to."

The ER? I hadn't thought of the ER. How high does a fever need to be to worry about it?

"I wish you were here."

Eww, I said the thing I hate to utter because I never want to make Nat feel guilty about being away. I also never want to turn into the needy woman who can't function without a man. There has been an understanding since the beginning of our relationship that I don't *need* him, I *want* him. I can handle him being away because I'm an independent woman with a mind of my own, but right now I would give my right arm to have him here to help.

"I know. I'm sorry the timing sucks. Call Mom. She's a pro at stuff like this."

See, I told you I should have called my mother-in-law, but I don't want to be a burden. My in-laws help enough as is. They take the kids whenever Nat and I have the need, and my brothers-in-law often fix things to save us the trouble of needing to pay a repairman. Not to mention, it's 11 o'clock at night. I never call this late. They'll assume it's an emergency.

"How is Megan feeling?"

"Fine as of when I put her to bed."

"Fingers crossed she stays that way. Keep me posted."

"I will."

We hang up, and I get a sick feeling in the pit of my stomach. I return to the crib and pick up my distressed son. Then I remember: Walgreens is open around the clock.

PART-TIME SINGLE MOTHERHOOD looks like full-time single motherhood when you lug your children out at all hours. I bet we make quite the picture entering the store like something the cat dragged in, the haggard mother with one kid screaming bloody murder and another who is Miss Cranky Pants because her mother woke her up to come to Walgreens.

The store employee greets us, but I can't hear a damn thing with Josh hysterical on my hip. I wish I had those earplugs I wear whenever I'm at a concert. I might have permanent hearing loss after this. The kid has healthy lungs, that's for sure.

We rush to the baby aisle. Or at least that was the plan. Megan drags her feet. No, a more accurate way of describing it would be as if her feet are glued to the floor. She refuses to move, her nonslip soles doing their job.

So, I have a beet red baby who's destroying my hearing on one hip while holding the hand of a stubborn preschooler whose body refuses to budge.

"Megan, please, the longer we are here, the longer it'll be before you get back in bed."

"No," she says, head shaking, curls flying.

"Why must you be so stubborn?"

Because she's my daughter, that's why. Who knows what other undesirable traits she's inherited from me?

"I wanna sleep."

"So do I, but your brother will keep crying if we don't get him the medicine he needs."

"I don't care."

Of course, she doesn't. I let go of her hand and, squatting, wrap my arm around her waist and pick her up. Jesus, she's heavy. Why didn't I get a shopping cart? Because I'm only buying one thing, that's why. We should be checking out right now.

Why the fuck did I have children? I could be at home right now jacking off or having phone sex. Instead I'm getting a hernia. And, oh, yeah, did I mention the snot and slobber in my hair? Yeah, there's that.

Somehow we make it to the baby aisle, and I find the infant pain reliever that comes with a dropper. Getting it off the shelf with no free hands is another matter. I squeeze my eyes shut and grimace. It seems easiest to grab it with the hand that's holding Josh. I inch closer to the shelves, hoping he doesn't kick and dump the product packages onto the floor.

"Can I help you?" the store employee says.

Not all superheroes wear capes. Some wear nametags.

"Yes, please," I say, raising my voice to be heard above Josh. "I need a box of the infant pain reliever with the dropper."

I back up, and the young man takes the medication off the shelf.

"Do you need anything else?" he says as if he does this all the time.

"No, that's it."

He walks us to the register. I can't dig through my purse to get my wallet without setting Megan down. She immediately sits on the floor and bangs her head against my leg.

The store employee hands me the medication, and I shove it and the receipt into my purse.

"Come on, Megan. Let's go home."

She doesn't budge. Holy shit, am I going to have to pick her up again? I'll never manage to lift her off the floor.

Josh cries so hard he makes himself gag, and I shift his body just in time for him to throw up on the counter. That's the third time today that's happened. Why do little kids always have to throw up?

"I'm so sorry," I say, wanting to crawl into a hole and die of embarrassment. "These things happen without warning. Do you want me to clean it up?"

I frequent this store often, and I don't want to get blacklisted.

The employee shakes his head. "I appreciate the offer, ma'am, but it looks like you have enough troubles as is."

Ma'am? I'm may be about a decade older than this kid, but if a wedding ring and two kids makes me a "ma'am," then guilty as charged.

"Thank you. I'm really, really sorry. My husband is away on a business trip, or else I would have come alone, and none of this would have happened." I stop and stare blankly. Why am I telling him this? "Again, I'm really, really sorry."

Please, Megan, get up. Don't embarrass me anymore than I already am. Maybe we share enough of a connection that she can read my thoughts, because she stands and begrudgingly walks with me to the car.

SCOOTER HOWLS THE MOMENT he hears Josh, and a frightened Maisie runs full speed past the door leading in from the garage and nearly trips me.

"Megan, go upstairs and get your PJs back on."

I should watch to see if she follows instruction, but because she's the more independent of the two children, I leave her to it. I take Josh to the dining room table and put him in his highchair.

Ripping open the top of the package, I measure out the appropriate amount of medication in the dropper. I learned with Megan how to do this quickly, although I think it might be a form of child abuse in some states. I put the dropper in Josh's mouth, hold his mouth shut and stroke his neck. It's the same method I use to give Scooter his heartworm medication. Josh fights me but swallows.

I take a step back and exhale, removing my jacket. Josh is still unhappy, so I don't bother to remove his jacket. I'll do that upstairs when I give him a bath. I walk to the coat closet and discover Megan fell asleep at the base of the staircase on the floor. Goddamn it. Josh can't be left unattended, so Megan needs to stay there for the time being.

When he feels well, Josh enjoys bath time and I hope tonight it'll have a calming affect. I take him directly to the bathroom and run the water. While we wait for the tub to fill, I strip him and take his temperature. It's 102 degrees. You'd think it was 1,000 from the way he's been carrying on.

I don't let more than a couple of inches fill the tub before I place him inside. Running my soapy hand slowly up and down his back calms him. He yawns twice and doesn't give me any trouble except when I run the washcloth over his face.

By the end of the bath, Josh, naked and quiet, follows me from the bathroom to his bedroom and surprisingly doesn't fall once.

"Mama," he says, outstretching his arms.

I pick him up and place him on the changing table. He yawns and doesn't fuss much while I dress him in a clean diaper and sleeper. I lie him in the crib and quietly leave the room, the white noise machine piping out the roar of ocean waves.

I drain the tub, take Josh's jacket to the closet and his dirty clothes to the laundry room. Now, onto Megan.

I shake her. She doesn't respond to the first few shakes, but when she awakens, she sobs. Oh, no, no, no! She's going to get her brother going again. I pick her up and carry her to her room. She's capable of changing her own clothes, but I help anyhow to speed up the process and shorten this hissy fit as much as I can.

"Goodnight, Megan," I say once she's tucked back into bed.

She's crying, so I skip kissing her. She'll be asleep soon and won't remember any of this. I leave her room and, exhaling, lean against the wall outside her door. Exhaustion hits me, but I can't go to bed. I need to take a shower to wash the baby snot out of my hair.

Remind me again why I had children. Oh, yeah, because I love their father. And I'd do it all over again in a heartbeat.

Speaking of their father, I should probably call Nat and give him an update, although I can't remember which time zone he's in. Now, where did I put my phone? My purse?

I find my phone, not in the purse pocket where I normally put it, but at the bottom of my bag. I was so frustrated earlier, I simply threw it in. I dial Nat.

"Everything okay," he says. "You're not at the ER?"

"The ER? No."

I forgot he suggested a trip to the hospital if necessary. I update him on what happened since our last phone call.

"Holy shit. You had a fun evening. I'm sorry I wasn't there to help."

"It's okay," I say, checking the pets' dishes to see if they need filled before bed. "I handled it. It was stressful as hell, but both kids are asleep. I'm exhausted, though, and Megan has preschool in the morning."

"Why not call her off? That way you all can sleep, and you don't have to drag Josh out when he's not feeling well."

"That's a good idea," I say, locking the door to the garage and turning off the lights with a flick of a switch. "It's not like she'll have homework to make up."

"You going to bed?"

"Soon."

I remember the medication bottle and, in the dark, retrieve it from the dining room table. I'll put it in the kids' bathroom in case I need it in the middle of the night.

"Think of me if you can," he says. "I'll be thinking of you."

"I always think of you when I'm in bed. I imagine you beside me with your arm holding me close. It's that sense of security that lulls me to sleep."

"I think I'll share in that daydream tonight, too. I miss holding you close. I love you."

"I love you, too."

We tell each other good night and hang up. I start up the stairs, the muscles in my thighs feeling like I've run 10 miles. Can't go to bed yet. I need to wash the baby snot from my hair.

Chapter 23

Our First Real Milestone

November 12, 2008

"Happy anniversary, Honey," Nat says when we enter Wendell's Lounge in Santa Fe for pre-dinner cocktails.

Santa Fe might sound like a strange place to travel for our anniversary, but I've been wanting to come here ever since I saw it on a TV travelogue. We could have gone back to Vegas, but Vegas doesn't scream romance no matter how many wedding chapels it has. Here there's the desert, the mountains, the rich history, Spanish style buildings, Native American culture.

Five years ago, I was seven months pregnant and got stuck in my dress. Talk about sexy. Not. Today, I squeezed myself into a little black dress paired with shoes that have silver straps and chunky, clear heels. The long sleeve dress actually is a New Year's ensemble, and little silver threads shimmer in the light.

I place my hand on his sports jacket's lapel. "A happy anniversary to you, too."

We make eye contact, holding the gaze for a few seconds. He glances away, almost shyly, before telling the hostess about our reservation.

She walks us to a small pub table by the fireplace. I wanted someplace intimate, so later we can get intimate, and, yes, you know what I mean. It's nice to see that I've gotten my wish. Well, the first part anyhow. A pub table means tall chairs, and we are not tall people. Nat manages to sit, but he's six inches taller. I need to step on the bottom rung of the chair like a vehicle running board to hoist myself upward. I land on the seat with an unceremonious thump.

"Here, I thought I outgrew a highchair," I say, crossing my legs and setting my purse on the table.

"Maybe I should have picked you up," Nat says with a wink.

I laugh. I'd rather have everyone focus on us because we're such an attractive couple, not because I can't easily sit on a chair.

"I'm not budging from this spot. I don't want to have to do that again."

We order cocktails and an appetizer.

Nat smiles and leans forward, placing his hand on my knee. "You look fucking hot in that dress. I can't wait to see you out of it later."

I bob my head. "I think there is a 99 percent chance that will happen."

He looks confused. "Why not 100 percent?"

"There's always that small possibility I might drink too much and get sick like I did at Greg and Katrina's wedding."

"You drank that much because you were bored." He squeezes my knee. "You aren't bored with me, are you?"

"Never," I say, reaching under the table for his inner thigh. "You always excite me."

"Nice to hear it."

I wonder how the kids are doing and resist the urge to check my phone. I gave specific instructions that no one should disturb us unless the house burns down or someone dies. Still, there always is that lingering doubt over the kids' wellbeing, especially after what happened during Josh's illness, an illness he gave to Megan, by the way, and then she gave it back to him.

"It's even more important now," he says as if reading my thoughts, "that we take time for the two of us. You hear stories of couples who drift apart after having kids, and I never want that to be us. What we have going is too special to ruin. I want to feel this way about you forever."

We interlace fingers, and silently gaze into each other's eyes.

"There is little danger of us becoming a statistic because we do take time to nurture our relationship," I say. "It's especially important because we're separated more than the average couple."

The waitress brings our drinks, followed not long after by the appetizer.

Nat lifts his glass. "A toast to the next five wonderful years."

"To the next five." I clink glasses with him. "But you know we've been living together for six. That's almost like being married."

He smiles at the memory. "We acted like newlyweds. Everyone thought we were crazy, told us we were moving too fast."

"They were the ones who were crazy. We knew what we wanted," I say, shoving a piece of bruschetta into my mouth.

I'm busy chewing, yet he observes me as if I'm the most beautiful thing in the world. "I still want you. I want you just as much as in the beginning."

I swallow and hope nothing's in my teeth. "I feel the same way."

He smiles. "I'm happy to hear that."

I would hope he would be happy to hear that. If he weren't happy, something would be wrong, right?

I set what's left of my bruschetta on the plate in front of me. "We're made for each other."

Ugh, did I read that in a greeting card somewhere? It sounds like a greeting card. I hope he doesn't notice how corny that sounds.

He takes a sip of beer and slowly sets down the glass. "I think you're right. I can't imagine being with anyone else."

That makes two of us.

AT 7 O'CLOCK, WE GO next door to Wendell's seafood restaurant. Our table is situated beside a picture window with a scenic view of the Sacramento Mountains, Sierra Blanca and Lake Mescalero. I resist the urge to take out my phone and snap a photograph.

I peruse the menu. This place is expensive, but you only have a five-year anniversary once. Well, most people do. Okay, some people do.

I don't notice the waitress until she speaks. "These are for you, ma'am."

There's that "ma'am" shit again. Am I that old? I look up to find her holding a crystal vase filled with red roses. She places them on the table and walks away without explanation.

"I wonder who those are from," Nat says.

Very few people know we're here. Maybe it's a mistake. I open the card. It reads:

To the most wonderful woman,
I couldn't ask for a better wife. Thanks for being mine. I love you.

Happy 5th wedding anniversary.

I set down the card and stare at Nat in astonishment.

His eyes light up. "Remember when we were first dating, how I brought you a red rose a night?"

"Remember? Of course, I remember. I still have them. I put them in the phone book and pressed them flat. They're wrapped in plastic wrap and stored for safekeeping in our wedding guest book."

"I didn't know you kept them."

I never told him because most men would find it a silly, not to mention outdated, feminine pursuit to press flowers. I didn't even know we were going to stay together in those days. I thought it was some fun to break up the drudgery of my life until he went back on tour. Yet I kept them.

"How could I throw them away? You gave them to me."

He taps one of the petals with his fingertip. "Now you have more for your collection."

I smile. "I think this time I'll press them behind glass and hang them on our bedroom wall as art, then every time we see them, they'll remind us of tonight."

"That sounds like a great idea."

"Well, thank you, Honey. This was a surprise."

My cheeks burn and the corners of my mouth upturn when I return my attention back to the menu.

"Oh, one more thing." Nat pulls a box out of his jacket pocket. "I have one more surprise."

He hands me the box, and I take it, hand slightly shaking. Inside is the turquoise necklace I admired at a Native American market earlier today. I loved it, but I wasn't keen on the price and opted to think about it.

"When did you buy this?" I say, not believing I'm holding the same necklace.

"Remember when I said I had to go to the bathroom and you waited by the front door? That's when."

"Oh my, clever boy." I replace the lid and set the box on my purse. "You spoil me. Thank you again."

He looks pleased with himself. "I spoil you because I love you."

"I love you more."

"It isn't a contest."

"Maybe not." I pick up the menu. "But now you've set the bar extremely high for our 10th. By the time we reach our 25th, you'll be buying me a yacht."

He picks up his menu. "Not a yacht. A private jet."

I actually wouldn't mind a private jet. If we had one, we'd never need to be separated for weeks at a time. But I know it's a silly fantasy. I wouldn't want to see the expenses associated with a jet when I don't understand why he hangs onto his sports car, a car built for two.

"The kids will be grown by the time we have our 25th anniversary," I say. "I'll have more free time than I know what to do with."

I probably shouldn't have said it. What I was thinking was the kids will be off on their own and I'll be home alone when Nat's on tour. It'd be like the beginning of our relationship, only worst because I'd be a lonely empty nester. You know what, it doesn't matter how I meant it, I still shouldn't have said it.

"Well, then," he says, "I'll need to find a way to occupy your time."

"I WANT TO THANK YOU again, Honey, for tonight," I say, setting the flowers and the necklace box on the hotel room nightstand. "You made it special."

Nat removes his jacket and tosses it aside. "It was special because our relationship is special," he says, taking me hand and squeezing it.

We gaze into each other's eyes for a moment before he pulls me close, pushes hair from my cheek and kisses me passionately.

His hand slowly moves down my back, sending tingles of anticipation through me, and comes to a rest on my ass.

"Go into the bathroom, take off your hose and thong and come back," he says, pulling up my dress. "Keep the stripper shoes on."

"The stripper shoes?" I say, insulted on my shoes' behalf.

"They have clear heels. That's what I'm going to call them."

I fulfil his request, returning to find him completely naked, cock standing at attention.

"Come dance around my pole," he says with a smile.

It's so corny I burst into laughter. I can't help it. But I don't laugh long. Holy shit. I need that cock inside me. I crave it.

I throw my arms around his neck and grind against him. His tongue tangled in mine, he pushes me against the dresser. I need him pressing into me. Badly. He picks me up and sets me on the dresser. I move my knees apart, clench his shoulders and hold on tight as that hard dick is inserted exactly where I want it.

I moan, my heels clonking against the dresser drawers with each thrust. I should hold my legs still, I suppose, considering we're in a hotel and walls are thin, but who gives a fuck?

Clonk, moan, clonk, moan.

Hips moving at a brisk pace, his tongue overpowers mine.

Clonk, whimper, clonk, whimper.

My nails scratch his back like a bear clawing a tree. Holy shit. That must have hurt. I'll apologize later.

I wrap a leg around his waist. This slows the pace somewhat, although the heel of the other foot still clonks against the wooden drawer.

There's a wild glint in his eyes. He's a wild beast. Ride me. Ride me hard! Our eyes lock. I lick my lips. He hovers his near mine, the skin barely touching, before we again kiss.

A bead of sweat falls off his chest and lands in my cleavage, prompting him to pull out and stand back looking proud of himself, my pussy juice glistening on his cock. I hop off the furniture, lifting my arms so he can help me shimmy out of my dress.

He drops it and my bra to the floor, and I am left wearing nothing but my stripper shoes. I turn, bend forward and give my ass a shake.

"Oh fuck," he says. "Get your ass on the bed."

I unbuckle my shoes and toss them to the floor before crawling onto the bed and spreading my legs, inviting him back inside. He's on me in a flash, sliding into my sopping wet pussy with little effort. I have to admit, this bed feels a lot better against my bare ass than that dresser. I didn't realize how much until now.

While his cock plows my field, I instinctively place my hand on the back of his head. There's a lot less hair to run my fingers through since he cut it, but I don't care. A moment later, I abandon his hair, running my hands down his back, fingertips grazing his skin, until I reach his ass and give it a firm squeeze.

Our moaning and groaning is our anniversary serenade.

He pulls out and, without being prompted, I flip onto my stomach. He enters from behind, his hot body against mine. Balanced on his hands, every thrust Nat takes pushes his lower abdomen onto my ass, which rubs my clit against the bed. I clench the closest pillow, feeling like I could cry.

He lowers to his forearms, and his chest presses into my back. I exhale, feeling a bit like a sandwich. Just when I can no longer catch my breath, he cums, the muscle vibrations making my pussy tingle.

I'm so sensitive, it won't take long for me to cum. I slip my hand between my body and the mattress and rub my button. His hand joins mine, and I gladly let him take over. His nimble fingers know exactly what to do. My ears ring, my body grows hot, my ab muscles tighten, and my pussy contracts around his cock.

He pulls out and plops beside me. I take a deep breath, roll over and lie my head on his sweaty chest.

"Do you think we'll fuck like this in another five years?" he says, caressing my hair.

I smile. "Absolutely. Why would we not?"

"I dunno. Age. Kids. Life."

I grimace. "Geez, you make it sound like we'll be old and depressed."

"Not old and depressed, but they say your sex life changes as you get more responsibilities."

I tiptoe my fingers up his chest. "Normal couples maybe. We're not a normal couple."

"Well, let's say I was home more and we were more normal. What then?"

I lift my head and make eye contact. "But that's not possible. Financially we can't afford for you to be home more often."

"Not now, but in the future. Just pretend. If I was home more often, do you think we would still fuck like this?"

I kiss his shoulder. "Well, I will. I don't know about you."

He smiles. "I will always want you. Didn't I prove that today?"

"You did." I lie my head back down. "I am confident we will always fuck this way."

He runs his hand down my arm. "If we would have more kids—"

I lift my head. What? More? More!

"You need to quit with the what-ifs. We will always have a passion for each other. We were meant to be together."

"Yes, we were. Happy anniversary, Honey."

"Happy anniversary."

He kisses the top of my head, and I relax against his shoulder.

Chapter 24

He Touched It

December 16, 2009

I've been attending Dramatic Sneezer concerts on and off since 2002. Nat looks hot, per usual, and it would be very easy for me to get distracted. Very easy. Very, very easy. But, at the same time, I attend these concerts now with our children. Forces me to keep my horniness under control.

And tonight we have some drama. Well, kid-level drama. Megan asked why she can't wear earplugs like grown-ups, and I told her it's because they don't come in her size. To be defiant, she keeps taking her headphones off, and I must remind her to put them back on. She doesn't understand she'll go deaf if she keeps it up. She also doesn't understand that most little girls don't get to do this. Josh is too young to question, but I've had a difficult time getting him to keep his headphones on, too. He sees Megan fiddling with hers and thinks it's okay to do the same.

I finally got them to leave their headphones on and watch the concert. Not a moment too soon either. A new album, *Outdated Technology*, is coming out in months, and I listen with apprehension to see how the audience will react to unfamiliar songs, but they appear to like them.

Standing here on the side of the stage, it's easy to forget that the kids are here. Well, that Megan is here. Josh is getting heavy. I shift him from one hip to another. .

A tired Megan stands beside me. At some point, I think we're going to need to bring lawn chairs for the kids. Two hours is a long time to ask kids to stay still, interested and standing.

Eventually, she sits on the floor. My arms are killing me so I set Josh on the floor beside her, and he makes himself comfortable near my feet.

I stretch my arms, flex my hands, and blood returns to sore muscles. I need to start lifting weights or something. Man, one toddler shouldn't make me ache like an old woman.

"Are you having a good time?" Nat says to the audience. "Here's one I know you'll recognize."

The crowd applauds, shouting a response to the question then goes apeshit when they hear the first cords of "Fighting Words," the song that made the band famous. It's amazing the affect music has on people. The best I ever can expect from one of my fans is an email.

I glance at the floor. Megan sits cross legged, singing half heartedly to the lyrics. She'll sleep well tonight, I'm sure of it. Josh, however, is not there. I wrinkle my brow, turn and look around. I don't see him anywhere. What the fuck? He's not here!

Where is he? How far could he have possibly gone? Someone that little doesn't realize things can hurt him. He doesn't know you shouldn't trust strangers. Oh, Jesus, how could I lose my son?

Pins and needles overcoming me, my heart speeds up. I'm going to faint. I rest my forehead in the palm of my hand and try breathing deeply. This can't be happening. It can't be happening.

Someone tugs on my sleeve. I open my eyes, hoping to see Josh but it's Megan. She points, and my gaze follows her finger. There's Josh. Phew. He's safe. Oh, my God, he's safe, but holy shit, he's on stage running around and laughing! Josh runs behind Nicole and Jerome, stops to wave at Kaleb and runs to Nat.

I think this might be the closest I've come to an out of body experience. It's as if I'm a witness to what's happening yet powerless to stop it. What am I going to do? How can I get him to come back? I wave, trying to coax him back, but he either doesn't see me or is having so much fun he ignores me.

Ah, shit, Nat's going to kill me. While I ponder what to do, Megan also runs on stage. What? Why did she do that? I thought younger siblings followed the older ones, not the other way around.

I swallow. If Josh is on stage and Megan is on stage, then guess where I'm going. I take a deep breath and follow. The music stopped a couple of minutes ago, and everyone's attention focuses on the toddler stage crasher.

Megan went only as far as her aunt on stage left and is easy to catch, but Josh hugs Nat's leg.

"How ya doing, Buddy?" Nat says, picking up Josh.

Josh responds by playing with the strings on the neck of Nat's guitar.

I have failed, totally failed, to watch the kids. Let me retrieve Josh and get out of here. Nat is no doubt pissed.

Clenching Megan by the arm to ensure she stays put, I make my way to stage center.

"I'm sorry," I say, placing a hand on Nat's shoulder. "I'll take him."

Josh strums, and Nat beams.

Nat doesn't answer, turning instead to the audience, "Houston, this is my son. My daughter. And my beautiful wife."

Oh, shit, there's a lot of people in that crowd. I smile nervously.

"He can't control his unruly family," Nicole says to the audience.

I want to get out of here as quickly as possible. I think Megan does, too, judging from how she eyes the audience with fear. I let go of her arm and place my hands under Josh's armpits. Nat hands the baby over, and we get the hell off stage.

"Do you want to hear another song, Houston?" Nat says while I usher the kids off stage.

The audience reacts enthusiastically, and the music resumes.

Nat is going to be pissed. He's going to be sooooo pissed.

I take the kids to the dressing room. They're done. This, in essence, punishes me more than them because I don't get to see the end of the concert. I remove Josh's headphones and motion for Megan to remove hers.

"Okay, Buddy," I say to Josh, "you're going into time-out. Running onto stage is a no-no."

I set him on a chair then turn my attention to Megan.

"Sit."

She sits, resting her head on the back of the chair.

I bend down to her level. "Megan, you can never, ever run onto the stage without permission. When Daddy's on stage, he's working. Understand?"

She nods. "Yes, Mommy."

"So what did I just say?"

"Never run on stage unless Daddy says so."

Um, close enough.

"Are you sleepy?"

She nods. I take Josh out of time-out and wait. Oh, Nat is going to be so pissed. My heart races. I really wasn't anticipating an argument during this trip. Bummer.

TOMORROW WILL BE A busy day. We're taking the kids to the beach in Galveston as an early Christmas gift. Josh has never been to the ocean, and his reaction will be precious. I was really looking forward to it, but I won't be able to enjoy it with this, this, thing hanging over my head.

I keep waiting and waiting, but nothing has been said about me failing to control the kids. Why is Nat torturing me like this? That's so unlike him. If something's on his mind, he says it. I'm so fidgety I can barely sit still.

"I'm sorry the kids ran onto the stage earlier," I say when the movie we're watching goes to commercial.

I can't force myself to make eye contact, focusing my gaze on the foot of the bed instead. Nat crosses and uncrosses his ankles, making the covers move. I swallow.

"I think Josh is going to be a guitar player. Did you see how he played with the strings?"

He thinks Josh is going to be a guitar player? What does that have to do with what happened? I look at Nat. He wears a goofy smile. Daydreaming or something.

"He's not quite 15 months," I say. "He likes anything that makes a sound. Or has flashy lights."

"It would be fantastic if he took an interest. I could teach him. I'd be something we could do together when he gets older."

"I'm sure that would be great. Years from now. But did you hear me? I said I was sorry."

He rolls onto his side. "I heard you. It was surprising, yeah, but weird things happen on tour sometimes. Can't get pissed off at every little thing that goes wrong. Sometimes I screw up a song, or there are equipment failures, or it rains during an outdoor show. Whatever. That's just the nature of playing live. Gotta let things roll off your back."

I'm not sure if I feel relieved or sick. "I thought you'd be furious."

"It's not like they destroyed any equipment or got hurt or anything. The audience loved it. They'll remember tonight's show, for sure. Did you watch Josh? He went straight for the guitar."

Has Nat completely lost his mind? Here I am apologizing for letting our children run wild and all he cares about is the fact Josh touched a guitar?

"*I've* touched guitars before. Doesn't mean I'm going to spontaneously start playing."

"Yes," he says, running a fingertip up my chest, "but when you touch it, it means something else entirely."

"Oh, does it now?"

"Don't you remember the first time you touched mine?"

I swallow. I don't think we're talking about an instrument anymore. The movie comes back from commercial, but he's lost all interest.

"I do remember," I say, playing along. "The neck was long and wide, and the head... It had to be tuned just right for the desired affect."

His fingertip reaches my collarbone, makes a U-turn and starts moving downward. "Those heads can be incredibly sensitive."

We make eye contact.

"Yes, they can be," I say, his finger passing my waist.

"That's why I don't let just anyone touch mine. She has to have a gentle yet confident touch."

His finger reaches the top of my thigh beside the pubic bone.

"You have such nimble fingers," I say, breathe shallow.

"It comes from years of practice."

Our lips collide.

His nimble finger continues its tour of my body, separating the top of my pussy lips and flicking my clitoris. I twitch uncontrollably, whimpering as his tongue intertwines with mine.

I separate my thighs to give him greater access, and he moves his finger in a circle over my clit, making me feel like I'm going to die in the best possible way.

He stops to wet his finger with my pussy juices and enhance the sensation. I moan, but he stifles my sounds with his tongue. The kids are sharing the room with us, after all.

I grab a handful of sheet. I need him inside me, yet I must cum.

"Cum for me, baby," he whispers in my ear. "Cum for me."

He continues circling. I feel it building. My back arches and my eyes roll back. The muscle spasms begin, and I growl like an animal.

I push on his shoulder until he lies flat and straddle him. His eyes widen. He wonders what I'm about to do, I can tell, but surely he must know. I release his hard cock from his underwear via the fly, lift up my nightgown and maneuver my pussy down.

Placing my hands on his chest, I pump until I establish a rhythm that pleases us both. I'm surprised Nat's groans haven't awakened the kids.

After several minutes, I pull my nightgown over my head and toss it aside. Somehow he senses I'm tired, and grasps my ass, one cheek in each palm, to take over thrusting.

I collapse onto his chest, thighs smarting, and insert my tongue through his parted lips, but soon I break the kiss, place my chin on his shoulder and moan in his ear.

He wraps his arms around my back, pressing my boobs into his chest, and thrusts a few more times before having muscles spasms of his own. I gasp, clenching his shoulders, and squeeze my pussy muscles around his now semi-hard cock. I should pull off him, but I don't want to.

"Anytime you want to touch my guitar," he says, grinning, "all you have to do is ask."

"Now is not the time for corny jokes," I say. "But, yes, I love strumming your guitar."

I pull off him and snuggle under his arm.

"Corny joke? I mean it. I enjoy when you touch my guitar. Guitar means penis."

"Yeah, I get it." I run my hand up his chest. "Big day tomorrow. The kids'll have fun."

"I just had fun."

"So did I."

We laugh as the end credits play on the TV movie.

DECEMBER 17, 2009

"We're at the beach," Nat says, turning off our rental car's engine "Are you excited?"

"Yeah!" Megan hops off her booster seat and grabs her plastic bucket and spade. "I'm going to build a sandcastle."

"Are you?"

"A huge one."

A stiff sea breeze smacks me in the face when I open the passenger door. It's not swimming weather, that's for sure, but it's a hell of a lot warmer than home. I open the backdoor and attempt to strap Josh's sunglasses behind his head, which is easier said than done because he keeps taking them off.

"That's great, Sweetie," Nat says, opening the other back passenger door and taking Megan's hand. "Maybe you'll find some cool things on the beach to decorate it with."

"Oh, like dead crabs and stuff?"

Nat laughs. "Well, maybe not that cool. Let's stay clear of animals."

I carry Josh on my hip and our pile of towels on the other, and we make our way to the beach. Josh has been to Lakeside Park and Beach back home in Vienna-on-the-Lake. That's on Lake Michigan, but he's so young I'm sure he doesn't remember. When Megan saw the ocean for the first time, she tried playing patty cake with it. I, of course, was 23 when Nat took me to the ocean for the first time. Just like with concerts, the kids don't realize how lucky they are to be able to make trips like this.

Megan rambles about the beach and decorating stuff at preschool, and Nat listens with undivided attention. Or he's a good actor. I can't tell.

"Mama," Josh says and points. "Ball."

In the distance two teenagers play volleyball with a beach ball. I didn't bring ours, even though it packs flat, because I figured it'd end up lost.

"Very good, Joshie," I say. "Are you ready to see the ocean?"

He says nothing, probably doesn't understanding the question.

"How about here?" Nat says to Megan about 12 feet from the water's edge. "I think this is an excellent sand-castle-building spot."

We stop and make a blanket out of towels. Megan tosses off her sandals and runs to the water to fill her bucket. I set Josh on his butt and remove his shoes.

Nat and I each take one of Josh's hands and we hoist him to his feet. He takes a tentative step into the sand and promptly cries.

"What is it?" Nat bends to Josh's level and sifts some sand with his fingers. "It feels weird, but sand is fun."

Josh shakes his head, tears streaming down his face.

"Look at Megan. She's having fun."

Megan returns, dumps her bucket into the sand and runs back to the water for more.

"Want to play with Megan?"

Josh continues to cry.

"Let's not push it," I say. "He can sit with us on the blanket and maybe go play when he's ready."

Nat and I make ourselves comfortable while keeping a watchful eye on Megan. Quieting, Josh stares, mesmerized, in the direction of the roaring waves. Maybe he remembers the sound from his white noise machine.

"Do they have toy guitars?" Nat says.

I shift my gaze temporarily to him. "Yeah, I suppose."

"I want to get Josh one for Christmas."

My heart drops. "I already finished the shopping and wrapped everything."

He smiles. "I'll be home in a few days. I'll go. It'll be fun."

"The stupidest shit you find entertaining when you haven't been home in a while. You'll be waiting in line for an hour."

"I'm sure I'll hate it, like, five minutes in, but I miss ordinary stuff sometimes. What could be more ordinary than buying my kid a Christmas gift?"

I nod. "Yeah, sure."

I know this has nothing to do with holiday shopping and everything to do with what happened yesterday. Nat's still convinced Josh is going to become a guitar player. I suppose most fathers have dreams for their sons, but I think he's grasping at straws with this one. Babies have an interest in, well, everything.

"Good idea or what?" Nat says.

If it makes him happy, why not?

I smile. "Yeah, it's totally a great idea."

Josh stands and steps gingerly on the sand. We applaud and congratulate him.

Chapter 25

Can't a Mom Have Some Privacy?

February 14, 2009

What woman wouldn't want to spend Valentine's Day with her husband? Well, I guess I shouldn't say that. After six and a half years and two kids, many women probably would wish their husbands were away longer.

I suppose the fact Nat is away on yet another day for lovers plagues my unconscious mind because an orgasm wakes me from a highly erotic dream. Huh, now I have a solution for that scene that's been giving me writer's block.

I roll onto my back and stick my hand between my legs, giving my button a quick rub. Oooh, yes, that feels good. I rub again, slowly using the edge of my nightgown to create a tickling sensation.

I pull up my knees and spread my legs. I need cock badly. Seeing as Nat isn't here, I'm forced to settle for the next best thing. I toss off the covers and rummage through the nightstand until I find my fake cock. It needs washed before use, so I run to the bathroom and quickly clean it.

When I return to bed, I stick that fake cock inside my pussy as far as it'll go and move it back and forth.

I close my eyes and try to remember my dream so I can type it out later. The hero's hard cock plunges into the heroine's wet pussy. She hasn't been this sticky in ages. He's been away – army deployment – and she hardened her heart, but now the only hard she wants is between her legs. She moans from pleasure, clawing at his back, while his muscular body thrusts. Reaching down, she grabs his ass.

I moan and decide to fuck myself before I make myself cum.

The hero lifts his head to gaze into the heroine's eyes. He—

The door creaks open. No, not in the fantasy. I lift my head and look between my legs at the open door. It's Saturday and the kids usually sleep, but Megan and Josh stand there, Scooter panting between them.

"Mommy?" Megan says.

"Mommy," Josh mimics her.

If you'd have set my ass on fire, I couldn't move faster. I sit and pull my nightgown to my knees, concealing the fake cock.

"You're supposed to knock when you come into this room," I say. "Megan, take your brother and go play quietly in your room. We'll have breakfast after I cum. Come downstairs."

She says nothing, takes Josh by the hand and leaves. Scooter follows.

"Close the door," I say firmly.

Her hand reaches for the doorknob, and the door closes. I exhale. She better follow instruction. Normally she does, but not always. It depends on her mood and whether she wants to be stubborn or not. I'm not taking any chances. I get up, the cock still in place, and lock the door.

The mood ruined, I don't really care about my fictional characters anymore. All my characters so far have been couples who face some sort of separation. I pulled that from real life. I've gotten used to this life, but it has its drawbacks. Not being able to fuck my husband when I want, for example. And I want his cock now. This facsimile, however, will need to do.

I sigh, lie back and resume the position. With a deep breath, I close my eyes and move the cock again, slowly at first then faster.

A moan escapes my parted lips. I move the cock faster. It makes a sound as it glides back and forth, doing its job. With my free hand, I use my middle finger to stroke my button in circles. When the orgasm finally comes, it's Nat who is on my mind.

I take a deep breath and pull the fake cock out, tossing it onto the bed. I'm not taking any chances. I'll wash it and put it away. In the past, I could leave it until I was certain I was finished with it. Sometimes it stayed in my bed for days. But the kids are getting older. Speaking of which, I'm registering Megan for kindergarten this afternoon.

The kids better be playing quietly in Megan's room. Oh, I hope she doesn't ask questions. Josh is too young to articulate his confusion, but Megan is a different story. She observes and sometimes questions when you least expect it, but hopefully she didn't see enough to wonder. I hope. Jesus, how will I explain it otherwise?

NAT SENDS LARGER BOUQUETS when he's away compared to the ones he buys when he's home as if larger makes up for his absence. I know that makes me sound ungrateful. I am grateful he remembers these occasions and plans ahead so the bouquets arrive on time, but if it's a choice between a vase of flowers and having him home, I'm selecting him every time.

I know a lot of women's husbands aren't romantic at all. Tiffany's live-in boyfriend/common-law husband Dennis never remembers Valentine's Day. Of course, in fairness, that's her doing. She thinks Valentine's Day is called the day for lovers, yet the focus is on the woman. She says the focus needs to be balanced or else it's sexist. She says I shouldn't care Nat's gone because that makes me emotionally dependent on a man. She thinks too much.

I balance Josh on my hip and keep a careful eye on Megan while we wait in line to register her for kindergarten. Where does the time go? It seems like only yesterday I found out I was pregnant with her and now— Oh, shit, wait. I did bring her birth certificate, didn't I? We'll never make it back before registration ends if we need to go home for it. I unzip my purse with my free hand and riffle for the documents we were told to bring along.

"Mommy, what are you doing?" Megan says.

I glance at her. "I'm checking to make sure I have everything we need."

She nods. "Mommy, what were you doing earlier?"

My body goes cold. "When earlier?"

"When you were in bed."

I swallow. I was afraid that was what she meant.

"I, um, I miss Daddy and sometimes when I really miss Daddy... Never mind, what I was doing. You should always knock before coming into Mommy and Daddy's room."

She squeezes her brows together. "But what were you doing?"

"Nothing you need to worry about, Sweetie."

I find the birth certificate and just in time because we're next. I hand the young, blond woman at the table the documents.

"Hi," she says to Megan in a voice so bubbly it's sickening, "what's your name?"

The woman is speaking to Megan, but Megan is focused me. "The thing you had between your legs. What was it? And why?"

The smile on the young woman's face fades, replaced by something else. "Oh, my."

If it were possible to crawl into a hole and die right now, I would.

"I'm not sure what you saw, Megan," I say, "but you should always knock before you enter Mommy and Daddy's bedroom."

"Oh, yes," the young woman says, "it is important to follow the rules. In kindergarten, we have classroom rules that must be followed, too."

Megan says nothing, and the woman hands me a clipboard. I avoid eye contact when I take it. The form asks for child's name, address, birthday, parents' names along with address(es), phone numbers and occupations.

Josh grabs the pen and the top of the clipboard, making it impossible for me to write a damn thing. I set him on the table and fill out the form as quickly as possible.

The young woman takes the clipboard, scrutinizing the form. She returns our documents, which I shove into my purse. Good. We can go. I pick up Josh. I want to go and never see this woman again. Ever. She knows too much.

"So," she says to Megan, "what is it like having two creative parents?"

Goddamn it. I want to get the hell out of here.

Megan shrugs. How the fuck would she know what it's like? She doesn't know the difference.

The woman continues. "What do your mom and dad do?"

I bite my tongue and taste blood. Ugh. That's a loaded question. What does your mom do? She sticks objects up her pussy.

Megan, however, is smart enough to know the woman refers to occupation. "Mommy spends a lot of time using a computer, and Daddy plays a guitar. He screams a lot on stage."

The woman smiles. "He screams a lot?"

"When he sings," I say. "Is this going to take much longer? My son needs a diaper change."

"Poopies," Josh says, proud of himself.

Thought I made that up, didn't you? Nope. I can smell it strongly. Might be diarrhea, and he's balanced on my hip. If we don't get to a bathroom soon, my coat might be ruined.

"Well," the woman says, "we do encourage diversity in our district. We welcome you and your family to Vienna-on-the-Lake Consolidated District 130."

Megan says nothing. She probably still wonders what I was doing earlier. Or maybe she wonders why districts in this state have such fucking long names. I was educated in Sterling Community Unit School District 5.

"Thank you," I say for her.

I grab Megan's hand. As we make our getaway, I hear the young woman greet the next child. If she ends up being Megan's teacher in the fall, I'm going to have a fit.

Always lock your door before using a fake cock. Lesson learned. They don't warn you about these things in parenting books.

MY PHONE RINGS WHILE I strap Josh into his car seat. Goddamn it. The timing is off for everything today. I quickly finish, climb into the driver's seat and slam the door to block out the harsh wind. I answer on the final ring before voicemail picks up.

"Hey, how are things going?" Nat says.

"Oh, we just finished registration. Everything's taken care of."

"I can't believe our baby is old enough for real school."

"I know. Crazy, right?"

"Put me on speaker phone." I put him on speaker, and he continues, "Megan, Sweetie, are you excited about kindergarten?"

She stares into the distance for a second or two. "I don't know. Mommy wrote on a paper, and a woman asked me stuff."

"Oh. What else is happening today? Anything fun?"

She beams. "We're having heart cookies later. And Mommy had something between her legs earlier and won't tell me what it is."

My cheeks burn. Why won't Megan let the topic die?

"Oh?" He fights an urge to laugh. "She did? How do you know?"

"Joshie and I saw her in the bedroom. Mommy says she misses you, but she won't tell what the thing is."

"I miss Mommy, too, and I'm sorry I can't be home today. The thing is magical. Mommy can't talk about it or else all the magic goes away."

A magic dildo? Well, I suppose it is magic in a matter of speaking. I'd rather have Nat home, but a plastic cock and heart shaped cookies with our kids are going to have to do.

Chapter 26

It's My Party

March 7, 2009

Nat and I plan to celebrate him being home by enjoying a quiet dinner together alone. He requested I wear something nice, so I opted for thigh-high hose attached to my lingerie garter belt and no underwear. I have plans to seduce him when we get home, and no underwear is part of the seduction plan, but holy shit it's cold outside with nothing on under my dress. I guess I should have thought this through for longer than two minutes.

He told me a new place opened downtown that we should try, but the building ahead is far from new. It's the oldest restaurant in town.

"Cooper's is the restaurant you wanted to take me to? I thought you were taking me somewhere new?"

Nat smiles and clenches my arm. "Well, it has new management. Besides, there are some good memories here. As I recall, you sucked me off in the basement."

I smirk. "I did do that. And as I recall, you enjoyed it very much."

"I always enjoy when you suck me off."

I lie my head on his shoulder. "Maybe, if we have a nice dinner, I'll suck you off again."

"No, not tonight. It's your birthday. I'll eat you until you squirm."

I laugh. "Sounds like a plan."

Nat opens the door for me, and I step inside the vestibule. Two things immediately strike me: First, warmth, although it's going to take a while for my limbs to thaw. Second, I don't see any lights.

"Are you sure they're open tonight?" I say. "It looks awfully dark in there."

"I made reservations, so they have to be open. Maybe they tripped a fuse."

I wrinkle my nose. "Tripped a fuse?"

He shrugs. "I don't know. We'll find out." He opens the door that leads into the restaurant. "See. It's unlocked. They gotta be open."

We step inside, and I take Nat's hand. It really is dark in here, as if the place is haunted or someone is going to murder us. The hair on the back of my neck stands on end.

"This is really creepy. Let's just go. We can come back some other time."

The lights flicker on, and a bunch of people yell "surprise!" in unison. The restaurant is full of people and "30" balloons. I grip Nat's hand, scared more shitless now than I was when I thought the joint was haunted.

"Happy birthday, Honey," he says. "I wanted to give you a birthday you'd remember."

"Yeah."

That's all I can think to say. He's stunned me speechless. I seduced him with a crotchless teddy for his 30th birthday, and he gave me a surprise party for mine. Oh, I'm going to need a stiff drink. I swallow, and it hurts.

Before I can process everything or react, I'm rushed by friends and family. Oh my God, did my family rent a bus to get here? They're, like, all here: my siblings, my parents, Yiayia, my nieces and nephews, my aunts and uncles, my cousins and their spouses and children. My in-laws are here, too, and my high school and college friends.

How was Nat able to contact all these people? I spot Shawna, and there's my answer. All he had to do was contact her and Vanessa, and they probably did the rest.

"Mommy!" Megan pushes her way through a gaggle of cousins and hands me a teddy bear wearing a party hat. "Happy birthday."

I caress her hair. "Thank you, Sweetie."

Josh follows her. Megan pokes him in the shoulder blades, and he raises his hand to give me a little balloon with a cartoon gift on it.

"Ba-oon, Mommy," he says.

"Yes, Buddy, balloon," I say, stooping to his level. "Thank you."

The kids run back into the crowd and when I rise to my full height, Maroula gives me a stifling bear hug.

"I still have two weeks to be 29. How does it feel to be an old woman?"

I laugh. "I thought I woke up feeling creaky today."

"That was from all the exercise you got yesterday," Nat says over my shoulder.

"Oh?" Maroula says, eyebrow rising. "Started a new workout routine?"

"You could say that," I say, fondly remember yesterday's fuck session.

"You have me curious. You'll have to tell me all about it later."

I smile and shake my head. Oh, no I don't. I write about those sort of fitness routines, but I don't freely talk about them.

Greg and Katrina are the last people to wish me a happy birthday. I wonder if they really wanted to come or if our parents made them. Yeah, I know Greg's pushing 40, but my parents can be very persuasive, and Greg always does what he is told.

"I hope you have a very happy birthday," Katrina says with an overly polite smile that I want to smack off her face.

I thank her. I'm sincere, even if she isn't.

"That wish is from both of us," Greg says even more stiffly than his cold wife. "Don't drink too much tonight. You know how well alcohol mixes with cake."

I narrow my eyes. "It's my party, and I'll drink if I want to."

Katrina purses her lips, and Greg looks disappointed I don't want to do as I'm told.

"Well, thanks for coming," I say and, blending with the crowd, get the hell away from them.

I find Nat talking to Brandon about, I don't know, creative stuff.

"What made you think to do this?" I say, joining them.

"I thought you would enjoy being the center of attention," Nat says.

I rub his cheek. "I always feel the center of attention in your eyes."

He smiles. "That's because you are. Do you want a drink?"

"Of course, I do. And make sure Greg sees me take it."

"Greg being an ass again?" Brandon says when Nat leaves for the bar.

"Yeah, he thinks he's being clever warning me that I can't hold my liquor."

Brandon shakes his head. "Try to finish your drink a good half an hour or so before the cake so you have time to digest."

"Thanks for the tip."

The restaurant staff sets out the buffet, and I feel guilty Nat probably spent a fortune throwing this party for me.

He returns with my drink, and I don't even bother to ask what type it is. I take it and sip. Whiskey sour. Not bad even if it is more sour than whiskey.

"I can get you something else if you want," he says after I wrinkle my nose.

As tempted as I am to have Nat wait on me hand and foot, Greg glares. I'll keep the drink.

"No, it's fine. Looks like it's almost dinner. Are we late or something?"

Nat shakes his head. "No. Why?"

"We only got here a short while ago, and they're already serving dinner."

"That's because of all the kids. If someone needs to leave early, they can."

I cross my eyes and wag my head to give Greg the false impression I'm already drunk. "You've thought of everything, haven't you?"

Nat smiles. "Maybe. We'll see what you say by the end of the night."

I want to answer with something dirty, but it's so loud in here I'd need to shout, and what I want to say is for his ears only.

A hand touches my shoulder, startling me, and a bit of my drink spills on my hand.

"Jesus, Mom, what did you do that for?" I say, turning around.

Mom purses her lips. "How was I supposed to know you two were so deep in conversation? You talk all the time. You should mingle. All these people are here for you."

They are, aren't they? I've had family birthday parties before, of course, when I lived in Sterling. Yiayia and Papou would throw me a party at Costas' Place every year. It wasn't anything fancy, just dinner, cake, presents and dancing. All Economos family functions include dancing. This is the first time I've had a party that also includes my friends, or my in-laws for that matter.

"I will, Mom. Give me a chance. Besides, it's dinner time."

"You should go first," she says with a smile. "You are the guest of honor."

I'm amazed how quickly Mom goes from one extreme to the next. I'll use her change in mood as an excuse to make my escape. I try to be graceful and casual, but Megan and Kendra run by and nearly knock me over. Oh shit, why do they need to do that when I'm wearing heels and no underwear?

I hope someone will be watching the kids tonight. I'd like to have fun. I am the guest of honor after all.

I take a plate from the end of the buffet line. I suppose being first I also get my choice of table, don't I? I know I'm safe from Greg or Katrina wanting to sit with me, but what about Mom and Dad? I said I wanted to have fun and – don't take this the wrong way – I love my parents but they ain't fun. Really, I suppose, the people I should sit with are my old college friends. I haven't seen most of them since my wedding.

I plop a scoop of rice on my plate and try to take a look at who's behind me in line. No one will deny me sitting with Nat, I wouldn't think, but who will sit with us? It better be someone who doesn't care if I squeeze his thigh under the table.

I MINGLED. NOT BECAUSE Mom told me to but because I wanted to thank everyone for coming. Shawna, my in-laws and my college friend Sarah Kim, who lives in Geneva, are the only guests who didn't need to drive hours to get here, and I wanted everyone to know I'm grateful they made the trip.

"Having a good time?" Nat says, rubbing my back.

I nod. "I am. Thank you."

"Wanna take a break?"

"A break?"

Who takes a break from a birthday party?

He smiles. "A trip down memory lane. I know of a great stockroom downstairs."

I catch his drift and turn to Sarah. "If you excuse me, I'll catch you later."

"Sure." She laughs. "I've lost Sean somewhere, so I had best go find my husband."

Hand in hand Nat and I go downstairs. We manage to avoid the people wandering the halls outside the restrooms and head straight for the stockroom where I sucked Nat off in '02. A single light near the main light switch illuminates it.

We close the door and immediately our lips collide. It's my birthday, so I expected fun today. I planned to initiate it. I expected it would come later in a more private place. Remember I complained I was cold? I'm not cold now. I'm hot, very, very hot.

I run my hands down Nat's back. He pulls up my skirt with one hand, caressing my thigh with the other.

"You're ready for me already?" he says, grazing my pussy lips with his fingertips and discovering my lack of underwear.

"I'm always ready for you."

His fingers penetrate, and I gasp. I fumble with his pants' button until it releases and push down his jeans. Underwear mid-thigh, he pushes me against the wall. The cinderblock is cold, but I don't care. I wrap my leg around his, allowing him to slip his hard cock inside my wet pussy, and grab two fistfuls of shirt when he starts thrusting. With each thrust, my back moves up the wall slightly. My hair is going to be a mess after this. Don't care about that either. I love this position because dick rubs my clitoris with every motion. Our lips part, and we make eye contact as best we can in the dark.

He groans and I moan for maybe 10 minutes. Then the door opens.

"You can't be in here," a restaurant employee, a young dude, the kind I might have went for 15 years ago, says before turning on an overhead light. "Whoa. And you certainly can't be doing *that* in here."

Nat presses into me, maintaining my modesty, I suppose, but not his. His ass is visible for all to see. That's what he gets for wearing a long sleeve t-shirt instead of a button-down.

"I did rent the place for the evening," Nat says.

The employee averts his eyes from Nat's bare ass by focusing on me, bringing back that creepy feeling I had when we first got here. Why is he staring at me like that?

"Yeah, yeah, but, but, you just can't. Health code violations and all that."

"A generous tip for your discretion."

The employee nods. "Sure. Yeah. Just don't be down here too long. If my boss sees you, he'll throw you out."

The young dude leaves, and we laugh.

"Where were we?" Nat says after the door clicks shut. "Oh, yeah, I was fucking your brains out."

I gasp, the muscles in my back tensing as I'm once again pushed against the wall, his hot, swallow breath blowing in my ear. He picks me up, and I wrap my legs around his waist, moaning in concert with his thrusts.

I'm so sensitive I could cum this way. I have a couple of times before – and by a couple, I mean two – most notably when Megan was conceived. The memory of that night passes through my mind. If I concentrate enough, maybe, just maybe, I can cum this way again. That would an awesome birthday gift.

I close my eyes and focus on the sensation. His thrusting grows faster, and my moans louder. *Focus. Goddamn you.* We cum in unison, cock and pussy spasming together. Happy birthday to me!

AFTER WE RETURNED UPSTAIRS, most of the kids were whining, some even crying, a consequence of it being past their bedtimes. The sugar rush of birthday cake put most of them, including mine, temporarily back in a good mood, so I took the opportunity to sit at a table near the buffet and open gifts. Josh sat beside me, entertaining himself playing with wrapping paper and bows.

By the time I finished the gift pile, I was as cranky as the kiddos. How many goddamn times did Mom need to take my photo? I swear she took one photo per card or gift, sometimes multiple shots from different angles. I'm so glad guests are beginning to leave. I put on a smile and fake it until my annoyance wears off.

"Did you have a good birthday?" Nat says.

I give him a kiss. "I had a wonderful birthday. Thank you."

"You're very welcome. You deserve it." He smiles. "I have one more surprise for you. My parents are keeping the kids overnight, so we have the entire night to ourselves. What should we do with all our free time?"

I put my hand on his arm. "I can think of two or three ways we can end my birthday with a bang."

"I was hoping you would say that."

I smile. "Oh, yeah?"

"Oh yeah." He lowers his voice and says in my ear, "Thanks for not wearing any underwear today, but I'd like to see you out of this dress."

"As soon as we get home. As soon as we get home," I say and wink.

ROCK STAR MOM

Chapter 27

Last of Her Kind

May 13, 2009

"What do you mean she fell down the stairs?" I say, voice rising sharply. "Why wasn't someone watching her?"

"Why would someone be watching her?" Mom says over the phone. "She's been perfectly fine and mobile. No health issues before this."

"But she's 92."

"Age doesn't matter. She wanted to remain independent, and we all agreed that was what was best as long as she could be independent. Family is nearby in case of an emergency. Petra found her when she went to walk Theophilus."

"Okay."

I feel faint. How would you feel if you just learned your last remaining grandparent is in the hospital? All I can do is picture her at the bottom of the stairs, body in a mangled heap, her dog going crazy, and my cousin finding her.

"I need you to listen to me," Mom says. "Yiayia fractured her hip. She needs surgery. It's a dangerous operation for someone her age."

My hand trembles. "Dangerous?"

"I'm calling you and Vanessa so you can come home."

"Wh– why do we need to come home?"

"Because this is very serious. Anything can happen, and we have to be prepared for the possibility."

I don't answer and instead save my manuscript and spin my chair away from the computer. My eyes focus on the swing set in the backyard. When Yiayia was here in March, I took her on a tour of the house and yard. She stopped by the swing set and said we finally made it because four generations of our family have been born in this country and it took four generations to get a backyard playground. The fact that was her measure of success made me laugh.

"Can you come tomorrow?" Mom says.

Tomorrow? I swallow. "I'll talk to Megan's preschool teacher when I go pick her up."

"I don't know why you felt the need to enroll her in preschool. It's bad enough she's starting kindergarten in the fall. Five is too young for a child to be away from her mother."

"With only one child home during the day, it gives me more time to write."

I don't tell Mom that over the course of this phone call I lost track of that one child. He left though the open office door. I get up.

"More of those stories of yours?" Mom says as I step into the hall. "I'll never understand why people buy that shit."

"It's escapism, Mom. Same as any other novel."

Josh isn't in the great room. Damn.

"If you say so. So I can expect to see you tomorrow?"

"I'll have to get someone to take Scooter. And I'll need to get Maisie's automatic food and water feeders out and the extra litter box."

Mom sighs. "Yes, I understand you have preparations to make. Will we see you?"

My hand shakes again. "Yes, I'll come, but I can't stay for days and days waiting. I'll come back if necessary."

"It's a three hour drive. Why not stay longer?"

"Because," my voice cracks, "you're asking me to be on death watch. You haven't called it that, but that's what it is. I refuse to put my children through that."

Josh isn't in the half bath or the walk-in pantry. Shit.

"Suit yourself. I have to get back to the hospital. Your father is flying in later."

I should ask her when Dad's retiring – he turns 69 this year – but maybe Shawna is right, and my parents enjoy being apart.

"Good luck." I place my foot on the bottom step of the staircase and hear a *brong* sound. "I'll see you tomorrow, Mom. Goodbye," I say and hang up.

Brong. The sound comes from the opposite direction of where I'm headed. Sure enough, the basement door is open.

There's no game room or home theater in our finished basement. About a fourth of it is the kids' playroom, and the rest is Nat's domain. He writes down there and stores expensive equipment.

I go down the steps and turn the corner. Josh plays one of Nat's electric guitars. Plays in the sense someone plays with a toy, not an instrument. He bangs on it and pulls the strings.

"Joshua!" I grab the guitar from him, unsure what, if any, damage has been done. "You can only touch this if Daddy is with you."

Josh bursts into tears. I'm sorry my tone was harsh. That's the stress coming out. I really don't want to go to Sterling, especially to see a loved one in the hospital. I don't want that image in my mind. I'd rather envision Yiayia spry and happy when I saw her at my birthday party.

I pick up Josh and caress his hair. "Shush. You have to learn to follow the rules. You can't play with things that aren't yours. You could break them."

"Gee-ta," Josh says, and I think he means guitar.

At least, he knows what it's called. Maybe Nat is right and Josh will take up the guitar, but that will be several years down the road. Today, I have a trip to Sterling to plan with two kids who will get cranky from a disrupted routine.

I kiss Josh's forehead. "We're going to be making a trip tomorrow. Proyiayia is hurt badly, and we are going to visit her. We have things to do to get ready. You can be my helper."

He whimpers, his fit ending. I set him down and take his hand.

"Great, Buddy. You're a great helper. Let's go upstairs."

He says nothing and allows me to lead him to the staircase. I leave the guitar where it is. I'll worry about it later. It's one that Nat modified, so I know he can fix any damage done, but hopefully a 20 month old can't do much damage.

When we reach the ground floor, I pull our suitcases out of the coat closet. Josh takes his little Thomas the Tank Engine suitcase and rolls it around. He thinks it's fun, I guess. I think of Nat and how I'd like to tell him what's going on, but he's overseas and I need to wait until he calls me at our scheduled time. God, this sucks. This must have been what it was like for Mom, not being able to reach Dad during the pre-mobile phone days, not that he ever scheduled a time to call her.

Why didn't Dad call? Didn't he care how we were doing at school, or how the extended family was doing, or if Mom cheated on him, or the house burnt down, or anything? At the time, I didn't think anything of it because I didn't know any different, and there was plenty of family nearby. Yiayia often made baklava and if we were lucky, she was waiting at our house or Thea Ilena's to treat Vanessa, Phil, Maroula and me after high school. Why she chose us, I'm not sure. Maybe she felt sorry for us because our other grandmother was ill and couldn't do anything with us. Phil, being a guy, always ate the most, and Yiayia would ask about our day and tell us what it was like going to high school in Peoria during the Great Depression.

"Choo choo," Josh says, running in a circle.

I guess he's pretending to be Thomas or one of the other trains.

"Come on, Buddy. Let's go pack."

We go upstairs.

MAY 14, 2009

"Come here, *koukla*," Yiayia says, and Megan runs to the hospital bed.

"Proyiayia," she says, "does it hurt?"

Megan looks a bit intimated by all the hospital machinery. I am, too, honestly. All of this reminds me of when Papou Petrakis was going through his cancer treatments or when Yiayia Petrakis was in and out of the hospital with her MS.

"Oh, they have me on medicine," Yiayia says. "I'm as comfortable as I can be."

The heart monitor beeps slightly with every thump of her heart. I force a smile – I am happy to see my grandmother, after all, just not like this – and set Josh on the bed near Yiayia's hand, so she can touch him. He's suddenly quiet and looks as if he might cry. You and me both, Buddy.

"How many great-grandchildren do I have now?" Yiayia says to me.

"I don't know," I say quietly.

"Well, let's see. You have two children. Vanessa has three. Chris has three. Greg one. Maroula three. Phil two. Persephone two. How many is that so far?"

Really? She's isn't going to go through all 14 grandchildren, is she? I swallow. Whatever makes her happy. She's having surgery in the morning.

"I dunno. I'm terrible at math."

"That's 16. Now, where was I? Anastasia has yet to marry. Petra has one. Minerva four. Narcissa two. Alexander three. Kostas one. Tom two. I have 29 great-grandchildren. I'm proud of all of you." She turns back to Megan. "How is preschool?"

"I didn't go today because we came here," Megan says.

"Oh. And where is *Baba* today?"

Megan looks up at me with large eyes.

"Nat's in Europe," I say. "Probably enjoying the *biergartens*."

I don't know why I said that. Makes it sound like he's on a European drinking tour.

"You're strong like your mother to have your husband away from home so much," Yiayia says. "Mine was away six days a week, but he was always downtown at the restaurant."

I don't feel strong. I really don't.

MAY 19, 2009

"I told you you should have stayed in Sterling," Mom says, tone dripping in disappointment.

"My home is in Vienna-on-the-Lake, and I told you I wasn't going to hang out in Sterling on death watch. Yiayia was fine when we were here last week."

Mom stops pacing her living room only long enough to glare at me. "What's so important in Vienna-on-the-Lake? Lord knows it isn't your husband. He's away, per usual."

My cheeks burn. This coming from a woman whose husband has been away for the better part of 40 years.

"Our house. Shawna. Scooter. Maisie. My manuscript. Megan's preschool."

Mom makes a dismissive motion with her hands. "Ack, preschool. So they can teach her what? How to sit in a circle and sing nursey rhymes?"

I take a step forward, but Vanessa blocks my way.

"None of this is productive," she says. "What is the prognosis?"

"They're unsure," Mom says. "She simply isn't healing like the doctors anticipated. That's why it's important that you stay here and don't keep crisscrossing the state."

"I'm going back to Vienna-on-the-Lake tomorrow," I say.

Mom resumes pacing. "I warned you. I told you surgery is dangerous for an elderly woman, especially with a broken hip, so it's not like you hadn't been forewarned."

"Okay! I heard you the first five fucking times you told me today. I'm going to crisscross the state again, because I'm not going to wait here simply because something might happen."

"You should have moved back home when you were pregnant with Megan like I asked you to. No, instead you married *him*, even though he's probably cheating on you. In Europe for work, my ass. He's probably off with a mistress or two."

I take a step forward, and again Vanessa blocks my way.

"Out of my way. Out of my goddamn way!" To Mom, I say, "He is not cheating on me. Why do you keep insisting that? What did Dad do to you?"

Mom and Vanessa both stare at me. Nessa looks frightened while Mom looks dumbfounded. What? She actually thought I believed Nat is cheating on me when there has been no indication whatsoever?

"This isn't about your father," Mom says. "It's about you crisscrossing the state when you should stay near family."

"Then why bring up Nat cheating on me? You realize he isn't, don't you? He treats me and our kids like we're the center of the universe. No. You're projecting your shit on me. I'm sick of it. Go to therapy or something, but leave me out of it."

"You should stay here in Sterling when Yiayia is in the hospital."

I turn to Vanessa. "Smell that? That's all the shit in here."

I turn and hightail it to the stairs.

MAY 23, 2009

"Megan, Sweetie, come sit with me."

I pat the mattress beside me on my old bedroom bed. Yes, we are back in Sterling. To say Mom said "I told you so" is an understatement. I should start staying at other relatives' houses. Anyway. Megan lets go of the doorknob, the stuffed animal under her arm sagging, and plods toward the bed.

"Kendra just got here," she says, sadness creeping into her voice.

"I know, but I'm sure she's tired and a little cranky from the long drive. Let her rest and eat something. By the time you go back downstairs she'll be ready to play."

"Okay."

She plops on the bed. I smile at her, even though my stomach hurts.

"Um, Megan, uh."

Megan knows about death to an extent. She's seen dead bugs, dried leaves, wilted flowers, that sort of thing, but I'm pretty sure she has no concept of how things die or even that it happens to animals and people.

She eyes me with confusion. I best get this over with.

"Do you know what death is?"

Megan looks even more confused. "It's when bugs lie on their back with their legs up."

She lies back on the bed, arms and legs in the air.

"Um, yeah, dead bugs do do that. But it happens to animals and people, too. Everything alive eventually will die."

"Everything?" she says, voice uncertain. "Even you and Daddy?"

I feel like I'm going to throw up, "Some day. But not until we're very old. Like Proyiayia. She's very sick. We're going to go to the hospital later with Thea Vanessa to say goodbye. The hospital only allows a certain number of people in the room at once, so Theos Brandon will take Noah, Parker and Kendra after we go."

"Why do we need to say goodbye? Where is she going?"

I swallow. "When things die, their bodies stop working. Their heart stops beating. They stop breathing and thinking. They can't move. They're just a body. No personality. They can't talk or anything. People bury bodies in what's called a cemetery, and there's a ceremony called a funeral where everyone who loves that person comes to see them off. The wake is the night before. That's when everyone comes to see the body and comfort everyone who is sad."

"Oh. Is Proyiayia going to die?"

"She is. When we go to the hospital, I want you and Josh to kiss her goodbye. Okay?"

Megan nods. "Okay."

"If there is anything else you want to tell her, this afternoon is the time."

"I'll color her a picture."

I smooth Megan's hair. "That's a good idea, Sweetie. She'll like that. You can go play with Kendra now."

"Okay, Mommy."

I manage to keep the tears out of my eyes until Megan leaves the room. I mean, I know Yiayia is 92 and can't live forever, but no matter how many years you have with someone you love, it's never enough. I don't care that I'm 30 and have a family of my own. I lost my other grandparents before I was 20. I didn't understand then what it's like to love a child unconditionally or to doubt my own parenting abilities. I'll always need my grandmother's love and wisdom. The fact I'm aging is reason to need her even more. That's selfish, and I know it. But I have many questions, and it's too late to ask them. So many questions.

Dishwalla's "Counting Blue Cars" enters my head. I haven't thought of that song since high school. My friends and I used to sing it along with the radio or just because, and Yiayia hated it because it refers to God as a female and she thought it was sacrilegious.

We're who we are because of our friends and family, and I'm about to lose someone who made me who I am.

MAY 27, 2009

It was a post-op infection that took Yiayia in the end. Chris and Phil think we should sue the hospital, but these things happen with shocking regularity so I doubt there's a case. If they want to talk to an attorney to feel better, then so be it.

The funeral and luncheon are mercifully over, but as is Orthodox tradition, we'll be back in 40 days to commemorate our matriarch's life.

I exhale. Vanessa shifts her weight on the bed beside me. Maroula, sitting on the chair that belongs to our old desk, stretches her legs.

"I still can't believe it," Vanessa says, wiping her nose with a tissue. "This all happened way too quick."

"Things will never be the same," Maroula says. "I'm used to seeing her nearly every day."

I'm not sure what to say. I haven't seen Yiayia regularly since high school.

"It's gotta be worse for Petra, though," Maroula says, "considering she lives in the lot behind her."

That's the downside of living so close to family. Sterling is such a small community, square mileage-wise, that I suppose it's no wonder the entire family lives in such close proximity. Papou used to call it Micro Hellas because so many of us lived in the same part of town. The Hardwicks are also close knit but their houses aren't right on top of each other, so Nat has no point of reference when I talk about growing up close to everyone.

Vanessa places her head in her hand. "What a horrible way to go. Promise me, if my time comes before yours, that you'll kill me first and won't let me suffer."

Maroula gasps.

"I love you, but I'm not going to prison for you," I say.

Vanessa looks hurt. "I would for you."

"No, you wouldn't."

"And where is Nat today that he couldn't join you?" she says, pissed I didn't agreed to euthanize her.

She's trying to hurt me. She knows damn well where he is and that I'd rather he was here. I want to lean on him like she does Brandon.

"Spain."

"Spain? He's in Spain?"

"Yes, he's in fucking Spain. Do you want me to call the tour schedule up on my phone and prove it to you?"

Maroula stands. "Enough. We buried our grandmother today. Do you have to argue today of all days?"

Vanessa shakes her head. "No, I'm sorry. I haven't been sleeping well."

We fall into silence for a minute or two.

"I wish I had asked her about motherhood," I say, breaking the silence. "There are so many things I'd like to know, but I didn't think about them until it was too late."

"Like what?" Maroula says.

"I'd like to know if she ever felt like a failure, among other things."

Vanessa wipes her nose. "I thought you'd want to know what it was like raising kids during World War II or something. Why do you want to know that?"

"Because I feel like a failure."

Maroula sits and wraps her arm around me. "Megan and Josh are great kids. Why do you feel that way?"

I tell them about the kids running on stage a few months ago and about Josh being rough with Nat's guitar the day Mom called to tell me Yiayia was in the hospital. I don't tell them about the kids walking in on me masturbating, but it's on my mind. There are other examples, too, of the kids misbehaving. Dozens of examples.

"Well, they've never gotten hurt, have they, or hurt someone else?" Maroula says.

"No."

"Then what have you done that's so bad?"

Vanessa upturns the corners of her lips. "You're not a negligent mother. And as for the behavior, you have to keep in mind that we grew up with strict parents. It's perfectly fine to be more laid back than our parents were."

"Then why do I feel so terrible?" I say.

She shrugs. "Self doubt?"

"I still feel like a failure."

Maroula hugs me. "You're not. Someday you'll have granddaughters sitting around lamenting the fact they didn't ask you enough questions when you were alive."

"Uh, thanks, I guess."

"No problem."

We exchange hugs and have a good cry.

Chapter 28

A Big Girl Now

August 31, 2009

Megan holds a fake mouse on a string above Maisie's head. The old cat swats on occasion but only when the toy comes near her paws. She'd much rather sleep on the couch than play.

"Come on, Maisie, you can do it," Megan says in a way that makes me think she believes Maisie is unconfident as opposed to old.

I set the cereal box on the counter. "Sweetie, you're going to be late. Maisie will be here when you get back."

Megan hangs her head. "Okay, Mommy," she says, putting the toy on the coffee table.

She climbs onto one of the stools at the kitchen island and sticks a spoon into her cereal. Beside her, in his booster chair, Josh sticks his hand inside his cereal bowl and spills half the contents. Thankfully, I serve his without milk and he eats his mess.

I glance at the clock. We have less than 10 minutes before the bus is scheduled to arrive.

"Do you need to go potty?" I say. "If so, now is the time."

Megan shakes her head and continues eating.

Josh reaches down and tries to feed Scooter a piece. He laughs when the dog, tail wagging, stands on his hind legs.

I move Josh's hand away before Scooter takes the cereal. "No. Scooter can only eat doggie food. You'll make him sick."

"Doggie."

Megan finishes, and I quickly put her bowl and spoon in the dishwasher. I have no appetite and didn't even attempt to eat anything.

I take Josh out of his seat. The moment his feet touch the floor, he chases Scooter who doesn't understand how he went from being offered a tasty snack to being chased.

I glance at Megan's white backpack decorated with pink hearts. "Daddy wants me to take some video of you this morning. And don't forget, he's going to call you after school so you can tell him all about it. And then after that, we're going to see Thea Shawna and baby Mia."

"Okay," she says, jumping from the stool and running to her backpack.

I grab my phone, tap the video app and hit record.

"Here we are on Megan's first day of kindergarten," I say. "We're about ready to go meet the bus."

Megan waves to the camera. I pan to the other side of the great room to catch Josh with Scooter then pause the recording.

"Come on, Buddy."

Josh follows, and I take his hand once we're on the porch. I'm not sure what to do with Megan. Does she want me to take her hand, or does she want to be independent? Will other kids laugh at her if they see her holding Mommy's hand? I should have asked her last night. Why didn't I ask last night?

"Why are you standing there, Mommy?" Megan says, stepping onto the pathway. "Come on."

Okay. No handholding it is.

"Um, sorry, Sweetie. I just thought of something. Let's go."

Megan leads the way. When it's nearly the bus's arrival time, I resume recording.

"We're at the end of the driveway waiting for the bus to arrive," I say to my phone. "It's due any moment."

Megan jumps. "I think I hear it."

"Maybe you do," I say, glancing in the direction the bus will come.

Our street is fairly quiet, so engine noises from big vehicles are rare. A second or two later the bus appears down the street.

"There it is, Mommy." Megan puts her face close to the phone. "Daddy, I see the bus."

The more excited she gets, the more my stomach turns. I really hope today goes well. Megan's totally unprepared for elementary school. There were only 15 kids in her entire preschool. In about half an hour, she'll be in a classroom of 24 in a building full of older kids. I always had relatives at my schools. I couldn't escape them. Megan has older Hardwick cousins, but none at her school.

I force a smile. I don't want her to sense my anxiety. "That's great, Sweetie."

Megan takes off for the curb before the bus even stops. "Bye, Mommy."

I take a step forward, ready to run after her if necessary. "Wait until the bus stops, Sweetie, so it's safe."

She stops when she reaches the sidewalk and waits, bouncing on her heels. When the bus stops and the door opens, she bounds up the steps without a moment's hesitation.

"Have a good day, Sweetie."

I wave with the hand holding the phone even though it's still recording, but it doesn't matter. The file is too large to text anyhow. Nat'll have to watch it next time we see him.

Josh tugs on my other hand, trying to release himself from my grip and follow his sister.

"No, Buddy, the bus is only for big kids. You're staying here with Mommy."

He stops tugging and watches the bus with interest, no doubt daydreaming about being older.

The bus pulls away, and I watch until it's no longer visible. Josh is remarkable patient. I know he's itching to continue chasing Scooter. We turn and head back toward the house.

I only vaguely remember my first day of kindergarten. Maroula and I were in the same classroom because kindergarten was only a half day then and we were in the afternoon class.

Back then, homeroom assignments were printed and hung on the school doors. In hindsight, that was a kidnapping waiting to happen, but that's the '80s for you. We did a lot of stupid shit then. Remember riding around without seatbelts on and blacktopped playgrounds? Nuff said.

Anyway, Mom didn't want to send me, because there's no state law mandating it and five is too young to be away from a parent, blah, blah, blah, but Dad was starting to be away on business trips more often, and I think she needed a break from single parenthood. She or Thea Ilena drove us in the afternoon, but we came home on the bus with Vanessa, Phil and Persephone. Phil was in second grade, Vanessa in third and Persephone in fourth. She liked to boss us around, telling us where we could sit on the bus and all that. Greg was in seventh grade and Chris in tenth, and they always came home after us, knocking Persephone down a few pegs because she wasn't the oldest anymore.

Maroula and I were like two peas in a pod in those days. Being only two weeks apart, we always has a playmate. This came in handy when we were really young because Vanessa and Persephone didn't want to play with us when we were toddlers. I met Jenny in kindergarten. She was a Shapiro then and the first Jewish person I ever met. I thought everyone celebrated Christmas and Easter. Maroula was jealous and tried to fuck up the friendship, but Jenny remained my best friend until sixth grade when we moved on to middle school and I met Shawna.

Then again, maybe Megan will be fine. There won't be an Economos lurking in every corner to boss her around. She could meet her version of Jenny.

Josh and I enter the house, and I head straight for the laundry room to throw a load in the washer. It feels like the laundry never ends. No wonder Mom was constantly doing laundry with four kids in the house. Jesus, how did she do it? Sometimes I feel like I can barely handle two. Like when they walked in on me masturbating. Thank God, Megan was assigned a different teacher than the one who registered her. Otherwise, that would have made for some really awkward parent-teacher conferences.

Josh disappears for a few minutes, and when he joins me, he holds his toy school bus. He's made an association between the real bus and the toy. I'm impressed. I pick him up and set him on the dryer.

"Someone special has a birthday next month," I say. "Do you know who it is?"

Josh smiles and points to himself.

"Yes. It is you." I tickle his belly, and he giggles. "How old are you going to be?"

He holds up two fingers.

"Very good. Daddy has his birthday not long after yours. Do you know how old Daddy is going to be?"

Josh sets his bus on his lap and stares at his fingers. I can tell he's trying to calculate how old a grownup would be.

"It's okay, Buddy. It's higher than you can count," I say, which makes Nat sound ancient, I know, but Josh can't count to Megan's age either. I don't want him to try too hard and getting frustrated. "He's going to be 33."

"Whoa."

I shut the lid on the washer and put it on regular cycle.

Josh wheels his bus back and forth beside his leg. "Vroom. Vroom."

"What do you want for your birthday?"

"Gee-ta," he says without looking up.

Although Nat hasn't used the nickname in a while, Josh certainly is his mini-me. Josh already has the toy guitar Nat bought him for Christmas. Don't tell me he wants a real one.

"Anything else?"

"Car."

Car? Yep, Josh certainly lives up to his middle name. He's never seen the movie *Cars*, but that would probably be a great theme for his birthday party. I have a looming book deadline, but I don't feel like making revisions today.

"Well, Joshua Nathaniel," I say, putting emphasis on the Nathaniel, "let's go party planning."

I know Josh has no idea what that means and probably wouldn't care if he did. Besides, Party City isn't open yet, so we need to bide our time. I really should do some writing. I have that looming deadline after all.

I lift Josh off the dryer, and he takes his bus into the great room. Maisie watches him from the couch but doesn't budge when he comes near her, even when he practically runs over her tail with his toy. I sit, and Josh runs his bus up my leg.

"Vroom vroom."

"Do you remember the song 'The Wheels on the Bus'? We used to sing it to you when you were a baby."

He looks at me but says nothing other than vroom vroom.

I sing the first stanza.

Josh smiles. Yes, he does remember, or he simply loves songs about things on wheels.

I tweak the next stanza. "The wheels on the bus take Megan to school, Megan to school, Megan to school. The wheels on the bus take Megan to school. All through Vienna-on-the-Lake."

Dumb, I know, but Josh seems to like it.

The school bus, the real one, is probably still picking up kids. I swallow the lump in my throat. I hope Megan finds her classroom. I hope she isn't bullied by the big kids. I hope she doesn't feel overwhelmed and wants to come home. My baby is growing up and needs to start learning her way in the world, but at the same time I want to protect her.

Josh giggles. I turn my head and see his bus between Maisie's paws. It looks like she's holding it, and he thinks it's hysterically funny. It's cute. I smile and caress his hair. He needs a haircut.

"Someday you'll meet a woman who'll love to run her fingers through your hair when you— Oh, never mind. That's years from now. After you're grown up. Twenty years at least. Bet you'll look good in longer hair just like Daddy did. Course, he looks good in shorter hair, too. So, now the question is: Do we cut your hair before your birthday?"

Josh sits and hugs me.

"No," he says.

It's so hard to believe my second baby is nearly two. Where did the time go? I know that this is what is supposed to happen, but it makes me feel somewhat useless. Pretty soon neither child is going to need me for much of anything, other than laundry, cooking and driving their asses around. It'll be uncool to hang around Mom yet alone hug her.

And when did that happen? When did my identity become wrapped up in one word – mom – the thing I never wanted to be?

I wrap my arm around Josh and give him a bear hug.

Chapter 29

Our Sacrifices Weren't in Vain

January 12, 2010

I feel bad the kids aren't here, but it's the middle of the school year, and kindergarten isn't preschool. Children can fall behind if you pull them out, and I refuse to be one of *those* parents who pulls their kids out of school for a vacation. Although, technically this isn't a vacation. It's three days, and Nat works one of them. So instead, I've become one of *those* parents who leaves town for no damn reason and drops the kids with family.

Although I do have a damn reason. A pretty good damn reason, too. I've never been to Hawaii, so when Nat asked me to join him, I had to come. One, how could I say "no" to him? It's not as if I see him everyday. Two, this opportunity may never come again. I'd regret it if I didn't. Still, I wonder what the kids are doing, then I remember how late it is back home and I have my answer.

Not far from our table, hula dancers sway to the beat of two drums for the amusement of restaurant goers. Look how thin their waists are with their flat-as-a-board stomachs. I'm jealous. Maybe I should take up the hula or belly dancing. After two kids, my belly is less than flat. Don't get me wrong, I've very grateful I'm still a size two, but I think that's more because I'm short with a small build than it is because of the size of my stomach. Actually, I don't remember ever having a super flat stomach. No, I was gifted with a high, round ass.

I glance beside me. Nat hasn't gained an ounce since the day we met, yet he ate more of his Kālua pig than I did. How is that fair? Oh, I know. It isn't. I swelled up like a watermelon twice while he stays skinny as a rail.

Eh, I'm just cranky because I'm tired. It was a long flight and with the time change and all.

I take a sip of my Mai Tai and discover I've nearly finished it. My eyes cross for a minute, my focus back on the dancers. I wonder if the big dude spinning the flaming torches ever set anything on fire? I mean, how do you learn to do that anyway?

Why don't we have luaus in Illinois? I really am tired. I'm talking nonsense. We need to get up an hour earlier on weekdays than we did during preschool to get Megan on the bus. It's actually the same time I had to get up when I was working outside the house, but for whatever reason that extra hour is kicking my ass. Then add jet lag onto that. It's almost 11 local time, making it – holy shit – nearly 3 a.m. Central. I yawn.

"How long do you want to stay?" Nat says, finishing his beer.

"Well, we're done eating, so we can go anytime, I guess."

I finish my Mai Tai then lean, lei swinging, to touch his thigh. "Thanks for asking me to come here with you."

He smiles, touching my leg. "How could I not? I knew you'd enjoy it. I just wish the kids were here. Want sex on the beach?"

"No, I don't want another drink."

"No. I meant an actual fucking on the beach."

A fucking on the beach? I stifle a yawn. We're in a strange city. Who knows where it is safe to go, and I'd rather not worry about getting arrested or becoming a crime victim.

"Let's go to the pool instead. Then we can go straight to bed afterward."

"Not what I had in mind, but I suppose that could be fun."

"Of course, it can."

I'd rather go to bed. Somehow, though, I think I can manage the energy to go to the pool with him. After all, it should be relaxing.

THE WATER IN THE OUTDOOR pool is still surprisingly warm. I wish Illinois had weather like this year around. I'd never complain. Ever. Instead, we get three months in the 80s if we're lucky.

The pool is empty except for us. Might be because it's the off season, I suppose, but I can't say that for sure. Maybe it's because it's pushing midnight.

I lean back in an almost a 45 degree angle against the side of the pool and close my eyes. The water bobs near my head and shoulders. I should probably change positions before I fall asleep and drown, but the water feels great against my sore muscles.

Gooseflesh raises on my arm as fingers caress it. I open my eyes. Nat stands beside me, gazing at my face. Oh, good, this is one time it's advantageous to have a husband who can't keep his hands off of me. He won't let me fall asleep and drown. No, I shouldn't have said "one time." I love the fact he can't keep his hands off of me. I don't want him to keep his hands off of me.

Fact is, for all my bluster about how I don't need a man, I want one, the years have made me dependent on him. He is the main source of our income. More importantly, I don't want to raise our children alone. I do most of the time, but he talks to them on the phone every day and spends as much time with them as he can when he's home. Plus, he can keep up with me sexually.

He grins. "I forgot how sexy you look in a bikini."

"How could you?" I say as if he's insulted me.

"Memory doesn't do you justice."

I straighten my posture and rub his calf with my foot. "Doesn't it, now?"

"No, it does not. You're hot and beautiful and sexy." He moves closer and caresses my shoulder, water rolling down my skin in large drops. "Remember what happened in California?"

"Yeah, I got pregnant."

His hand stops mid-motion. "Yeah, um, I wasn't thinking about that. I was referring to the hot tub."

I point behind us. "Security camera. We didn't need to worry about that in the hot tub, what, with all the bubbling water and all."

"Well." He again caresses my shoulder. "That's only an issue if you want to get naked."

I'm confused, or the brain isn't working quickly enough to figure it out. There were only three things we did in that hot tub: have a polite conversation with strangers, snuggle and fuck. And we didn't get naked for any of it.

He moves the crotch of my bikini bottom aside, and I gasp when his fingertips separate my pussy lips.

"Here's what I'm thinking. If the camera is there, we stand in that corner." He points. "The pool will hide us somewhat. We move your swimsuit aside, like I just did, and mine has a fly, and bang, we bang. So what do you think?"

Somehow I doubt there is only one security camera. But it is a plan, and I've heard most cameras aren't monitored. The footage gets taped over every 24 hours if there's no reason to consult it. The entire pool area is deserted, so no one could report us.

It's so late back home that if we don't do this now, I'm going to collapse from exhaustion. I stifle a yawn and press my lips into his, my tongue darting into his mouth.

I hug him because if I don't, I'm liable to lean backward and conk my head on the concrete. This, at least, keeps me upright and from doing something stupid and drowning.

Nat, of course, knows none of this. He thinks I'm reacting in the heat of the moment, not conducting a self-preservation measure. His response to my boobs-into-chest move is to run his hand slowly down my back until it reaches my ass. He grasps the cheek.

Meanwhile, the tip of the middle finger of the hand that's been hanging out between my legs for the past couple of minutes outlines the opening of my box. He carefully circles, my back stiffening and a tingle of anticipation running up my inner thighs. The finger penetrates in an equally methodical movement. First, only the tip enters, but he continues to move his finger in a circle until it's in up to the first knuckle, then the second and then.... He finger fuck me as if that finger is a cock that hasn't gotten laid in ages. I'm awake now!

I need to satisfy my curiosity and plunge my hand down the front of his swim trunks, stroking his cock until he's so aroused he breaks our kiss.

"Let's move to the corner," he says, kissing my neck behind the earlobe. "I need to fuck you."

Well, it's not surprising in the slightest that he's hard as a rock. The memory of the hot tub in California probably made him instantly horny.

This pool has an unusual shape and it's deeper for some reason in the corner where Nat thinks the security camera will have the worst view. The tiles read 4'5" which is too deep for my liking for what we're about to do.

He kisses me, continuing what we started, and I wrap my leg around him. We hopefully look like nothing more than an amorous couple in security cam footage, but we're about to fuck with our clothes on. Oh, this is weird. Have we ever done this before? Partially undressed sure but not— Oh!

I claw at his back the moment his cock enter my pussy. So much fabric blocks the way – my bikini's crotch, his swim trunks – yet he manages to thrust.

Oh, fuck, that feels excellent, even if my swimsuit pushes on my pussy lips. Slow and steady, his swollen dick glides back and forth. He's being cautious, I can tell, trying to keep up the façade that we're only making out.

I break the kiss. "Fuck me till you cum, then let's fuck again upstairs."

What? Why the hell did I say that when I'm exhausted? The moment my body hits a mattress, I'm going to want to sleep.

He nods, so transfixed by what he's doing that he can't speak. I guess me saying that made him forget all about being cautious, because all of a sudden his thrusts become energetic and I'm pushed into the pool wall. It's conflicting to have such pleasure in my pussy and such pain in my back.

I throw my arms around his neck, trying to keep us cheek to cheek but it's not working so well. His face is higher above the water line than mine. Water splashes against my shoulders and neck, coming dangerously close to my mouth and nose. Chlorine burns my nostrils. Holy shit. Maybe I'm going to drown after all. Drowned by fucking. I don't want to die this way. What will the kids say when they're older? At the same time, if he kills me, I hope it traumatizes him so much he can never fuck anyone else.

I hang on tighter, practically choking him. I step off the bottom of the pool and wrap my other leg around his waist then cross my ankles. Now I know why I suggested fucking upstairs. So this could be a quickie.

He groans, the pace of thrusting increasing. He pushes into me, the muscle contractions strong, and kisses my forehead. I cry out.

"You're okay. I've got you," he says inadvertently pushing my shoulder blade into the concrete.

I'm trembling. I hang onto to him, forgetting all I need to do is put my feet down and stand. He tries to withdrawal but can't because my ankles are crossed, toes interlaced.

"Honey, you're okay. Put your feet down. You're really tired. Maybe we should just go to sleep. There's always tomorrow."

I nod, finally releasing my grip and setting my feet down. Our bodies separate. I stand fully upright, getting myself as far above the waterline as I can. Next thing I know I'm enveloped in a tight hug.

"That was supposed to be fun," he says, the sound of his heartbeat in my ear.

"It was, but the water was so close to— I didn't want to inhale or swallow it."

I relax in his arms. Maybe I did panic a bit. He's right. I need to sleep. It'll be fine in the morning. What's important is that we're together.

"If you want to swallow," he says, holding me, "I'll give you something to swallow."

I slap his back.

DESPITE HOW RUNDOWN I was when we went to bed, I only slept until 10 o'clock. Ten Central. You know what time that is Hawaii Time? Too goddamn early. So I woke Nat up to get him up. After that, I was finally able to rest.

We decide to go walking, hand in hand, on the beach. The warm sand under our toes reminds me, in a weird way, of how it's freezing back home. The sun glistens off the waves as they crash into shore, and I stare, memorized by their roar. I could stay here all day and not get tired. I laugh to myself. What a dumbass statement. Sounds like something I would have said as a teenager, discovering the world for the first time.

"I'd like to run something past you," Nat says, breaking the trance.

I turn my gaze from the water to him. "What is it?"

"Now don't get offended or anything. You're doing an awesome job. But I've been monitoring our bank accounts for the past three years."

Three years? I'm our household's bill payer, but we both have access to our joint bank accounts via the internet. I wrinkle my brow, and my sunglasses partially slide down my nose.

"How can I not be offended? If you trust I'm paying everything on time, you wouldn't need to monitor things from a distance. Or do you think I'm making purchases behind your back?"

"Will you let me finish? That damn Economos temper of yours."

"Petrakis, actually. It comes from Mom."

"Whatever. As I was trying to tell you, I've been doing this for a reason. Even with buying the house, having to replace your car and Josh coming along, we are the most financially secure we've ever been. It seems to me that we've finally reached the point where I don't need to tour nearly as much."

A tingly sensation overcomes me. "Oh?"

Obviously, I wasn't expecting that.

"We've sacrificed to get to this point. I've missed milestones and things in the kids' lives that I would have wanted to be around for, and I know it's a burden on you to be a single parent much of the time while trying to write and take care of the house and Scooter and Maisie. We've sacrificed in our relationship, too, being apart so often."

"I knew what I was getting into from the beginning, and so did you." I squeeze his hand. "How would it work if you toured less often?"

"I talked it over with everyone, and we think we can swing six week tours with at least two weeks of a break in-between. Just think about it, we can take real family vacations, and I can be home more often to spend time with you and the kids."

"Is that what you wanted to run past me? Did you think I'd say 'no'?"

He nods. "That's what I wanted to run past you. I mean, if you prefer it, we'll continue touring like we've always done. I know you value your independence and all. Maybe you enjoy the current arrangement, for all I know."

I laugh. "You're talking out of your ass now. Of course, I'd rather have you home more often. It's great you've figured out a way to balance work and home without us starving."

He pulls me close, and we kiss.

"Your books have helped us, too," he says. "We probably still could have swung it otherwise, but it would have taken much longer, because you'd be working a 9-5 and we'd be paying for daycare."

It makes me feel good to hear him say that. I'd blush if I weren't probably already getting a sunburn.

"Glad I could help. So when can you start this new schedule?"

"After this tour ends. That's why I asked you to come out here. Who knows when or if we'll ever play in Honolulu again, so I wanted to share this experience with you."

I rub my knuckles against his cheek. "I'm glad you did. I'm excited to have you home more often."

He smiles. "The kids will be excited, too."

I return the smile. "Yes, they will."

Megan, especially, will be excited. She always comes home from school a little chatterbox wanting to tell me all about her day. She enjoys board games, too, and she's becoming competitive to the point where she hates losing, and I never let her win which has made her more competitive. Why she's inherited all my negative traits, I'll never know. It'll do Josh good to have a male influence around more often.

We kiss again. This time, his tongue dances in my mouth. I love his tongue. I love his lips. I love him. I love the life we created together.

Thank you for reading *Rock Star Mom*. I hope you enjoyed it. If you have a moment, please help other romance readers discover their next book by leaving a review of *Rock Star Mom* on your favorite retailer's website.

Keep exploring the world of *The Rock Star's Wife* by visiting the official website at https://rockstar.melinadruga.com/ for character bios, to learn more about relationships and the music industry, listen to Cassandra's playlist, and more.

Want to stay updated on future rock star romance books?

- Follow me on Instagram: www.instagram.com/melinadruga/[1]
- Follow me on Facebook: www.facebook.com/MelinaDruga[2]
- Follow me on YouTube: www.youtube.com/c/MelinaDruga[3]
- Follow me on Pinterest: www.pinterest.com/MelinaDruga[4]

The Rock Star's Wife companion playlists can be found on Spotify at https://open.spotify.com/user/
312s3lke7maxj3lyupbfy73pwpr4?si=b39b968de23847dd

Finally, in addition to rock star romances, I have published historical fiction and nonfiction. You can learn about my older books on

- My website: www.melinadruga.com/[5]
- Goodreads: www.goodreads.com/MelinaDruga[6]
- BookBub: www.bookbub.com/profile/melina-druga[7]

Thanks again, dear reader, and I hope to meet you again in the pages of another book.

---

1. https://www.instagram.com/melinadruga/

2. https://www.facebook.com/MelinaDruga

3. https://www.youtube.com/c/MelinaDruga

4. https://www.pinterest.com/MelinaDruga

5. http://www.melinadruga.com/

6. https://www.goodreads.com/MelinaDruga

7. https://www.bookbub.com/profile/melina-druga

A Preview of Sex & Surprises

Book five in The Rock Star's Wife series

September 23, 2010
      10 a.m. …

Deadlines don't stop because I'm horny, even if I do write erotica. My third book came out earlier this year, and I should be writing the fourth, but instead I'm pacing the great room. Why? Nat will be home at any moment.

He hasn't been gone that long, relatively speaking, thanks to his new schedule, but absence still makes the pussy grow wetter.

I hear something outside and rush to the window. Sure enough, a taxi idles in our driveway. My heart races watching Nat remove a suitcase and duffle bag from the truck and make his way to the house.

Well, I can't stand here gawking at the window. I need to do something. What? Shit. Think. I lean against the foyer's console table. This way, my new long sleeved dress will be the first thing he sees when he walks through the front door. I call it a dress, but I couldn't wear it on the street without being arrested. Its sheer black lace with nothing underneath and a hem mere inches below my pert, round ass. It hugs every curve, and I feel fucking sexy.

I hope Nat thinks I look sexy. Do you suppose he will?

The door unlocks. My heart races so quickly, I might faint. I suck my lips to plump them. I should have put on lipstick. Why didn't I put on lipstick? I run my fingers through my hair to give it an unkempt look. No, wait. I shouldn't have done that. What if it looks like I just rolled out of bed? I don't have time to fix it. Shit! I don't have time to fix it!

The door opens.

"Welcome home, Honey," I say, shaking the back of my head slightly in a vain attempt to fix my hair.

"Good to be home," he says, dropping his luggage and closing the door.

Understandably, his focus is on getting in the house. That luggage is heavy, and I don't want the entire neighborhood seeing my womanhood. I move my shoulders back and my chest forward, subtly trying to make my boobs perkier.

"I'm happy to see you."

The door locked, Nat turns and drops his keys. They slam on the tile floor with a thunk and a jingle.

His eyes widen. "You, um, wow."

"Speechless, are you?"

A smile crosses his face. "Uh, yeah."

I think he likes it. I smile and lick my bottom lip, twisting my tongue.

He crosses the foyer in three steps and grabs me so hard it knocks the wind out of me. Our lips meet for the first time in six weeks, tongue entering through parted lips. I wrap my arms around his neck, rubbing my body against his. The fabric of his jeans grazes my clitoris, which I've nicknamed my button, and sends little waves of pleasure up my hips.

It doesn't take long before I'm sitting on the console table, legs spread and his body between them. I claw at his back while his cock thrusts in and out of my sopping wet pussy as if it's the first time.

No, correction, this is a thousand times better than our first time because I know what kind of lover I have on my hands. First times can be passionate and steamy (ours was), but there always is an element of the unknown. You don't know what sort of lover your partner will be or what turns them on. Remember, all those years ago, how badly I wanted Nat inside me? I never wanted a man so much. Times haven't changed much, have they?

The table shakes, bumping against the wall like Morse Code. Ten minutes ago, the vase fell over, dumping its contents onto the floor. I break the kiss, let out a moan so loud it causes our black Scottie Scooter to howl, and wrap my legs around Nat's waist. He grasps my hips and continues thrusting faster, faster, faster.

I press the back of my head into the mirror hanging on the wall behind me and squeeze my shoulder blades together. He's going to cum in three, two, one. I feel the muscle vibrations when he stops thrusting and pushes his cock as far inside as it'll go.

Out of breath, we make eye contact and smile.

"Holy shit," he says. "Now, that that's over with, I suppose I should unpack."

"You made quite a mess in here," I say, gesturing to the floor where Scooter loudly laps vase water.

"I could use a beautiful assistant in the bedroom," Nat says, "to, you know, help me unpack."

There is a glint in his eye that I like. That I really like.

"That could be arranged. But what's in it for the assistant?"

He smiles. "Oh, she will be fully compensated, but the work is long and hard."

11:43 A.M. ...

"Scream for it, baby! Scream for it!"

From this vantage point – on my shins and forearms, ass in the air, boobs jiggling, hair flying – all I can see is his dick plunging in and out and his balls swinging. I shout in pleasure with every thrust, our bodies making a slapping sound whenever they collide.

Nat reaches forward and plays with my button. Oh my God! My eyes cross, and I clench the fitted sheet as my body begins to twitch. He knows to stop before I cum and pushes his body into mine until I collapse onto my stomach.

The thrusting continues and, even though he only paused for a few seconds to allow time to change positions, my pussy is so sensitive it feels fucking incredible. I close my eyes, his groans loud in my ear and his body pushing against my ass.

My clitoris rubs the mattress with every push of the ass. I grow hot, my ears ring, and I cum. I grimace as my ab muscles harden.

Nat orgasmed once this morning, and we've been at it this time for nearly an hour. When he pulls out and flips me into missionary, it's obvious he's tired.

My thigh muscles quiver as of I've been doing squats all morning, but I gladly allow him to penetrate again and he cums not long after.

"You wore me out," he says, wiping sweat off his forehead and collapsing beside me.

"Sleep for a while." I sit. "I'll go get some writing done."

He pulls me down beside him, eyes pleading. "I'd rather you stayed here with me."

I place my hand on his cheek and nod. "Of course. I'll stay as long as you want."

12:38 P.M. ...

Nat stirs, and I open my eyes to find him peering at me. He awoke earlier than I expected. I didn't sleep but rested, going over in my head what I want to type out next time I tackle my manuscript. My thigh hurts from laying on it too long, but his arm is draped over me and I didn't want to disturb him by rolling over.

I smile. "Did you sleep well?"

He kisses my forehead. "I always forget how great it feels to be in my own bed until I'm back. Back here with you."

"Great," I say, gazing into his brown eyes so full of expression. "I'm happy to have you back. I miss you when you're gone."

"Do you?"

"Of course. Why wouldn't I? I love times like this."

He smiles that gorgeous smile and runs his fingers through my hair near the temple, pushing the unkempt mess off my face.

His lips graze my forehead. "I love it, too. Nothing better than being naked in bed with you."

I stick my hand under the sheet and fondle his inner thigh, brushing his balls. Nat doesn't complain. The average man who has known his wife for eight years, has two children and just got back from a lengthy business trip would complain he's tired or that he's already fucked me twice in a short timeframe. But you know what my man does? He takes my hand and directs it to the shaft of his cock covered in dried pussy juices.

"You know what I like, baby," he says, breath growing shallower.

Our eyes locked, I stroke his cock until it hardens. His hand sits on my hip. I've been told I have curves in all the right places, and he enjoys rubbing his palms over those curves. His touch stimulates me like none other.

When I can't stand it anymore, I gently push him onto his back. He knows what I'm about to do. How could he not? His eyes on me, I straddle him.

"I'll do all the work," I say, slipping my pussy down on his cock. "You just lie there and enjoy yourself."

He positions his hands on my ass. "Fuck me, baby. Fuck me."

I start pumping.

2:13 P.M. …

I cum and feel as if I'm dying. Dying from pleasure. My body convulses five or six times before I catch my breath.

Our bodies intertwined in spoon position, I don't want to move and I get the feeling he doesn't either, but we have responsibilities.

"I gotta go pick up Josh," I say, glancing at the clock on the fireplace mantel, "and Megan's bus will be here not long after I get back."

"Aww. I could stay here all day," Nat says, caressing my curves. "I hate the idea of you having to put clothes on your luscious body."

"I know. Part of me misses the days when we could stay in bed all day. But, in case you forgot, we have kids, and I have to pick Josh up. He gets anxious if I'm late, and I barely have time to get dressed as is."

He withdrawals and plops on the floor. "I suppose that means I need to get dressed, too."

I laugh. "Only if you want to avoid having to answer your kids' uncomfortable questions. Either way, they'll be happy to see you. They drew all sorts of pictures for you as a welcome home."

He smiles, but it's a less mischievous grin than earlier. "I'll be happy to see them, too. I promise I won't say a word about how you and I have done nothing but fuck since I got home."

"Here, I was worried that you might." I stand and a combo of cum and pussy juice rolls down my leg. I point to it. "I guess I should wear underwear. What will the other moms think?"

He folds his hands behind his head and doesn't look ready to budge from the floor anytime soon. "That you're a horny MILF who got laid four times since the start of the school day."

I laugh. "Yeah, that's what they'll think. What's today by the way?"

"The 23rd. Why?"

The 23rd? For some reason, I was thinking it was the 19th. If today is the 23rd, then I'm exactly mid-cycle. If, if.... Shit. It's too late now to do anything about it. I swallow so hard it hurts and hope I haven't gone pale.

"No reason," I say, shaking my head. "I just couldn't remember. I have a phone conference with my agent in a couple days. She'll want to know how the next book is coming, but we can talk about that later. I really do need to go pick up Josh."

I walk toward the staircase, glancing at the fireplace before ascending. Nat watches my ass.

7:58 P.M. ...

"Bedtime," Nat says, closing *Frog and Toad Are Friends* and setting it down on the loft's side table.

Megan clasps her hands in front of her chest. "Another one, Daddy. Pleeeeeease."

Josh squirms on Nat's lap. "Daddy, I like stories."

"I know, Buddy." Nat smooths Josh's hair before kissing his head. "That was the third story. You know you're supposed to go to bed after one story. You got two bonus stories. You have school in the morning. You need to go to sleep."

"Awww," the kids say in unison.

Nat stands, setting Josh on his feet. Megan shimmies off the couch and grabs her stuffed animal from the cushion next to her.

He takes our pouty offspring by the hand and leads them to their bedrooms to tuck in while I wait in the hallway. The moment he closes

Megan's door, I wrap my arms around his neck, push him against the wall and intertwine my tongue with his.

It sure the hell is sexy watching Nat with the kids. Oh my God, it turns me on. I've been watching him all evening. First when the kids got home and presented their drawings, then when he played hide and seek with them while I made dinner, their cute conversations during dinner, and finally bedtime.

After a minute or two, my hands move to their intended target. I unbutton and unzip his pants, shoving my hand inside. He whimpers.

"Any interest in going to bed early?" I say.

"I'll go anywhere with you if you keep stroking my cock like that."

We retreat to our bedroom, and it doesn't take long before we shed the clothes we've been forced to wear when the kids were around. Now I'm the one pinned against a wall, his cock thrusting, my foot propped against the side of the dresser for support.

He shushes when I moan louder than intended. The last thing we need is one of the kids knocking on the door to investigate the strange noises coming from our room. This should be our cue to move to the bed and change positions, but we don't.

Eventually, though, my foot slips one time too many, and he pulls out. I take a few steps and rest my forearms on the dresser. He fucks me from behind, eyes wild, while we watch our reflections in the mirror.

It's weird watching yourself be fucked, so I focus on his image instead. Damn, he's enjoying himself.

I want to kiss him. I mean, I really, really want to kiss him. I love those lips. I crave those lips.

Several minutes later, he pulls out and follows me to the bed. I lie down, spreading my legs as far as they'll go, and moan with glee when he plunges back into me. I wrap my legs around his waist and claw at his back. I hope he fucks me all night. I want to be fucked all night.

SEPTEMBER 24, 2010
    Midnight ...

We rarely use our soaker tub. It's a waste of space, really. The jets aren't as relaxing as our actual hot tub, but it does the trick on sore muscles. And my muscles are as sore as they would be if I did a full body workout. I lean against Nat, the water line moving back and forth across my breasts.

The timer shuts the jets off, and the water settles into calmness, but stillness lasts mere minutes. One thing leads to another, and we find ourselves doing a variation of reverse cowgirl.

"I don't like this position," I say, squeezing my pussy muscles around Nat's cock. "I can feel you, but I can't see you or touch you."

He groans. "Change positions then."

I pull myself off him and turn, pressing my chest against his. Water droplets roll down our wet shoulders, and I maneuver my hips down onto his cock.

I begin pumping. Water splashes around us and onto the floor.

4:23 A.M. …

My right leg draped over Nat's left hip, our faces graze in the dark and his stubble scratches my cheek.

"Did you miss me while I was away?" he says.

"Of course, I missed you," I say, lips millimeters from his. "I've already told you I missed you."

"You didn't just miss fucking me?"

"No. I could ask you the same question."

"I enjoy being on tour, but I enjoy being home with you even more."

"Good. I want you home with me."

Why is he feeling vulnerable now of all times? I don't have much time to ponder. He thrusts harder – well, as hard as possible while scissoring anyway – and I gasp before pressing my lips into his. He hugs me tight, and I run my fingers through his hair.

7:11 A.M. …

Nat pulls out and collapses out of breath onto his pillow. I snuggle against him, and he wraps his arm around me. Exhausted, I close my eyes and feel myself relaxing to sleep.

"Shit, it's time to get the kids up," he says. "Time flies when you're having fun."

"I want to sleep," I say, my eyes closed. "Someone kept me up most of the night. How I'll get any writing done today, I have no idea, but I have to. I did nothing yesterday."

"It was well worth it, wasn't it? Besides, as I recall, you were the one who wanted my body."

I slap his chest. "Yeah, like you didn't enjoy it."

"I told you yesterday, you're a MILF. All the other moms are jealous."

"Yeah, sure." I force my eyes open and discover he's gazing at me with that look that's a combo of lust and admiration. "They'll really be jealous of the dark circles under my eyes and the disheveled hair I don't have time to brush."

He laughs. "You just proved my point. They'll all know you look that way because you were fucked multiple times. Well, that and because you're walking funny."

"Uh huh. Sure."

I get out of bed, leg muscles twitching. Maybe I will be walking funny. The kids won't notice. The moms on the other hand... I burst into giggles at the thought that they'll know I'm a fuck machine. I'm rather proud of it, too. If only because it turns my husband on.

He props himself up on an elbow. "What's so funny?"

"I'm just so fucking tired. Everything is funny."

He gets out of bed. "I'll wait for the bus with Megan. You take Josh to preschool and make all the other moms jealous."

I throw my pillow at him. "Stop fucking saying that."

"Why? It's true. Their husbands probably don't even touch them anymore. If they have men in their lives to begin with."

I sigh and roll my eyes.

9:12 A.M. ...

Josh safely at preschool, I return home. I'm exhausted, and all I want to do is sleep, but I must force myself to write. The conference with my agent is tomorrow. Plus, I need to count my days to determine if I fucked up royally. I've been trying not to think about it, but I saw several moms at the school with babies and it reminded me.

I find Nat in the great room drinking coffee and wearing nothing but his bathrobe. I narrow my eyes. He was fully dressed when I left.

"Did you take a shower?" I say, disappointed he didn't wait for me.

He sets his coffee cup on the kitchen counter and walks toward me. "No. I've been thinking about how you said you were going to write today."

"What about it?" I say, eyelids heavy.

"Well, I really don't think you're going to get any writing done today either," he says before grabbing me and sticking his tongue in my mouth.

Other Rock Star Romances by Melina Druga

The Rock Star's Wife Series

Ever wondered what happens when sex, family drama, and enough rock & roll to deafen a small country collide? Buckle up, buttercup, because *The Rock Star's Wife* series is about to blow your eardrums.

Sexual Awakening

CASSANDRA "CASSIE" Economos has a full plate: There's Kurt Cobain, for starters – a permanent fixture on her bedroom wall and in her teenage heart. Then there are her friends. Oh, and let's not forget her big, fat, gloriously dysfunctional Greek family. And simmering beneath it all is a burning desire to escape to Chicago.

But hold on, because Cassie's about to add another item to her ever-growing list: sex. There's just one tiny, insignificant, Mount Everest-sized problem — Cassie is strictly forbidden from dating. Her family, bless their well-meaning, overbearing hearts, has a list of rules longer than a CVS receipt.

But Cassie is determined to break free from the shackles of her family's rules, and, armed with a healthy dose of teenage audacity, embarks on a hilarious and often cringe-worthy journey into the world of dating. Expect awkward encounters, disastrous dates, and enough mortifying moments to make you want to crawl under a rock and never come out.

With a quirky cast of friends cheering her on, ambitious dreams tugging at her heart, and a whirlwind of humorous misadventures to navigate, Cassie grapples with the complexity of desire and identity. Will she be able to balance the expectations of her family while discovering her true self?

So buckle up, grab your headphones, and get ready to laugh, cry, and maybe even cringe a little as Cassie navigates the messy, hilarious, and ultimately unforgettable journey of growing up, falling in love, and finding her place in the world.

Sexual Awakening is the first book in *The Rock Star's Wife* series, following Cassie through the rollercoaster of life from her awkward teen years to her (hopefully) more sophisticated 40s. With music as a constant backdrop, Cassie will explore the profound connections that shape her life, both romantic and platonic.

https://books2read.com/Sexual-Awakening

Mr. Right is Myth

Cassandra "Cassie" Economos is starting fresh at the University of Illinois. Navigating the waters of college can be tricky, especially with Kelly, her former majorette teammate from the dark ages of high school, pushing her to step into the dating scene.

Cassie's heart isn't ready — after all she's still sporting a Jason-induced heartbreak (the jerk actually insulted her!), and perpetually wondering if Todd, the one who got away, was actually "the one." Cassie's dating life is flatter than a week-old soda, but Kelly is on a mission to drag Cassie out of her romantic funk and into the chaotic world of college dating.

When Cassie reluctantly dips her toes back in, she discovers that sometimes the search for love can feel like an endless rock ballad of disappointment. After a string of lackluster romances, epic fails, awkward encounters, and enough cringe-worthy moments to fuel a thousand therapy sessions, fate finally introduces her to a seemingly perfect match.

But let's be real, folks. This is Cassie we're talking about. There's always a catch. Is he secretly a vampire? Does he have a collection of porcelain dolls in his basement? Or maybe he just chews with his mouth open. Whatever it is, you know it's gonna be good.

Mr. Right is a Myth is book two in *The Rock Star's Wife* series, a hilarious and heartwarming journey that follows Cassandra from her awkward teen years to her (hopefully) slightly less awkward 40s. Buckle up for a rollercoaster of romantic mishaps, platonic shenanigans, and a soundtrack that'll have you dusting off your old mixtapes. Because let's face it, life is a song, and sometimes you just gotta dance to the beat of your own slightly off-key drum.

https://books2read.com/MrRightisaMyth

Rock Star Romance

ONE YEAR. NO DATES. Doctor's orders. (Okay, her orders, but still). After a spectacular heart implosion, Cassandra "Cassie" Economos needs time to focus on important things like adding to her iTunes playlist and mastering the art of ordering takeout without making eye contact. But when the mundane routine begins to gnaw at her spirit, an unexpected invitation to a Fourth of July cookout beckons her to step out of her comfort zone. Little does she know, it's not just the sizzling burgers that will ignite her summer.

Enter Nat Hardwick, the magnetic frontman and lead guitarist of up-and-coming metal band Dramatic Sneezer. (Yes, you read that right.) With his ridiculously long sideburns and piercing gaze, he's everything Cassie thought she didn't want. He's so, so not her type. But in one electric moment, their worlds collide, casting a spell neither can resist, and sparks fly faster than cheap fireworks.

Suddenly, Cassie's carefully constructed single life is under siege. When the tour bus rolls in and the glittering lights beckon Nat away, Cassie must confront the shadows of their burgeoning romance. Can love survive Nat's relentless tour schedule, screaming fans and distance, or will their connection fade like the echoes of a last encore?

Find out in *Rock Star Romance*, book three in *The Rock Star's Wife* series, following Cassie through the rollercoaster of life from her awkward teen years to her (hopefully) more sophisticated 40s. With music as a constant backdrop, Cassie will explore the profound connections that shape her life, both romantic and platonic.

Are you ready for a front-row seat to Nat and Cassie's wild ride? https://books2read.com/Rock-Star-Romance

Rock Star Mom

THE ROCK STAR'S WIFE is back and better than ever in *Rock Star Mom*.

Cassandra "Cassie" Economos, once a wild child with a penchant for disappointing her parents and making questionable dating decisions, is now Cassandra Hardwick, suburban mom extraordinaire. Yes, that Cassandra, the one who swore she'd never trade her dreams for a house in the suburbs. But here she is, folks, living the dream... or at least a dream. It involves more sippy cups than tequila shots, but hey, who's counting? (Cassie is, constantly.)

Cassie's married to Nat Hardwick, the ridiculously talented frontman of (the equally ridiculously named) Dramatic Sneezer. Nat is off touring the world, serenading screaming fans while Cassie battles rogue Cheerios and the existential dread of being a stay-at-home mom.

But don't feel too sorry for her. Cassie's got a secret weapon: her best friend Shawna. Shawna, bless her chaotic soul, has moved nearby, bringing with her a much-needed dose of sanity. And if that wasn't enough to keep her busy, Cassie's also trying to launch her career as an erotica writer. Because what better way to spice up suburban life than with a little... ahem... creative expression?

Just when Cassie starts to get comfortable in her new role, a surprise drops like a power chord from hell. Let's face it, life is a song, and sometimes it's a little off-key. But that's what makes it worth singing along to.

So, buckle up, get ready for laughter, tears, and maybe a few awkward moments as Cassie navigates the hilarious, messy, and utterly unpredictable world of motherhood, marriage, and the occasional erotic fantasy.

This is book four in *The Rock Star's Wife* series, so if you haven't already, go back and read the first three! (We're not judging, but you're missing out on some serious drama.) Follow Cassandra from her teenage years to her (gasp!) 40s as she stumbles, falls, and occasionally triumphs in the game of life.

https://books2read.com/rockstarmom

Sex & Surprises

CASSANDRA "CASSIE" Hardwick, erotica author extraordinaire and mother of two, thought she had it all figured out. Her husband, Nat Hardwick, the ridiculously talented (and sneeze-prone) frontman of Dramatic Sneezer, was finally coming home! Years of shrewd financial planning means fewer tours, more romance, and maybe even a chance to remember what each other looks like without the aid of a pixelated screen.

Cassie envisions candlelit dinners, whispered sweet nothings, and maybe even a weekend getaway where they can rediscover their spark. But fate, as it often does, has other plans. Plans involving two blue lines, a jealous cousin with a talent for drama, and a whole lot of, well, surprises. Instead of romantic weekends, Cassie faces down a domestic invasion of epic proportions. Will she find the balance between her duties as a mom, an acclaimed writer, and a devoted wife?

Sex & Surprises, the fifth installment of *The Rock Star's Wife* series, proves that even when you think you've got it all under control, life has a way of throwing you a curveball. Or two. Get ready for laughter, love, and a whole lot of ... well, you'll just have to read it to find out!

https://books2read.com/sexsurprises

Family Upheaval

CASSANDRA "CASSIE" Hardwick, everyone's favorite rock star's wife, is back! And this time, be prepared for family drama of epic proportions! You see, Cassie's best friend since sixth grade, the ever-fabulous Shawna, embarks on a journey to uncover her birth family.

And being the supportive BFF that she is, Cassie decides to spit in a tube, too. Thinking she'll maybe discover a distant cousin who knits sweaters for cats or something equally "thrilling," Cassie's blindsided by results that will challenge everything she thought she knew about her own identity.

Meanwhile, in the Hardwick household, things are never dull. Cassie and her rock star hubby, Nat (aka Dramatic Sneezer frontman and lead guitarist – yes, the name is still ridiculous), must navigate the wild ride of their children's growing pains. They're growing up, which means more hormones, more angst, and more questionable fashion choices.

Family Upheaval, book six in *The Rock Star's Wife* series, is about to take you on a wild ride!

Between the chaos of family drama and the pulse of rock 'n' roll, the unexpected becomes reality!

Let's face it, life's too short to be boring. Especially when you're married to a rock star. And you just discovered you're related to... well, you'll just have to read the book to find out! (But trust us, it's good. Like, "hide-in-the-bathroom-to-avoid-your-family" good.)

https://books2read.com/familyupheaval

The Pandemic Diaries

THE COVID-19 PANDEMIC brings chaos and cabin fever to the Hardwick household. Cassandra "Cassie" Hardwick faces the ultimate test: Will her family survive close quarters without losing its mind?

Remember concerts? Music festivals? Yeah, Cassie's husband Nat, frontman of Dramatic Sneezer, does, too. Now, instead of serenading screaming fans, Nat's instituted a strict safety bubble. The kids are stuck inside, doing remote learning, and let's not forget the great toilet paper shortage of 2020.

Join the Hardwicks as they navigate the hilarious, heartwarming, and occasionally hair-pulling realities of pandemic life. From Zoom meetings gone wrong to family game nights that devolve into epic battles of wills, *The Pandemic Diaries* is a laugh-out-loud reminder that even in the face of global crisis, love, laughter, and a whole lot of alcohol can get you through anything.

Book seven in *The Rock Star's Wife* series throws you headfirst into the bewildering world of lockdowns and hand sanitizer, revealing that sometimes the greatest challenges lead to the sweetest melodies.

Get ready to laugh, cry, and maybe even recognize a little bit of your own pandemic experience in this relatable and utterly charming addition to *The Rock Star's Wife* series. Because let's face it, we all went a little bit crazy during lockdown. The Hardwicks just did it with more guitars and slightly better hair.

https://books2read.com/pandemicdiaries

Rock Star Parents

IN THE THRILLING CONCLUSION to *The Rock Star's Wife series*, the world slowly emerges from the shadow of the COVID-19 pandemic. Cassandra "Cassie" Hardwick, wife of Nat Hardwick, the charismatic frontman of the legendary band, Dramatic Sneezer, faces her biggest challenge yet: her kids growing up.

Megan is diving headfirst into her first serious relationship, the kind that makes Nat reach for his shotgun (figuratively, of course). Cassie desperately clings to the last vestiges of her daughter's innocence. Good luck with that, Cassie! You'll need it.

Joshua's decided that strumming a guitar is far more appealing than, say, algebra. He's formed a band, naturally. And he's also discovered girls. Think hormones, questionable lyrics, and a garage that smells suspiciously of teenage angst and stale pizza.

Sweet, precocious Sophie officially enters the wonderful world of puberty. Cassie feels a little like she's aged approximately 75 years overnight. And Nat? Well, let's just say he's started carrying around a Taser. Again, figuratively.

And then there's Matthew, the baby of the family, whose innocence is slipping away far too quickly. Cassie's trying to savor every last moment of his childhood, knowing that all too soon, he'll be trading in his dinosaur toys for... well, probably a guitar. It's genetic, after all.

So grab your air guitar, crank up the volume, and prepare yourselves, people, because this ain't your mama's minivan carpool drama. This is rock and roll parenting, baby! Because in the world of rock and roll, anything is possible. Even surviving parenthood. (Although, some days, it feels like a miracle.)

The Rock Star's Wife series follows Cassandra from her teen years into her 40s as she navigates relationships (both romantic and platonic) — all with music playing a prominent role. Get ready for a wild ride filled with laughter, tears, and maybe just a little bit of head banging.

https://books2read.com/RockStarParents

Companion Books to The Rock Star's Wife Series

Christmas Surprise

IN THE ENCHANTING WINTER of 2000, prepare for a holiday season so chaotic, it makes *Home Alone* look like a silent night.

Cassandra "Cassie" Economos finds herself at a crossroads as she returns home from the University of Illinois for a much-anticipated winter break. She ponders the unspoken words that hang between her and her boyfriend, Corey Fuchs.

Corey, bless his heart, does love Cassie, he just can't seem to articulate it, mostly because their lives are diverging faster than a pair of figure skaters after a wardrobe malfunction.

Meanwhile, Cassie's cousin Phil, a man whose romantic gestures usually involve accidentally setting things on fire, is planning to propose to his girlfriend, Jennifer Anderson, but must navigate the frantic waters of familial expectations and thwart their well-meaning but intrusive plans.

Jennifer, a woman of saintly patience, adores Phil, but she's starting to suspect his family views her as slightly less desirable than a fruitcake at a Weight Watchers meeting. Can their love survive the Economos clan's well-intentioned but utterly disastrous interference?

Told from four perspectives, *Christmas Surprise* is a high-spirited holiday romp featuring characters from *The Rock Star's Wife* series. Grab your hot cocoa and cozy up for a Christmas celebration like no other. Expect meddling relatives, awkward mistletoe encounters, and enough Christmas cheer to power a small city.

https://books2read.com/RockStarChristmasSurprise

Holiday Homecoming

STEP INTO THE FESTIVE whirlwind of *Holiday Homecoming*, a heartwarming romantic comedy set during Thanksgiving and Christmas 2002.

Cassandra "Cassie" Economos is braving Thanksgiving with her family, solo. That's right, folks, she's back at the familial nest without her rock-god boyfriend, Nat Hardwick of Dramatic Sneezer fame. Why? Because touring, that's why! Prepare for the third degree, Cassie, because "frontman for a band called Dramatic Sneezer" doesn't exactly scream "stable life partner" to the Economos clan.

Meanwhile, Nat is on the road, crafting a heartfelt surprise to prove just how much Cassie means to him. He's determined to prove to Cassie (and her skeptical family) that his heart beats only for her. Will his surprise be a hit, or will it crash and burn like a poorly timed guitar solo?

But wait, there's more! Cassie's cousin Phil is wrestling with his own holiday drama. His wife, Jennifer, is facing a blast from the past in the form of her long-absent father. After a decade of radio silence, he's back, stirring up a whole cauldron of complicated feelings. Can Phil navigate this emotional minefield and keep the holiday spirit (and his marriage) intact?

Told from four perspectives, this story revisits characters from *The Rock Star's Wife* series. It

serves up the holidays with a side of family dysfunction, a heaping helping of romance, and a generous sprinkle of rock-and-roll. So grab a plate, pour yourself a drink, and prepare for a holiday season you won't soon forget!

https://books2read.com/holidayhomecoming

Holiday Headaches

STEP INTO THE WHIRLWIND of the 2004 holiday season with *Holiday Headaches*, a collection of three short stories featuring characters from *The Rock Star's Wife* series that prove the holidays are both a blessing and a headache!

First, meet new parents Cassandra and Nat Hardwick whose world is turned upside down when their 11-month-old gets sick. Forget sugar plums. Visions of fever reducers and frantic Google searches dance in their heads. Will they survive their first holiday parenting experience? Spoiler alert: probably. But not without a few near-meltdowns and a whole lot of baby wipes.

Then, buckle up for a fender-bender of festive frustration with Phil and Jennifer. Their holiday cheer takes a detour when an impatient Chicago Blackhawks fan rear-ends Jennifer's car. Suddenly, visions of sugarplums are replaced with insurance adjusters and rental car agreements. Can they salvage their holiday spirit, or will this accident turn into a full-blown Christmas catastrophe?

Finally, Vanessa and Brandon grapple with the most terrifying holiday monster of all: credit card debt. Between three growing kids and unexpected bills, their spending has spiraled out of control. Will they be able to rein in their finances before Christmas morning, or will they be facing a mountain of bills bigger than Santa's sack?

So grab a cup of cocoa, curl up by the fire, and prepare to laugh your way through these relatable and ridiculously funny holiday tales. Just try not to spill your cocoa along the way.

https://books2read.com/HolidayHeadaches

The Christmas Gift

AS THE TWINKLING LIGHTS of the holiday season approach, the Economos family is anything but merry. Following the tumultuous events of *Family Upheaval*, Daria Economos finds herself grappling with her husband's betrayal, her heart heavy with hurt as Christmas looms like a fruitcake-shaped asteroid. Daria's not sure if she wants to deck the halls or deck her estranged husband.

Determined to bring joy back into their fractured lives, eldest son Chris rallies his siblings —Greg, Vanessa, and Cassie — and sets out on a heartfelt mission to transform their mother's holiday into something special. He envisions a Norman Rockwell painting come to life, complete with caroling, a perfectly trimmed tree, and a family dinner where everyone smiles politely and pretends their lives aren't crumbling faster than a gingerbread house in a hurricane.

Of course, things don't exactly go according to plan. Can the family find a way to forgive, to laugh and to rediscover the true meaning of Christmas amidst the chaos? Or will this holiday season be remembered as the year the Economos family finally imploded, leaving behind only a trail of tinsel, tears, and slightly singed Christmas cookies?

Get ready for a heartwarming holiday adventure filled with dysfunctional family dynamics and the enduring power of love (and maybe a little bit of ouzo) to get you through even the most challenging of times. Just try not to choke on your Christmas ham. We warned you.

https://www.amazon.com/dp/B0DF2DB21P

Standalone Stories

I Don't Hate You

ROCK STAR CHASE WHEELER trades his glittering life in the spotlight to return to the quiet embrace of his small Wisconsin hometown, compelled by his beloved grandmother's final days.

His hometown also holds Alexis McNeil, the woman whose heart he shattered, the mother of his son, Cody. Immaturity and insecurity drove a wedge between them, leaving behind a wreckage of unspoken words and broken promises. Now, standing on the precipice of unimaginable loss, Chase is forced to confront the consequences of his past.

Alexis has built a life for herself and Cody, a life carefully constructed to keep the pain of Chase's abandonment at bay. But beneath the surface, the years haven't erased the memory of their passionate connection and the embers of love still glow.

Grandma Wheeler sees the unspoken truths. Her dying wish is simple: for them to find their way back to each other, to heal the wounds of the past and build a future for Cody. She knows that beneath the layers of hurt and resentment, love still flickers, a love that deserves a second chance.

The road to reconciliation is paved with obstacles. The scars of the past run deep, and the insecurities that once plagued their relationship resurface. Can Chase prove to Alexis that he's a changed man, that he's worthy of her forgiveness and love? Can Alexis let go of the pain and resentment and open her heart to the possibility of a future with Chase?

Passionate, raw, and real, I Don't Hate You weaves a emotionally charged story about second chances, the enduring power of love, and the courage it takes to confront the past and embrace the future.

https://books2read.com/IDontHateYou

My Best Friend's Brother

HAYLEY HANCOCK HEADS back to Rochester, Minnesota, for her high school best friend Cheyenne Cox's wedding. But returning to Cheyenne's world is like stepping into a different dimension. The Cox family oozes old money, and Hayley can already feel the judgmental stares and thinly veiled condescension. She needs a lifeline, a distraction, anything to make it through this ordeal with her sanity intact. And then she sees him.

Connor Cox. Cheyenne's younger brother.

No longer the bothersome teenager she once knew, Connor has transformed into a striking, confident drummer. The attraction is instantaneous, a magnetic pull that neither of them can deny. As wedding week unfolds, stolen glances turn into lingering conversations, innocent touches become electric sparks. They find solace in each other's company, a shared understanding that transcends the social barriers that separate them.

But a romance between Hayley and Connor is complicated, to say the least. Cheyenne, caught up in her own wedding whirlwind, is oblivious to the simmering chemistry between her best friend and her brother. The Cox family, with their rigid expectations and judgmental eyes, would never approve of Hayley. And Connor, despite his undeniable attraction to Hayley, has responsibilities and commitments.

Will their star-crossed romance blossom despite the weight of social expectations?

Get ready for a steamy, heartwarming, and utterly addictive story about unexpected connections and the courage to defy expectations. My Best Friend's Brother is a rollercoaster of emotions, filled with, sizzling chemistry and a love that just might conquer all.

https://books2read.com/FriendsBrother

Midlife Melody

AFTER YEARS OF SACRIFICE and hard work, Holly Leftwich has achieved a major milestone: she's a homeowner. And not just anywhere, but in Cincinnati, Ohio, a city she chose specifically for her vibrant daughter, Ainsley, a gifted guitarist who has landed a recording deal.

Once the notorious frontman for a wildly popular metal band, Spencer Everlong was the embodiment of every rock star stereotype imaginable. But those days are history. Haunted by his past and the damage he inflicted, Spencer has worked tirelessly to re-invent himself.

Holly and Spencer's connection is undeniable, a spark that ignites with every stolen glance and whispered conversation. But their budding romance is threatened by the ghosts of Spencer's past. Old habits die hard, and some people are not willing to let him forget. As Spencer tries to navigate his new relationship with Holly, he finds himself battling not only his own demons, but also the lingering consequences of his former life.

Will their love be strong enough to overcome the obstacles in their path and create a midlife melody that resonates with hope, healing, and the promise of a brighter tomorrow?

A story about second chances, finding love when you least expect it, and the healing power of music. Sometimes, the greatest love stories are the ones that are forged in the fires of adversity, the ones that rise from the ashes of the past, and the ones that remind us that it's never too late to find your happily ever after.

https://books2read.com/MidlifeMelody

Sunny Rock Harbor

NESTLED ALONG THE PICTURESQUE shores of Lake Superior, Sunny Rock Harbor is a place where the air is filled with the sweet promise of fresh beginnings and the summer sun dances on the water.

Devon Dixson, a rock star whose career hit a sour note, leaves behind the gritty streets of Detroit in the hopes a change of scenery will re-ignite his creative spark and banish the persistent cloud of depression that clings to him. But the picturesque landscapes and tranquil atmosphere of the Upper Peninsula prove to be no match for his inner turmoil. He's still just as lost, just as uninspired, and just as profoundly sad.

Paige Purdy, the spirited co-owner of a quirky souvenir shop, is determined to escape the shadows of her past. However, the small-town gossip mill is relentless, and half the town seems convinced she should reconcile with her ex-boyfriend. Paige is resolute in her desire for a fresh start, a chance to define her own happiness.

A chance meeting on the beach leads to a comical, albeit disastrous, clash of personalities. Devon, brooding and cynical, clashes with Paige's down-to-earth, upbeat nature. Yet, beneath the initial friction, an undeniable spark ignites. Despite their differences, they find themselves drawn to each other, intrigued by the hidden depths they sense beneath the surface.

Will summer change the course of their lives forever? Dive into the magic of *Sunny Rock Harbor* and find out!

https://books2read.com/SunnyRockHarbor

About the Author

Melina Druga is a multi-genre author based in the Midwest. With more than 20 published books, including *The Rock Star's Wife* series, she has established herself as adaptable writer with the ability to write in multiple voices and literary styles.

Melina's writing journey began in childhood when she wrote her first "novel" as a 10 year old. Her spicy, contemporary fiction explores the challenges of maintaining relationships within the world of rock and metal. Her historical fiction captivates readers by transporting them to the founding of Canada. She draws inspiration from song lyrics and current/historical events and is passionate about pushing women's stories to the forefront.

When not breathing life into characters, Melina can be found listening to music, exercising, and spending time with family and friends. Her next book, Sex & Surprises (The Rock Star's Wife #5) is available for preorder.

Connect with Melina on her website or social media for behind the scenes content, writing updates, teasers, and more:

Website: www.melinadruga.com/

Instagram: instagram.com/melinadruga/

Pinterest: pinterest.com/MelinaDruga

Facebook: facebook.com/MelinaDruga

YouTube: youtube.com/@MelinaDruga

Goodreads: goodreads.com/MelinaDruga

BookBub: bookbub.com/profile/melina-druga

Rock Star's Wife companion playlists: open.spotify.com/user/312s3lke7maxj3lyupbfy73pwpr4?si=b39b968de23847dd

Read more at https://www.melinadruga.com/.

About the Publisher

Sun Up Press publishes both fiction and nonfiction titles.